The Sean O'Rourke Series
Book 6

Blood Flows in the East

by

Michael E. Cook

TELEMACHUS PRESS

This book is a work of fiction. Names, characters, places and incidents are either the product of the author's imagination or are used fictitiously. Any resemblance to actual persons, living or dead, or to actual events or locales is entirely coincidental.

Cover art and design by Telemachus Press, LLC with assistance from Beatrice Gallaugher

Published by Telemachus Press, LLC
http://www.telemachuspress.com

Contact the author at cookorourkeseries@gmail.com

ISBN: 978-1-948046-10-7 (eBook)
ISBN: 978-1-948046-11-4 (Paperback)

Version 2018.07.06

Table of Contents

The Sean O'Rourke Series

Book 6

Blood Flows in the East

CHAPTER ONE

The first thing Sean did the next morning was send a telegram to Judge Sharpton. It went as follows.

Federal Judge Sharpton
Federal Court House
St. Louis

Kid Evans and gang dead<<stop>>Abducted woman rescued<<stop>>over $80,000 recovered<<stop>>will put money in bank minus reward money<<stop>>reward money goes to Kathleen Jameson<<stop>>$30,000 stolen from Clancy Evans<<stop>>$5000 from bank in Missouri<<stop>>$10,000 from another bank in Missouri<<stop>>unknown amount stolen from Bill Thompson<<stop>>unknown amount from cattle rustling<<stop>>will distribute recovered money when hear from you

O'Rourke

Sean had the money stashed in his room. He took the money to the bank and explained to the banker about the money. Then he went to Kathleen's room at the hotel. Sam answered the door when Sean knocked. "Mornin', how's Kathleen doin'?" said Sean. "I got somethin' for her."

"Come on in," said Sam. "We was just havin' some coffee and then was gonna go have some breakfast." Kathleen was sitting on the edge of the bed sipping her coffee. She smiled at Sean and then went over and gave him a hug.

"Hope yer feelin' better," said Sean. "I got some reward money for you."

"Reward money! Why would I get that?" asked Kathleen.

"Cause you purty much caught that son of a bitch by yerself," said Sean. "Jeb just put on the finishin' touches. Jeb don't need no money anyhow. It's all yours." Sean handed the money to Kathleen. He counted it out as he gave it to her. "There ya be, $7000."

"Oh my, what am I going to do with all that?" said Kathleen. "Maybe I will have my own place soon."

"Maybe Sam can help ya with that," said Sean. "Looks like you two'r made fer each other. Well, I'll leave you alone now. Me'n Maggie got some serious things ta talk about." Sean gave Kathleen another hug, shook Sam's hand, and then left.

As soon as Sean was out of the room, Kathleen wrapped her arms around Sam. "Will you help me figure out what to do with this money?" asked Kathleen. "I was figuring on having my own place someday."

"I was hopin' that you'd go with me back ta Texas," said Sam. "I already got a place and I sure would like it if you were my partner. I want you for my woman Kathleen. I know we just met, but I got strong feelins' fer you. I think you got them fer me too."

"I do have strong feelings for you Sam," said Kathleen. "I was hoping that we could become more than just partners."

"You just say when and we'll git ourselves married," said Sam. "I understand there's a Justice of the Peace in this town. Are you sure you wouldn't mind bein' married to a lawman?"

"I like the idea of being married to a lawman," said Kathleen. "I know you're a good man and will protect me and our children— if we have children. I'd like to get married next week. I want to be pretty for you. Maybe some of the bruising will be gone by then."

"Kathleen, you'll always be beautiful to me," said Sam. "Nothin'll change that."

"I do love you Sam," said Kathleen. "Now let's get this money to the bank and then have some breakfast."

Maggie, Sean, Betty, and Michael sat down at their regular table and sipped coffee while they waited on their breakfast. Betty was the first to speak. "Michael and I have decided that we're going back east," said Betty. "We love you two and all the people here, but things have gotten worse lately. We would like to own a nice neighborhood pub maybe in Boston or a big city like that. We need a more peaceful place. Abilene will only get worse before it gets better."

"I fully understand," said Maggie. "I don't want our baby to be born here. I need some quiet too."

"You'll have that quiet," said Sean. "How bout we stick it out till the end of this season and then sell the place. We can go back to St. Louis for a while. We can stay there till the baby is grown some and then go wherever you want."

"What about that Federal Marshal's badge?" asked Maggie. "Would you be willing to give that up?"

"I think I could give it up for you and the baby," said Sean. "I've done my duty and then some. But you gotta remember darlin', I've made a lot of enemies. Lawman'r not, there could always be some trouble."

"I know that," said Maggie. "But I'm willing to take those chances. So Michael, is there a place back east that's for sale that you've been thinking about?"

"I haven't been looking yet," said Michael. "I'll be sendin' out some telegrams and maybe I'll put some ads in some papers back east sayin' I'm lookin' for a place to buy. If we haven't heard anything after a couple of months, then we'll head east anyway. Maybe we'll build a brand new place."

"What would you call your place?" asked Sean.

"I haven't thought about that yet," answered Michael. "I guess I better."

~~~~

Elizabeth Thompson decided she would sell all of her properties and then go back to Cincinnati. She would stay in Abilene till all of her places sold. Ads were placed in papers all over saying that there would be an auction. The places could be sold separately or together. Elizabeth would have the right to reject bids that she thought were too low. The auction would be held in a month. That would give any interested party plenty of time to check out the places.

When Alan Cooper's assignment with Elizabeth was terminated, he reported to his office that his assignment was finished.

He stayed with Elizabeth while he waited for his next assignment. At times he wondered if Elizabeth was just using him. Other times he was sure that she felt something for him. He knew that he was having strong feelings for her.

A week later, Alan received his next assignment. There was some politician in Chicago who wanted Alan as a bodyguard. This job would start in eight days. Alan figured it would take him three days to get to Chicago by train so he and Elizabeth made the most of those five days. On the first of those five days, they never left the hotel room except to eat. That evening as they lay holding each other, Elizabeth looked into Alan's eyes. "I want you to be with me," Elizabeth said. "You don't have to marry me. Whenever you have time between assignments, I want you to be with me."

"What if I don't want that?" said Alan.

"What do you mean? I know you have feelings for me," said Elizabeth.

"I do have strong feelings for you Elizabeth," said Alan. "I just don't want to be your man. I want to be your husband too."

"Oh Alan, I want that too," said Elizabeth. "I have hoped that we could be married some day. You know that you'll be marrying a rich woman, don't you?"

"I don't need your money Elizabeth," said Alan. "I just need you. Besides, I'm not a poor man myself. I inherited a lot of money and some properties in Washington D.C."

"So why are you a Pinkerton?" asked Elizabeth. "You don't need to work."

"I guess it's kind of like why Sean O'Rourke is a lawman," said Alan. "He doesn't need to work, but someone has to do what he does and he's good at it. I'm good at what I do and I like it. So when can we get married?"

"Jason Hunter is the Justice of the Peace in this town," said Elizabeth. "We can talk with him tomorrow if you'd like."

"I'd like that," said Alan. "I'd like that a lot. Maybe if I tell my boss I'm getting married, he'll let me have some time off."

"What about that Chicago politician?" asked Elizabeth.

"The Pinkerton's have plenty of good men," said Alan. "That politician'll be taken care of."

The next morning, Alan sent a telegram to his boss and asked for some time off to get married. He received a reply later that morning. The Chicago politician had changed his plans. Alan could have a month off. Instead of talking to Jason Hunter about the wedding, they stayed in their room and celebrated. The next day after breakfast, they talked with Jason about performing their wedding.

"You know what you folks might think about," said Jason. "I'm doing another wedding next week. Sam Waters and Kathleen Jameson are getting married. They'll be asking Sean if the wedding can be at Maggie's Place. We could have a double wedding."

"That would be nice," said Elizabeth. "We'll go over and talk with Maggie now. Thank you."

"It'll be my pleasure to get you two hitched," said Jason. Kathleen and Alan thanked Jason again and headed for Maggie's Place. When they got there, Sam and Kathleen were there talking with Maggie and Sean. They could see Maggie and Sean were happy to have Kathleen and Sam's wedding in the saloon. Hugs and kisses and handshakes were being exchanged. Elizabeth and Alan waited for a break in the action and then joined them.

"I could tell by all the hugs and kisses that you are having Kathleen and Sam's wedding here next week," said Elizabeth.

"Would you consider having a double wedding that day? Alan and I are getting married."

"Of course we can do it," said Maggie. "Everyone knew that you two would be getting married. We'll be glad to have a double wedding here. Kathleen, you and Sam don't mind do you?"

"Of course not," answered Kathleen. "It'll be a wonderful time."

"Let's all sit down and have a toast to your upcoming nuptials," said Sean.

"Nuptials, I've never heard you say that word," said Maggie. "It sounds strange coming from you."

"Well sorry, let's have a toast to their upcoming weddings," said Sean. They all laughed a little and sat down. Tom brought over a bottle and some glasses and they had their toast.

~~~~

The next few days in Abilene were very quiet. There were plenty of drunk cowboys and cattle herds, but it had been unusually quiet. Sean and Michael were worried that something was about to happen. Sam was beginning to think the same thing. He was a lawman and knew that with that many cowboys and that much liquor, trouble always comes. Even Alan thought it was too quiet. He and Elizabeth were on their way to the general store one day when Alan noticed four riders coming into town. They had two pack horses with them and all four of them were heavily armed. Each man wore a pistol belt and had another holster and pistol tied to his saddle horn. Each man had a repeating rifle and a long gun in scabbards on their saddles. Some shotguns were tied to the packs on the pack horses. They looked like they had been in the saddle for a good while. They stopped at one of the other saloons in town. They tied their horses and went inside. "I need to tell Sean about those men," said Alan. "They didn't come here for a church social."

"Why should Sean know about those men?" asked Elizabeth. "Everybody carries guns around here."

"Most of them do, but for most men, one is enough," said Alan. "I'll be telling Sean."

When they got to Maggie's Place, Sean and Michael were standing there looking out a front window. Maggie was over by the bar so Elizabeth went over to talk with her while Alan talked to Sean.

"I came to tell you about some men I saw coming into town," said Alan. "There was f—"

Sean interrupted him. "Michael and I saw them too," said Sean. "They look like bounty hunters ta me. Probly come here hopin' ta find the whereabouts a Kid and his bunch. They're gonna be disappointed. I'll wait a bit and then go over there."

"You want me to go with you?" asked Alan.

"No need, but thanks fer the offer," said Sean. "If there'd be any trouble, I can handle four of'em." Sean and Michael went over to their regular table and drank some coffee. Alan joined them. Elizabeth was still talking with Maggie. None of the men spoke. Sean finished his cup of coffee and then checked his two pistols and made sure they were fully loaded. "I'm goin' over there now," said Sean. "I doubt there'll be any shootin', but if ya hear shootin' and ya see them four runnin' out the door, you kill'em. Michael, git yer Winchester and give Alan my Winchester. You two wait here just inside the door." Michael got the rifles and Sean headed to the other saloon. Jeb went with him. When Sean got to the other saloon, he stopped and looked over the swinging doors. Jeb stayed to the side so he couldn't be seen. The four men were at the bar drinking whiskey. There was a big mirror behind the bar. Sean was sure that the four men saw him. Sean entered the saloon and moved to the right away from the doors. Jeb came in and sat down on Sean's right. Jeb had a very low growl going. Sean was about forty feet from the bar. He could see that the four men were watching him in the mirror.

"Well lookey here boys," said one of the men. "We got us the famous sharpshooter and lawman a watchin' us. He must figure we're bad men. What do ya want O'Rourke? And that's bout the ugliest dog I ever did see."

"I wanna know what you boys'r doin' here and don't insult my dog. He don't take insults too good." said Sean. "You got names?"

"Name's none a yer," said the man who was doing the talking.

"None a yer what?" asked Sean.

"None a yer damn business," said the man.

"Oh that's funny," said Sean. "That's so funny I might laugh so hard that I'll shit myself. Don't you think that's funny Jeb?" Jeb increased his growl a bit. "I figure you boys'r bounty hunters and yer here hopin' ta find out somethin' bout Kid Evans and his gang. Well boys, yer too late. Kid and his bunch'r in hell where they belong."

"Did you kill'em?" asked the man.

"I had some help," answered Sean.

"What about all that money they stole? Was any of it recovered?" asked the man.

"That's none a yer," said Sean. "None a yer damn business."

"Haw haw haw," said the man. "You know O'Rourke, these boys'n me fought fer the stars and bars. We was all sharpshooters. We never wasted no time like you shootin' Corporals and Sergeants. We went after big game. I'd a got ole Grant one time, but some stupid Lieutenant got in the way after I squeezed the trigger. I got me several Colonels and a lotta Captains. Ronnie down here on the left almost got Sherman onest. We all got us a passel a officers. We was after that bounty they had on you too. No one saw you after Atlanta. We figured you was hidin'."

"Look, I don't give a shit how many men you killed durin' the war," started Sean. "The war's over and while yer in this town, it better stay over. You look at me the wrong way or even make me think yer goin' fer iron, I'll shoot you dead. I'll kill you so fast you won't know yer dead till you don't wake up the next mornin'."

"Don't go gettin' so all high toney," said the man. "We all know how fast you are. You probly could kill us if we tried to pull on ya. We never come here ta git shot by you. We come here hopin' ta hear somethin' bout Kid Evans. I reckon we're too late. Ya got any new posters on anyone?"

"Nothin' that'd be worth yer time," said Sean. "Nobody's worth more than $50 right at the moment."

"Well I reckon we'll have us some more drinks and some food and then we'll move on," said the man. "Don't you worry O'Rourke, we're not gonna bushwack ya."

"Does yer momma know what you grew up ta be?" asked Sean.

"Does yers?" asked Ronnie.

"Nope, she doesn't," answered Sean. "My Ma and Pa was murdered by some white scum. I helped kill them scum. Now you boys make sure you stay away from me." Sean turned and left. He watched in the mirror in case one of the men would try and back shoot him. Jeb watched the four men until Sean cleared the door and then he followed him. As soon as Jeb cleared the door, the four men turned and continued their drinking.

"They was bounty hunters," said Sean as he entered Maggie's Place. "Just like I figured. They was after Kid Evans. They said they'd be movin' on after eatin' and gettin' some drinks. I don't trust'em. I figure they'll go after the bank. Looks like they put in a lotta time chasin' Kid and they don't wanna leave empty handed. I'll be keepin' an eye on'em."

"I'm here if you need me Sean," said Alan.

"Thanks, I might need me another good man," said Sean. "With me and Michael and you, we oughta be able ta handle things. Think I'll talk ta Sam too." The three men sat down at the regular table and had some drinks. Maggie and Elizabeth joined them. It wasn't long until Sam and Kathleen joined them. It wasn't another fifteen minutes and the four bounty hunters rode out of town heading west. Sean didn't want to upset the women but he figured they had a right to know what he thought could happen. He got right to the point. "Ladies, there was some bounty hunters in town a little while ago," started Sean. "They was after Kid Evans and his bunch. Now that they know Kid and his bunch is dead, I figure they'll be after the bank. Them boys was all sharp-shooters for the south durin' the war. That means they're good shots and they'd like ta see me dead too. I'm gonna wait a bit and then go track'em. I figure they'll set up camp a few hours from town. Hard ta tell when they'll come if they're comin'. Could be tonight or in a few days."

"I'll give a hand," said Sam.

"Why do you think those men would want to rob the bank?" asked Elizabeth.

"Cause they put in a lotta time chasin' after Kid," answered Sean. "That was a big reward fer him. Them fellas don't wanna come up empty handed. They know there's plenty a money in that bank."

"I know that," said Elizabeth. "I have a bunch in there."

"We all do darlin'," said Michael. "Sean and us'll make sure it stays there."

"I'm gonna get somethin' ta eat and then I'll be trackin' them fellas," said Sean. "I'll get back soon as I can."

~~~~

The four bounty hunters rode for about three hours and set up camp. The land was mostly all open plain with a few rolling hills. When they had their campfire going, the smoke could be seen from more than a mile away. The four men's names were Ronnie, Amos, Tully, and Saltie. Saltie thought he was the leader of the group. He was the one who had done most of the talking with O'Rourke. They had a bottle with them and they passed it around as they sat by the fire. "We're taking that bank in Abilene," said Saltie. "O'Rourke or no O'Rourke, we're takin' that bank. We come too far to come up empty handed. I bet that money that Kid and his boys took is in that bank. Plus Abilene's a cow town now. Gotta be lotsa money in that bank."

"So you think we can take O'Rourke?" asked Tully.

"We better if'n we want that money," said Saltie.

Sean started tracking the bounty hunters right after he had eaten. He took Jeb with him. It was almost dark when he spotted smoke coming from a campfire. He waited till dark and headed toward to campfire. There was a half moon so Sean could see fairly well. When he got within a quarter mile of the campfire, he dismounted and tied his horse to a small tree. Sean knew that with the half moon, he could be seen also, so he took his time and eased closer and closer to the campsite. When he got within a hundred yards, he got down and slowly crawled closer. He and Jeb stopped when they were fifty yards from the campfire. They laid down behind some small bushes and waited. Sean could see the four bounty hunters sitting around the fire. They were passing a bottle around. The bottle was passed one more time and then Saltie took the bottle and put it in some saddle bags. "That's enough whiskey fer now boys," said Saltie. "I got me a plan fer tamarra. When I git done tellin' ya, speak up ifn' ya think ya got a better idea."

"So we're really gonna take that bank?" said Amos.

"Yep, and we'll git O'Rourke too," said Saltie. "Now listen up. We'll git up at first light and head back ta town. Ronnie, you pick a good spot bout a half mile from town and wait. Me'n Tully'n Amos'll ride inta town. Tully here'll git hisself on a roof where he can see all a downtown, especially the bank. Me'n Amos'll take the bank. Tully should git a good shot at O'Rourke ifn' he heads out inta the street after us as we're gittin' away. Ifn' he don't git a good shot, then Ronnie'll git one when he comes a ridin' after us. Now Tully, don't take no shot lessn' ya git a good one. Ole Ronnie'll git'm if you don't git a good shot. We can all meet up right here. How's that sound boys?"

"It sounds all right ta me, but I hear O'Rourke's a smart man," said Amos. "I just bet he figures we're up ta somethin'. I bet he figures we're all mad cause we didn't git that reward money fer Kid. He could be awaitin' fer us."

"You worry too much ya dern fool," said Saltie. "So what if O'Rourke'd be waitin' fer us. We lived through the war didn't we.? We oughta be able ta shoot our way outta that town if'n we had to."

"I spose," said Amos. "I reckon we'll find out."

Sean heard all that he needed. He and Jeb slowly eased their way back to Sean's horse. When he got back to town, everyone was as Maggie's Place waiting for him. Sean tied Billy out front and went inside. "Well, what are they up to?" asked Michael as Sean entered.

"They think they're takin' the bank first thing in the mornin'," said Sean. "I thought up a plan as I was ridin' back ta town. First I'll tell ya what they're plannin' ta do. One of'em's gonna wait bout a half mile outta town. The other three'll ride in. One of'ems gonna git on a roof and cover the street hopin' ta git a shot at me if I come out into the street after'em. The other two'll take the bank. If the one on the roof don't git a shot at me, then the one outta town will when I chase after'em."

"So what's your plan?" asked Sam.

"Well, I'm the only one them boys seen," started Sean. "They don't know the rest of ya. I'm gonna go have a talk with that banker."

"He'll be asleep," said Maggie.

"He'll wake up fer this," said Sean. "Now Alan, you said you'd lend a hand. I could sure use you."

"You can count on me," said Alan. "Just tell me what you want."

"Well here's what we'll do," Sean began. "Alan, yer gonna pretend ta be the bank teller in the mornin'. Michael, you'll be settin' in the office pretendin' ta be the bank President. Sam'n me'll be somewhere on the edge a town so we'll see'em when they come ridin' in. We'll watch the one that breaks off and goes lookin' fer a good roof ta git on. We'll let'm git up there and git nice'n cozy. Alan, when them two come inta the bank, you'n Michael be ready. Don't hesitate. Soon as you see'em startin' fer iron, you kill'em. Don't be wastin' time tellin'em to stop'r anything like that. Them boys is killers'r they wouldn't be bounty hunters. Are you all right with this Alan?"

"I am," answered Alan. "If they're reaching for a pistol, then they probably will use it. I won't let them get the chance. I wouldn't want to widow Elizabeth again even though we're not married yet."

"What about the man outside of town?" asked Michael.

"We'll git him after we git the three in town," said Sean. "Me'n Jeb'll git'm. Now I'll go wake up that banker and tell'm what we're doin' in the mornin'. You all git some rest. We can meet back here for an early breakfast."

Sean woke up the banker and told him what would happen in the morning. The banker wanted to help, but Sean assured him that he wasn't needed. The banker gave Sean the key to the front door of the bank so Michael and Alan could unlock the door at eight o'clock when the bank would normally open.

Sean could tell that Maggie was a little upset by what was going to happen. "It'll never end will it?" said Maggie. "There'll be more dead men in the street tomorrow."

"We didn't invite them," said Sean. "We didn't ask them to come here and rob the bank. Please don't worry. It'll be over quick."

"I know," said Maggie. "But I'll still worry about you and Michael and the others."

"That's because you love us and we love you darlin'," said Sean. "Now try and git some sleep. Just let me hold you." Maggie cried for a few minutes and then was fast asleep. Sean fell asleep shortly after Maggie did. The next thing Sean knew, Jeb was pawing him and waking him. "Thanks boy. I reckon it's time ta git up," said Sean. Maggie raised up in bed to see what was happening. "You go on back ta sleep darlin'. Me'n the boys'll git some breakfast and then go ta work." It was pretty early and Cookie or Barbara weren't in the kitchen yet, so Sean got started on coffee and breakfast. The coffee was just about done when the other men started arriving. Sean got all of them a cup and then started on the food. He made them some ham and eggs and taters. As the men ate, they went over the plan again. They all knew what to do. About an hour before daylight, Sean and Sam went to the edge of town where they could see the bounty hunters coming in, but couldn't be spotted by them. Michael and Alan would wait till eight o'clock and then go into the bank and act like they were getting ready fo the day's business.

At a little before eight o'clock, the three bounty hunters came riding into town. One of them broke off from the other two. As soon as the two riders were past them, Sean and Sam followed the rider to see where he would go. The rider stopped behind the hotel where Bill Thompson had been killed. He tied his horse to a post and looked around for a way to get on the roof. It wasn't long until he was on the roof. It was the highest roof in town. "I'll work my way back over towards the bank and try not ta git myself spotted," said Sean. "You stay right here and stay low. Don't let'm spot ya. When them other two go inta the bank, there'll be some shootin'. When that shootin' starts, that one on the roof'll raise up enough where one a us can git a good shot at'm. Now don't do no shootin' till ya hear shootin' at the bank. And don't wait on me. If ya git a shot, take it." Sam nodded his head yes.

Sean was near the center of town hiding next to one of the other saloons. Michael and Alan had just unlocked the bank and gone inside. The two bounty hunters were riding slowly down the street toward the bank. They stopped in front of the bank and threw their horse's reins over a hitching post as they dismounted. One of them looked inside the bank and then stepped back. Alan was at his teller's window acting like he was doing some paper-work. Michael was in the office but could be plainly seen by anyone who entered the bank. Alan was acting like he was writing with his left hand, but he had a pistol in his right hand which was down to his side where it couldn't be seen. Michael had his pistol in his right hand on the desk. There was a pile of books on the desk so the pistol couldn't be seen. The two bounty hunters waited a moment outside and then entered the bank. Saltie entered first. Amos was right behind him. Saltie started towards the teller's window. Amos started towards the office. Both of them were drawing their pistols as they moved. Before the men had their pistols halfway out, two shots were fired. They were fired so closely together, they almost sounded like one. Saltie was thrown backwards and hit the floor dead. There was blood all over his chest. Amos was thrown backwards so hard that it knocked him back through the door where he fell dead on the sidewalk. Michael had put a bullet in his forehead.

When Sean heard the shots in the bank, he watched for the other man on the roof to raise up and take a look. Sean had the man in his sights and was about to squeeze the trigger on his Winchester when he heard Sam's Henry fire. The man came tumbling down off the roof and landed about ten feet in front of the hotel. Elizabeth had been in her room at the hotel and was staying out of sight. When she heard the third shot, she just happened to be looking out one of her windows. She saw the body of the dead man come flying down and land in the street. She knew Alan had told her to stay put, but she had to see if any harm had come to him. She left her room and took off running toward the bank. Alan, Sam, Sean, and Michael were out in the street now talking. Elizabeth saw Alan in the street and knew that he was all right. She went to him and hugged him hard.

"Well, looks like the undertaker'll make a little money today," said Sean. "I'm gonna git me some coffee and then I'll be after that last man."

"Maybe he heard the shootin' and took off," said Sam.

"That's possible," said Sean. "But I don't think he'd take off unless he knew what just happened and he's got no way a knowin' that yet. He'll be out there waitin'. I know that country. Me'n Jeb'll git'm." They all went to Maggie's Place and had some coffee. Maggie joined them. Sean could tell that she was having trouble holding tears back. There wasn't much talking. Sean finished his coffee and then he and Jeb headed to the livery.

"I'll be comin' with ya," said Sam. "If that man was a sharp-shooter, it wouldn't hurt ta have two of us. Besides, he's never seen me. He'll just figure I'm some lone cowboy ridin' along. Maybe I'll spot'm. He'll be lookin' fer you, not me."

"That makes sense," said Sean. "Make sure that badge a yers stays outta sight."

"It'll be in a pocket," said Sam. "Now let's get it done. I kinda like that horse a Michael's anyway. He needs rode more." The two men saddled up and headed west out of town. Sam headed straight down the trail and Sean swung way out to the left of the trail. Jeb went his own way. He knew what they were doing. The two of them would meet up behind a small rise that was about a mile from town. Sam was about a quarter of a mile from town when he thought he heard a horse whinny in the distance. He stopped and listened, but he didn't hear it again. He rode on. Another quarter of a mile down the trail, he saw some movement to his right. He kept riding but watched for the movement. It was Jeb. Jeb stopped and laid down. He would look at Sam and then look away like he was looking at something. He did this several times. "Ole Jeb's got'm spotted," Sam said to himself. "I'll go meet Sean and let'm know."

The two men met behind the small rise as planned. "Jeb's got'm spotted," said Sam. "He's back there just a little ways on this side of the trail." Sam pointed. "There's not much cover. He must just be in the high grass."

"Well take me ta where Jeb is," said Sean. "Then we'll see if we can spot his horse. If we spot his horse, I'll have you work your way around so you'll be behind his horse. I'll find him and start shootin'. He might git up and run fer his horse. When he does, take care of'm."

"You sure you'll find'm?" asked Sam.

"I might not see'm right off, but I'll put some lead in places where I'd be If I was him," said Sean. He'll either fire back and give his postion away or he'll run."

"What if he don't run'r shoot?" asked Sam.

"Then he's one brave son of a bitch," said Sean. "I got a lotta bullets fer this Winchester and I'm not afraid ta waste any. He'll shoot'r run."

They headed to where Sam had spotted Jeb. Jeb was still there. Sean got out his spyglass and looked around. He spotted the man's horse. It was tied to a small tree. There was some brush around the tree and the horse couldn't be seen very well. "You work your way over on the other side a that horse," said Sean. "I think I know where that fella is. You ride a ways and then git off yer horse. Walk on the horse's left side so he's between you and that fella. That way if he sees you, he won't have a good shot. I'll wait a bit and let ya git over there. Git as close to that horse as ya can. When ya hear shootin', be ready."

Sean waited for a while and then rode closer to where he thought the man was hiding. Jeb stayed right where Sam had first spotted him. Sean had a feeling now that he was being targeted. He kicked Billy in the slats and took off and slid down out of the saddle and hung on Billy's right side. Sean heard the bullet whiz by as he slid down. Sean peered over Billy's neck. He spotted the smoke from the man's rifle. Now Sean knew exactly where the man was. There was a rock that stuck up about three feet and was right beside the trail. Sean passed it just as the man had fired. Sean turned Billy around and headed for the rock. He got back up into the saddle and then slid to left side of the horse. When he neared the rock, he slowed Billy some and then dropped off at the rock. He pulled his Winchester from the scabbard as he dropped off the horse. Just as he got behind the rock, another bullet whizzed by. It clipped the top of the rock. Sean laid flat behind the rock and took as good a shooting position as he could. As soon as another shot was fired at him, Sean fired off ten shots from the right side of the rock. He worked the lever as fast as he could. He waited a few seconds and then emptied the Winchester. He got back behind the rock and began reloading. When he was about to crank off some more shots, he heard Sam's Henry fire. Then it was quiet. Sean waited and listened. "Got'm," shouted Sam. Sean got up and walked toward where the man had been. There was some blood on the ground. It wasn't a lot, but Sean had hit the man. Sam had let the man get up on his horse before he shot him. Sean knew this when he saw all the blood on the horse and saddle. "Are we gonna bury this fella?" asked Sam.

"I feel generous today," said Sean. "We'll put'm on his horse and take'm ta town. That way he can be buried with his friends."

CHAPTER TWO

I t was fairly quiet in town for the next several days. Michael and Betty had gotten a telegram about a pub that was for sale in South Boston. The price seemed reasonable and they were heading east right after the double wedding. Maggie seemed to be upset but she cheered up some the day of the weddings. Sean had always heard that pregnant women were sometimes easily upset so he figured that a lot of Maggie's problems were because of her condition. Of course he knew that in the short time that he had been a Federal Marshal, a lot of blood had been spilled and it didn't look like things would change.

Everyone had a wonderful time at the wedding. The wedding ceremony was at 1pm and the drinking and dancing went on till well after midnight. The saloon was closed to the public for the party and some cowboys got a little upset, but there were no serious problems.

Betty and Michael's train was leaving at 2pm. Maggie, Sean, Betty, and Michael had a big lunch together that day. Maggie made an announcement as they were eating. "I have decided that

I do not want to sell Maggie's Place," started Maggie. "I want to keep it. I have so many memories here. Some are bad, but most of them are good. I still do not want our baby to be born here. I think we should ask Tom if he would run the place for us."

"That's fine by me," said Sean.

"I think Tom'd do a good job," said Michael. "He's been with you since the beginning."

"I'll have a talk with Tom later today then," said Maggie. "Now you two don't forget to send us a telegram when you get to Boston. We want to know everything about your new place."

"So when will you and Sean be going to St. Louis?" asked Betty.

"I would say in maybe a month," answered Maggie. "The cattle drives should be slowing down some by then. Sara and Doug should be able to go back to St. Louis then too. Simon is healing fast and he'll be a big help to Tom. I just thought of something. I know we can send a telegram to Jug and Lolita about our move, but how can we let Jesse Strong know?"

"I doubt we can get ahold of Jesse unless we would actually ride down there," said Sean. "If we sent a letter to the man that's in charge of the reservation, there's no guarantee it'd get delivered. Jesse and all of'em down there know that if they ever need me, they can send a telegram to the Judge. There's a telegraph in a little town just north a their territory."

"So when will you talk to the Judge about your job?" asked Maggie.

"When we're ready to go ta St. Louis, I'll let the Judge know we're comin' and I'll talk to'm face ta face," said Sean.

A lot of tears were shed when Betty and Michael's train pulled out of town. "I'll sure miss them two," Sean said to Maggie.

"Couldn't ask for a better friend than Michael. Same fer Betty. I sure hope things work out fer them. Boston is a real big city. More folks there than I wanna see."

"I know what you mean," said Maggie. "St. Louis isn't near as big as Boston, but it's too big for us. After the baby grows some, we can figure out where we want to go. Maybe things will quiet down in Abilene. Maybe we'll come back here. We have all the time in the world."

"We'll have each other and the baby," said Sean. "That's all we'll need. How you feelin' darlin'? If yer up to it, I feel a little frisky." Maggie didn't say a word. She just smiled at Sean and led him back to their room.

Sam and Kathleen left for Texas a week after Betty and Michael left. Sam had sent a telegram to his deputy in Lonesome and told him he would be headed that way. His deputy told him to please hurry back. He had enough of being a law man and wanted to get started on his law practice.

~~~~

Alan and Sean became very good friends during the short time he and Elizabeth were in Abilene. Maggie and Elizabeth became close too. When Elizabeth and Alan left Abilene after the auctions, a lot of tears were shed again. Alan assured Sean that if his help was ever needed, he would be there. Sean said the same thing.

Maggie and Sean went to St. Louis about two weeks after Elizabeth and Alan had left. They stayed in a room at "The Palace" until they found a nice house to rent. After they moved into the house, they sent a telegram to Tom in Abilene and had him get their bathtub shipped to them. They were able to have it shipped by train so the tub was at their house a week after they moved in. The very day the tub arrived, they spent most of an afternoon soaking in it.

Maggie was really enjoying how quiet it was in St. Louis. After a couple of weeks, she began to worry that Sean wasn't happy. She encouraged him to spend all the time he needed at "The Palace."

Sean had talked to Judge Sharpton when they first got to St. Louis. He told the Judge that he was considering giving up his badge. The Judge told him to take a month off and think it over. "You are the best damn Marshal that any Judge could ever have," said the Judge. "No one can do what you do. If you decide to quit, there will be no hard feelings. I understand about family and the dangers that go with the job. You have been wounded so many times already. Take your time my friend and think it over. I'm sure Maggie has had enough of the killing and blood, but I'm sure she knows that it takes a good man to stand up against the outlawry that is choking our country. She knows you have been that man. She will stand by you whatever decision you make."

Maggie and Sean were sitting out on their front porch having coffee one morning when a letter came from Michael and Betty. They had gotten a telegram from them when they first got to Boston. It just gave them their new address and said that things were looking good so far. Maggie and Sean were eager to read this letter. It went as follows.

Dear Maggie and Sean,

Things went very well when we first got here and got the place going. We named the place "Betty and Michael's Pub." We live upstairs above the pub. We are finding out now that this whole city is full of corruption. They have a regular police force in this city. Every policeman who walks this beat thinks we should give them free drinks. They say if we don't, they'll start rousting our customers. Four days ago, two men came in here and told us we needed to buy some protection. We asked them "protection from what." They said "fires and such." I asked them who their boss was. They said they were their own bosses. I kindly asked them to get the hell out of the place. When they refused, I beat the hell out of them and threw them out. The next day, the police started rousting some of our customers. A day later, they told me the cost of my liquor license was going up and my shipment of whiskey was stolen. Then a day later, some fella came in here and said that if I gave his organization thirty percent of my profits, my troubles would go away. I also asked him who his boss was. He wouldn't give me his name. He just said he was a high official in the city. I told him to tell his boss to talk to me in person so I could break his face. Betty doesn't know I wrote this letter. I know she is afraid. I have talked with other people in town about the corruption and how to get rid of it. Most people are afraid to do anything about it. They say it's been that way here as long as they can remember and they just accept it. I cannot accept it and I intend to do something about it. Wish me luck.

Michael

"I'm afraid for them Sean," said Maggie after they read the letter. "I think something bad will happen. Maybe you could ask Judge Sharpton if he knows what Michael should do. Maybe he knows a Judge or some people in Boston."

"I'll go talk to the Judge right after breakfast," said Sean. "I'm worried about them too. I know Michael can handle himself, but things are different in a big city like that. He's just way outnumbered. You know if things get out of hand I'll be going to help him."

"I know that Sean," said Maggie. "You're a good man and they are our friends. I know you'll do whatever is necessary."

After Sean had his breakfast, he went to see the Judge. The Judge was in court and Sean had to wait a while. Sean let himself into the Judge's chambers and waited. The Judge didn't seem surprised when he saw Sean waiting for him. "Have your reached a decision?" asked Judge Sharpton.

"I won't be givin' up this badge just yet Judge," said Sean. "My friend and former deputy Michael is in trouble."

"Tell me about it," said the Judge.

"Well Michael and his wife Betty moved to Boston to get away from all the blood and violence," started Sean. "They bought a pub in south Boston. Things started out well, but now they are finding out that there is a lot of corruption in that city. The local police are giving him a hard time and demanding free drinks. Men are trying to get Michael to buy protection. They raised the price of his liquor license. Some organization tells him that if he gives them thirty percent of the profits, his troubles will go away. The leader of this organization is some high city official. Michael is trying to get things organized and get rid of the corruption. He said that most people accept it because it's been there for years. I'm worried about this. Michael could get himself hurt or killed."

"I've heard that there is plenty of corruption in that city," said the Judge. "It's that way in a lot of big cities. Political machines run things. I know a Judge in Boston. I'll see what he knows about the corruption and who he thinks the head man might be. Let's just hope he's not involved too. I'll send him a telegram today and I'll get with you when I get a response."

"I appreciate that Judge," said Sean. "Now I'll get out of yer way." They shook hands and Sean left. Judge Sharpton sent the following telegram to a Judge in Boston.

Federal Judge Ralph Compton
Federal Court House
Boston

Ralph<<stop>>can you tell me about corruption in your city<<stop>>former deputy of mine now a pub owner having trouble with local police<<stop>>organization trying to extort money from him<<stop>>protection rackets<<stop>>

Federal Judge Robert Sharpton
Federal Court House
St. Louis

Robert received a reply two hours later. It went as follows.

Federal Judge Robert Sharpton
Federal Court House

St. Louis

Robert<<stop>>corruption rampant in Boston<<stop>> organizations have very good lawyers and have not been able to get convictions<<stop>>councilman in south Boston is one leader we have not been able to convict<<stop>>suspected of arson extortion and murder <<stop>>name is Tom Flannery<<stop>>have heard that Chief of Police is corrupt but no proof<<stop>>hope changes happen next election

Ralph Compton

As soon as Robert read the telegram, he headed to "The Palace." He figured Sean would be there. Sean was there and he went to the Judge when he saw him entering the place.

"I've heard back from a colleague of mine," said Robert. "I'm afraid for Michael too." Sean took the telegram and read it."

"I'll be goin' ta Boston if somethin' happens," said Sean.

"You're a Federal Marshal Sean," said Robert. "You can go anywhere in these United States or the territories. I wouldn't let anyone know I was coming if I were you. I wouldn't even tell Michael. If you sent a telegram, it might get read before it got to him."

"Do you think the telegrams sent back and forth by you and that Judge in Boston could have been read by other people?" asked Sean.

"They could have," answered Robert. "Two judges talking back and forth about corruption is nothing new. Getting proof would be something new. Sending a new person to investigate

would be something new. Organizations like this are very confident in their ability to keep operating. They exist by intimidation,
fear, murder, and whatever it takes. There are never any witnesses to their crimes, at least any who would testify."

"Well you know that if somethin' happens to Michael and I go
to Boston, some people are gonna die," said Sean.

"I know you will do whatever is necessary for justice to be
done," said Robert. "When you are surrounded by corruption,
sometimes extreme measures are needed. Let's hope things will
be all right for Michael."

Sean thanked Robert and went home to tell Maggie about his
talk with the Judge. She was sitting out back with Jeb. Sean gave
her a kiss and sat down beside her. He gave Jeb a good pet. "Well
darlin', Robert says that Boston is full of corruption," started
Sean. "He sent a telegram to another Judge that he knows. That
Judge told him that the corruption was very organized and they
have not been able to convict any of them. One of their council-
men is suspected of arson, extortion, and murder, but they have
not been able to convict him. There is never anyone who can or
will testify."

"Well darlin', if you end up going to Boston, it's sounds to me
like you better get things cleaned up," said Maggie.

"I will darlin'," said Sean. "If anything happens to Michael,
some people are gonna bleed."

"What did the Judge say about you going to Boston?" asked
Maggie.

"He said he knew that I would do whatever is necessary so
justice is done," said Sean.

"Maybe if you do go to Boston, you could get Alan to help you," said Maggie. "He might be familiar with Boston. I know he's been all over the country."

"I'm sure he would be a big help," said Sean.

~~~~

Alan Cooper had been on assignment in Boston. His assignment was over now and he was looking forward to going home to Elizabeth. Alan went back to his hotel. He would spend the night and then catch a train back home in the morning. He had just finished his dinner at the hotel and was reading a newspaper when something on the second page caught his eye. There had been a fire on the south side. Three buildings had burned. One of them was a pub. The name of the pub was "Betty and Michael's Pub." There were two deaths caused by the fire. The remains of Betty and Michael O'Connor were found in the ashes of the pub. The cause of the fire is unknown. The remains were taken to the morgue.

Alan almost cried after he read the paper. He hadn't known Michael all that long, but he considered him a good friend. More importantly, Michael was Sean's best friend and he knew that Sean would want things taken care of. The next day, instead of leaving, Alan went to the morgue to take care of things. He also wanted to make sure that the remains were of Betty and Michael. When Alan arrived at the morgue, he told the attendant he was the victim's brother and wanted to spend some time alone with him. The attendant left Alan alone.

Alan had been an investigator for a long time and he knew what to look for at a crime scene. The first thing he did was make sure it was Michael's remains. The left leg was missing just below the knee and the body frame was big. This was Michael. Alan examined the skeleton as best he could. Some bones were missing or badly damaged, but the skulls of Michael and Betty were still intact. Alan examined the front of Michael's skull and found no evidence of anything except being burned. Then he turned the skull to one side. When he turned the skull it disconnected from the spinal column. Alan examined the back of the skull. There was a small hole at the base of the skull. Then Alan examined Betty's skull. There was a small hole at the base of her skull too. Michael and Betty had been executed. A small caliber gun was used. They were shot and then someone started the fire.

Nothing had been mentioned in the paper about foul play. The bodies were probably not examined. It was just assumed that they were lost in the fire. Alan said nothing about his discovery to the attendant. He told him that arrangements would be made and the remains would be picked up later that day. Alan would also have Betty and Michael buried and headstones would be placed.

Alan had all of this arranged and then went to a telegraph office. He knew Sean would want to know as soon as possible. He sent the following telegram.

Sean O'Rourke
The Palace
St. Louis

Sean<<stop>>Have been on assignment in Boston <<stop>>Betty and Michael dead<<stop>>fire<<stop>>

Have made arrangements<<stop>>take Maggie and meet
me in Cincinnati<<stop>>will explain

Alan

Alan also sent another telegram to Elizabeth telling her that
he would be headed home and that Maggie and Sean would be
visiting. He didn't explain anything in the telegram.

Sean was at the saloon when the telegram arrived. He sat
down and cried for a good while. Susie saw him and went over to
see what was happening. "Betty and Michael are dead," cried Sean.
"There was a fire. Maggie'n me'll be headed east." Sean was still
sobbing as he headed home. Susie started crying too.

Maggie started crying uncontrollably when Sean gave her the
news. They both cried together for a good while. Maggie finally
spoke. "Why would Alan want us to meet him in Cincinnati?"
asked Maggie. "I don't understand."

"I'm guessing he knows somethin' and he couldn't put it in
the telegram," said Sean. "We figured Michael would have some
trouble but we never figured they'd end up dead. Get some things
rounded up. We'll be going to Cincinnati. Then I'll be going to
Boston. If Betty and Michael was murdered, they'll be some people dyin'. Take plenty of money and clothes. We might be gone a
while."

Sean got started packing. He would take two pistols with him.
He would be wearing his shoulder holster. Sean kept the bowie
knife that the undertaker had cut out of an outlaw's skull. It was
the one that Bo Billings carried and Jesse Strong had shoved it
into Bo's skull. Jon always kept it razor sharp and it was still that
way. Sean made some straps so he could wear it under his jacket

without being seen. He also packed his Winchester and a sawed off double barreled ten gauge. Plenty of ammunition was packed.

There was a train headed east the next day at ten o'clock. Dan Taylor came over with a carriage and took them and all their luggage to the train station. On the way there, Sean stopped at the Federal Court House and let the Judge know where he was going. The Judge was in court so Sean left a note with the Clerk.

~~~~

It took longer than expected for them to get to Cincinnati. There were a lot of train changes and delays. When they arrived in Cincinnati, They hired a carriage to take them to Elizabeth's house. Maggie and Sean were amazed when they arrived. Elizabeth's house was what some folks considered a mansion. It was big and beautiful. Elizabeth greeted them at the door. Alan had not arrived yet. "Your place is just beautiful," said Maggie. "Words cannot describe it."

"Bill and I bought this place after we had been married five years," said Elizabeth. "We hoped it would be full of children, but we weren't blessed with any."

"I hope you don't mind Jeb bein' here," said Sean. "I figured he should be here with you while Alan and I go to Boston. I do figure we'll be going."

"Jeb is welcome here," said Elizabeth. "As far as you going to Boston, I don't really know much about what happened other than Betty and Michael were killed in a fire. Alan didn't explain anything at all."

"Well from what we understand, there's a lot of corruption over there," said Sean. "Alan probably thought it best not to say

too much in the telegram. You never know who you can trust. We
had a telegrapher once in Kansas City who was on some crook's
payroll. We got rid of him and the crooks. So Elizabeth, how do
you like being married to a Pinkerton?"

"I love Alan with all my heart and soul," said Elizabeth. "I
knew what he was when I married him. I accept it. Alan is kind of
like you Sean. He doesn't have to be a Pinkerton, but he's very
good at it and he likes it. Alan owns property in Washington D.C.
and he inherited a lot of money. He would never have to work
again if he didn't want to."

"That's sounds familiar, doesn't it?" said Maggie.

"Yes darlin', it does," said Sean. "Now why don't we talk about
other things or maybe you ladies can have some girl talk. I'll take
Jeb out back and maybe have a look around the neighborhood."

"There's some Irish whiskey in that decanter on the living
room table," said Elizabeth. "Glasses too. Help yourself."

"Thanks, don't mind if I do," said Sean. Sean poured himself a
drink and he and Jeb went out back. Sean could tell that Jeb
needed to do his necessaries. "Well Jeb, we're in the big city now.
Spose we'll hafta find a respectable place for you ta go." The back
yard was huge and there were plenty of big trees. Sean took Jeb to
the trees farthest from the house and told Jeb to get it done. After Jeb was done, Sean and Jeb walked around the yard and just
looked around. It was very quiet. Sometimes he could hear the
sound of a carriage going down the street. The street wasn't
paved, but it was brick. The sound of the horse hooves hitting the
bricks seemed to travel a good ways. Then he heard some small
children playing. They were in the back yard next door. Then it
got quiet. Sean spotted them and could see them whispering to
each other. They were looking at Sean and Jeb. "Come on over

and meet Jeb," Sean said to them. The children were two boys, probably around 6 or 7 years old. The boys were hesitant to come over. "It's all right boys," said Sean. "Ole Jeb won't hurt ya. He likes folks that like him. Come on over and say hi." The two boys came over very slowly. When Jeb sat down, he was taller than the boys. They were just amazed.

"Howdy boys. I'm Sean and this is Jeb," said Sean. "What's your names?"

"I'm Scotty and this is my brother Bobby," said Scotty. "Is Jeb really a dog? We never seen a dog this big."

"Yep, Jeb's a dog," answered Sean. "Don't know what kinda dog he is, but he sure is big. He's a good cow dog."

"What do you mean cow dog?" asked Bobby.

"Well have you boys heard a cowboys?" asked Sean.

"I think so," answered Scotty.

"Well cow dogs'r used ta help move cows around," said Sean. "Ya see boys, cows don't always wanna go where ya want'em to. That's where a cowboy and his horse comes in or a cow dog."

"We never seen you here before Sean," said Scotty. "Are you visiting?"

"Yes, my wife Maggie and I are visiting Elizabeth and Alan for a while," answered Sean.

"So if you're gonna be a here for a while, maybe we can play with Jeb sometime," said Bobby.

"All right by me, but you better ask your folks first," said Sean. "They need ta know that just cause Jeb is big, he's not a mean dog. He won't hurt nobody unless they're tryin' ta hurt him or me'n Maggie'r our friends."

"Can we bring our momma over right now and have her meet Jeb?" asked Scotty.

"Sure, go git her," said Sean. The two boys ran over to their house. About five minutes later, they came back practically dragging their mother.

"I hope my boys haven't been bothering you sir," said the woman. "I'm Mrs. Marsha MacDonald. Pleased to meet you."

"Sean O'Rourke ma'am, and the pleasure's mine," said Sean. "The boys been admiring ole Jeb here."

"I can see why," said Marsha. "I've never seen a dog like this one. What kind of dog is he?"

"Don't know about any breed," answered Sean. "He was being used as a cow dog when I got him."

"I can see how a dog that big could move cows around," said Marsha. "Now you said your name was Sean O'Rourke, didn't you?"

"Yes I did ma'am," answered Sean.

"I've heard of you," said Marsha. "My husband talks about you all the time. He's the Chief of Police here. Will you be here long? I know he'll want to meet you."

"Well Marsha, I'd be honored to meet your husband," said Sean. "But I need a favor from the both of you. Please don't spread it around that I'm here. If you've heard of me, you should know that trouble follows me around at times. Do you understand Marsha?"

"I do," answered Marsha. "I've been a cop's wife for a good while. We've had our share of trouble."

"So can the boys play with Jeb?" asked Sean.

"Sure, as long as Jeb don't mind," said Marsha. Jeb went over and sat down next to Marsha. He looked up at her like he was asking to be petted. Marsha petted him and then the boys were all over him. One of them got on Jeb's back and rode him around like a horse. Jeb even rared up for him. The boy came off, but came off laughing. "I see they'll get along fine," said Marsha. "Steven will be home this evening," said Marsha. "May I bring him over to meet you."

"Sure, and it was nice meetin' you Marsha," said Sean. "Believe I'll let Jeb and the boys play a while. I'm goin' in and see what the ladies are up to. Jeb, take care a them boys."

The women were sitting on a sofa in the living room talking when Sean went back inside. "Made me some new friends," said Sean as he entered the living room. "Ole Jeb's got some new playmates too."

"That'd be Scotty and Bobby," said Elizabeth. "They're good boys. Alan plays with them sometimes when he's home.

"I met Marsha too," said Sean. "She knew who I was and asked if she could bring her husband over to meet me. I said it was all right."

"Steven's a good man," said Elizabeth. "Some think he's young for a Chief of Police, but he does a good job and the city likes him."

"Maybe he'll have some advice for what I might have to do," said Sean.

"I'm sure he will," said Elizabeth. "Now we've been talking all this time and I haven't even shown you to your room. Let's do that and get you settled." Elizabeth showed them to their room and let them get settled in. Sean didn't unpack much. He knew he would be going to Boston. They had just gotten settled and were coming downstairs when Alan arrived. They were halfway down the stairs when the door opened and Alan and Elizabeth wrapped themselves together. Maggie and Sean stopped on the stairs and let them have a good hello. After about five minutes, Maggie and

Sean came down the stairs. Alan went to them. He gave Maggie a hug and a kiss and then gave Sean a good handshake.

"Let's sit down and have a drink while I tell you what I found out," said Alan. Elizabeth got Alan and Sean some whiskey and then got Maggie and herself some tea. "Well, first off, I'm sorry I couldn't tell you this in the telegram, but Betty and Michael were murdered," started Alan. "I didn't say anything because I wasn't sure who could be trusted."

"How do you know for sure they were murdered?" asked Maggie.

"Because I examined the remains at the morgue," answered Alan. "There were bullet holes in the back of their heads. The bodies were not examined by anyone. It was just assumed that they were lost in the fire."

"So you never let anyone know that they was murdered?" inquired Sean.

"No, as I said, I wasn't sure who could be trusted," said Alan. "Two other properties were lost in the fire, but there were no other injuries."

"Don't they have a fire department there?" asked Sean. "Wouldn't them fireman know if the fire was intentional or not?

"We'll be finding that out when we get over there," answered Alan. "I know for a fact that there is a lot of corruption in Boston. We'll have to figure out who we can trust."

"You know that some men are gonna die, don't you Alan?" said Sean. "If you're not all right with this, I can go by myself."

"I have no problem with killing if we know for sure the ones killed are worth killing," said Alan. "I had no problem at the bank in Abilene and I'll have no problem in Boston."

"Steven will be coming over this evening," said Elizabeth. "He wants to meet Sean. Maybe he'll have some ideas for you on how to catch the killers."

"He might," said Alan. "I'm sure there's been problems here with the same type of trouble. Steven didn't get to be Chief of Police for being stupid. I'd say he'll be some help. Don't worry Sean. We'll get the killers and probably some of their friends too. It'll be a lot different than it is over in Kansas. We're always out-numbered, but this time we'll be too outnumbered to count."

"Well, if ya cut the head off a snake, the snake dies," said Sean. "They'll just be a lot more snakes this time. I figure for every snake we kill, there'll be a couple wantin' ta take his place. We'll git'm. We'll git'm all."

"I'd like to spend tomorrow with Elizabeth," said Alan. "We can leave for Boston the day after tomorrow if that's all right with you Sean. I also need to let my boss know what I'm doing."

"Day after tomorrow'll be fine," said Sean. "That'll give them killers another day to think they got away with it. And you can tell your boss I hired you to help me investigate a murder. Now before I forget, I'll be givin' you some money. It's for takin' care of Betty and Michael. What do I owe you for that?"

"It wasn't much," said Alan. "I just had them put the remains in a medium priced casket and bury them. I had their names put on the headstones with the date of their deaths, and I told them that you might be getting with them to carve more things on it. All told, I only spent $100. That was for the plots, the caskets and burying, and the headstones."

"Well me'n Maggie sincerely thank you for all that," said Sean. "It was good that you were in Boston. If it weren't for you, we would never have known that they had been murdered. That is, unless we dug them up and had them examined." Sean handed Alan $150.

"That's more than enough," said Alan.

"Well you can buy me a drink while we're in Boston," said Sean. "Now if you'll excuse me for a minute, I'm goin' out back and make sure Jeb and them boys is still gittin' along." When Sean went outside, he saw Jeb and the boys laying in the shade under a tree. The two boys had their heads on Jeb and were using him for a pillow. They were all sound asleep. Jeb must have sensed that he was being watched. He raised his head up for a moment and looked at Sean. "Go on back ta sleep Jeb," said Sean. "I bet you'n them boys wore yerselves out. Nothin' wrong with a nap." Jeb put his head back down but didn't close his eyes. Sean was heading back into the house when he heard Marsha yelling for the boys to come back home. The boys didn't stir. Sean walked over to them. "Best wake up boys," said Sean. "Yer Ma's callin' ya. Probly bout suppertime." The two boys sat up and yawned a little. Then they got up and headed home.

"Can Jeb play again tomorrow?" asked Scotty.

"Sure, as long as yer Ma don't mind," said Sean. When Sean and Jeb went back inside, Elizabeth and Maggie were in the kitchen working on dinner. Alan had fallen asleep on a sofa. Sean didn't bother him.

They had just finished dinner when Steven showed up. He was very excited about meeting Sean. Alan had answered the door when Steven had knocked. Steven gave Alan a short greeting and then went looking for Sean. "Where is Mr. O'Rourke?" said Steven. "I've got to meet Mr. O'Rourke." Sean heard Steven and left the dining room to go meet him.

"Hello, I'm Sean O'Rourke and you must be Steven MacDonald," said Sean as they shook hands.

"Yes I'm Steven, and I must tell you that it's a great honor meeting you," said Steven. "I've heard so much about you. It sure is something for us to get a visit from a real lawman from out west. Listen to me. I sound like a little kid."

"Well it's not every day I get to meet the Chief of Police of a big city," said Sean. "And it wasn't that many years ago that Cincinnati was the west."

"That's true," said Steven. "So what brings you to our fair city?"

"A friend of ours was murdered in Boston," answered Sean. "Me'n Alan're goin' over there and take care a business."

"Aren't the police doing that?" asked Steven.

"The police may be on the take," said Alan. "There was a fire and our friends' remains were found in the ashes. The remains were taken to the morgue without being examined. I examined them and discovered that they had been executed. There were small bullet holes in the backs of their skulls."

"So when you discovered this, you did not tell anyone?" asked Steven.

"No, I didn't. I wasn't sure who I could trust," said Alan.

"We got a letter from them sometime before they was killed," said Sean. "Michael said the cops rousted his customers if he didn't give them free drinks. There was also some protection racket. They raised the price of his liquor license and then his shipment got stolen. Then some outfit said if he'd give them a big chunk a his profits, his troubles'd go away. The boss a this outfit was some political official. Michael said he was tryin' ta git folks organized to fight the corruption. They killed'm for it."

"Sounds like you'll have your hands full Sean," said Steven. "I know about corruption in city government. We've had trouble here too. Those people are highly organized and hard to get rid of, but it can be done. It just takes time."

"Well how would you recommend that we start?" asked Alan.

"The first thing I'd do is find out how corrupt the police are, and how far up the ladder it goes," started Steven. "The cops that I have known that were corrupt were not the brains behind an outfit. They usually take bribes to look the other way on things. Some beat cops think it's their right to get a free meal or a free drink at times and their supervisors look the other way when they do. I assure you, they don't do that here. The last cop in this town that took a bribe is in prison for 5 years. So anyway, I'd start with the police. I'd squeeze anyone I thought I could squeeze. You might get some names that way. If there is some protection racket, maybe you could grab one of the collectors and squeeze him. Find out if the newspapers are honest. Maybe if they were honest, you could get them to print some story about a certain person you think is dishonest and stir things up. Sometimes if you stir things up, mistakes get made. You just need to remember that these type of people are highly organized and they have eyes everywhere. Once they know you're there and what you're doing, they'll come after you. They'll shoot you in broad daylight in a crowd and not think a thing about it. They won't play fair so you can't either."

"I got a name from a Federal Judge in Boston," said Sean. "There's a Councilman who is suspected of a lot of crimes, including murder, and they have never been able to get him convicted. Witnesses are hard to come by."

"Well I'd still check out the police first," said Steven. "But since you have a name from a reliable source, I'd go after that person. Find out who works for him and squeeze them if you can. Maybe he's not the top boss. You men got your work cut out for you. Just don't give up. Try something and if that doesn't work, try something else. Sean, if what they say about you and your reputation is only half true, you'll get the job done. I know you will. Tell you what. Tomorrow, I'll send a telegram to the Chief of Police in Boston and ask him if there was an examination of the remains that were found in the fire. I'll tell him the deceased were friends of mine. His answer might let us know if he can be trusted or not."

"That would be a big help," said Alan. "Now how about an after dinner drink or two?"

"Sounds good," said Steven. "I'm hoping that Sean won't mind if I ask him about his life out west."

"I won't mind Steven," said Sean. "Alan, I bet you'd like to be alone with Elizabeth for a spell since you've been gone. Why don't you go be with her. I imagine Maggie's tired and would like to lie down. I'll see Maggie to bed and then I'll come back and talk with Steven.

Maggie was already asleep in their bed when Sean went for her. Sean went back downstairs to talk with Steven. "Maggie's with child," said Sean. "She's already asleep. I reckon carryin' a child around inside ya can wear ya out pretty good."

"Yes it can," said Steven. "Marsha was worn out a good bit of the time with our first boy. Wasn't so bad on the second one. She knew what to expect on it. So Sean, I want to hear all about things out there if you don't mind."

"We got plenty of whiskey so I don't mind," said Sean. They talked well into the night. Finally around midnight, Steven decided he better get home.

CHAPTER THREE

S teven sent a telegram to the Police Chief in Boston first thing
the next morning. He received a reply that afternoon. As soon
as he was off duty, he rushed home to show Alan and Sean the
telegram. The telegram went as follows.

Chief MacDonald
Cincinnati

A thorough examination of the bodies in question was
not done as foul play was not suspected<<stop>>bodies
were claimed by brother<<stop>>fire chief thought it
was odd that bodies were side by side as if someone laid
them there<<stop>>two other buildings were lost in
fire<<stop>>both were residential but all managed to es-
cape flames

Chief Munroe
Boston

"Sounds to me like the Chief is probably an honest man, but he didn't do what should have been done," said Alan after reading the telegram.

"That's what I think too," said Steven. "Any time there is a death, a thorough examination should be done on the deceased. Probably no one really wanted to examine burned and charred bodies."

"Well we'll find out if he's honest or not," said Sean. "We'll start at the bottom and work our way up. Steven, we thank you for your help. We'll be leavin' tomorrow mornin'. We'll see you again when we get back. If we need more advice while we're there, we'll send you a telegram."

"Glad I could be of some help," said Steven. "Now try to remember that Boston is not the wild west and you can't be having gunfights all over the place."

"There won't be any big gunfights unless someone else starts one," said Sean. "We'll take care a business on the quiet. I can do quiet when I hafta." They all shook hands and Steven went home.

~~~~

Sean and Alan left early the next morning. There were a lot of tears as they were leaving. "You get them Sean," said Maggie as the train pulled away. "You get them and you hurt them bad."

"I will darlin'," Sean yelled out the window of the passenger car. "Them sons a bitches'll never kill'r hurt anyone ever again."

When they arrived in Boston, Alan picked them out a hotel in south Boston. They got one room on the top floor. It was a corner room and had two beds. There was only one way to get to the room from the inside. Entry could only be gained from the outside if someone used a rope and dropped down from the roof or if they had a ladder that would reach four stories. When they checked in, Alan used his real name, but Sean checked in as Sean Thornton.

It was morning when they arrived at their hotel. After they had some breakfast at the restaurant in the hotel, they decided to take a carriage and ride around all over south Boston. This part of the city didn't look anything at all like Sean thought it should look. It reminded him of pictures of slums in London that he had seen in books. "How come it looks so dumpy?" Sean asked Alan.

"Probably because south Boston is where most of the Irish live," said Alan. "Most of them are poor and can't get decent jobs. A lot of places won't hire the Irish. They even put up signs that say "No Irish need apply.""

"What's that all about?" asked Sean. "Hell, I'm Irish. Does that make me different'r some kind a animal'r somethin'?"

"I don't understand it either," said Alan. "All I know is the Irish and the British aren't too fond of each other. Goes way back I guess. Don't know what that's got to do with anything in this country."

"I thought we kicked the British out some time back," said Sean. "I guess anytime someone's different, someone's gonna be scared of'em. Just like folks out west're scared a Indians. I guess some folks is scared a them Chinese too. Don't know why. I never heard of'em ever hurtin' anyone."

It wasn't long until they could see where there had been a fire. They had the driver of the carriage stop when they got next to the burned buildings. Sean and Alan got out of the carriage. "Driver, do you know anything about this fire?" Alan asked the driver.

"Just what I heard from other folks," answered the driver. "All I heard was that the owners of the pub were the only ones killed."

"Didn't that seem strange to you?" asked Sean. "There was folks in two other buildings and no one else got hurt at all."

"Yes, it does seem strange," said the driver. "But strange things can happen in a fire."

"Well you stay put for a spell," said Sean. "We're gonna have a look see around here. Don't worry, we'll get you paid. Ya might wanna get out of the middle of the street in case another wagon'r somethin' needs ta get by." The driver pulled the carriage to the side of the street and Alan and Sean started looking through the charred ruins of the pub. They had been looking at the ruins for around ten minutes when a beat cop approached them.

"All right you two, just what do you think you're doing there?" asked the cop.

"What does it look like we're doin'?" said Sean.

"Oh, so you're giving me some back talk are you?" said the cop. "Now get out of there before I run you in."

"I guess no one ever taught you any manners," said Sean. "First off, what is your name officer?"

"I'm Officer Clary," answered Clary. "Now who might you two be?"

"You got a first name Officer Clary?" asked Sean.

"Yes I do. It's Donavan," answered Officer Clary.

"Well Officer Donavan Clary, I'm Federal Marshal Sean O'Rourke and this fine gentleman is Detective Alan Cooper. He's a Pinkerton," said Sean. "Now Officer Clary, how many free drinks would you say that you were given at the pub here?"

"I don't know what you're talking about," answered Clary.

"Sure you do," replied Sean. "And how much free bread do you get from that bakery over there and how much free meat do you get from that butcher shop down the street."

"I do not help myself to free anything around here," answered Donavan. "I understand that others do, but I do not and never will. Did you say your name was Sean O'Rourke?"

"Yes I did," answered Sean. "And why don't you help yourself like others do?

"I wasn't raised that way," answered Donavan. "And I've heard of you. Everyone around here has heard of you," said Clary. "Why are you here in Boston?"

"So you say you've heard of me," said Sean. "That means you must know my reputation. If you know my reputation, then you know what I'm capable of. I'm gonna tell you somethin' and you will not breathe a word of it to anyone. If you do, bad things could happen. Now do you understand?"

"I believe I do," answered Clary. "Now why are you here?"

"Those two people who owned this pub were my best friends," said Sean. "Michael O'Connor was my deputy and Betty was his wife. They moved here to get away from all the blood and violence out west. They didn't die in the fire. They were executed. Someone shot them in the back of the head and then set the place on fire."

"How do you know they were shot?" asked Clary. "Everyone just said they were lost in the fire."

"I went to the morgue and examined the remains myself," said Alan. "There were bullet holes in the back of their skulls. The remains were not examined by anyone after the fire. Either the police or the fire department didn't bother with it."

"Any time there is a death, it is the responsibility of the police to find out the cause of death," said Clary. "If you want, I can find out who the officer was that investigated things."

"That would be nice, but if you start asking questions, you could end up dead too," said Alan. "Did you know that Michael O'Connor was trying to unite the people around here to fight the corruption?"

"I heard something about it," answered Donavan. "But no one said anything to me. Most people around here don't trust the police."

Alan kept looking through the ruins trying to see if he could find anything that would prove that the fire was intentionally started. As he was looking around, He noticed two men across the street watching them. He walked over to Sean and Donavan. "I think maybe we have some company," said Alan. "Those two fellas across the street have been looking at us pretty hard. Do you know them Donavan?"

"No, but new folks are coming here all the time," said Donavan. "Some of them are fresh off the boat."

"Well they seem pretty interested in us," said Alan. "Have you ever had to use that pistol you're wearing?"

"No, I've never had to draw my revolver, but I've had to use my billy," answered Donavan. "More times than I care to say."

"Well Donavan, I have an idea," said Alan. "I want you to take off walking your beat just like you always do. Sean and I will go the opposite direction you go. Maybe them two gentlemen will follow you. If they do, Sean and I will be following them. Don't let yourself get into a spot where you can be jumped. Do you understand Donavan?"

"I do," answered Donavan. "I'll be careful."

Officer Donavan was twenty five years old. He came to America in late 1860 after his parents died in Ireland. Donavan's father was a blacksmith and had taught Donavan the trade. When his parents died, he decided he would seek his fame and fortune in America. After he had been in America for a short while, he found out that it wasn't the land of milk and honey. The Irish were treated like dirt in a lot of places. Donavan was out looking for work one day when he saw a crowd gathering in an alley behind a pub. He went back to investigate. There was a bare knuckle fight going on. Two men were beating the hell out of each other and bets were being placed by the audience. When the fight was over, the winner yelled out that he would take on any challenger. Donavan sized the man up. He was maybe five feet ten inches and weighed maybe two hundred pounds. His arms looked fairly muscular, but he had the start of a big belly. Donavan was six foot one and weighed one hundred and eighty five pounds. He was strong as an ox. Donavan had been in a few fights as he was growing up and had always won, so he decided he would take on the winner. What's the worst that could happen? He could get knocked out and lose and not make any money. He didn't have any money anyway.

"What do I get if I win?" yelled Donavan as he walked over to the make shift ring.

"Twenty dollars," yelled out a man who was standing next to the winner of the fight. He had a bunch of bills in both hands. "I'm Paddy Cohan. And who might you be young man?"

"Timothy O'Clary," answered Donavan. He did not want to give his real name. "Twenty dollars huh. How much do you get if I win?"

"Depends on the betting. You got any money to bet on yourself?" asked Paddy.

"No, I'm flat broke," answered Donavan.

"Well then twenty dollars is a lot of money to you isn't it?" said Paddy.

"I guess so," said Donavan. "Let's get started." Donavan took off his shirt and waited for the betting to stop. When the betting was over, the fight started.

"Marcus of Queensbury Rules," yelled Paddy.

The two men squared off and sized each other up. The other man threw the first punch. It was a right aimed at Donavan's jaw. Donavan moved to his left a little and the punch missed. The man threw the punch so hard that he was a little off balance when he missed. Before the man had pulled his right arm back, Donavan hit him in the ribs with a left hook. It buckled the man a little. Before the man could get straightened back up, Donavan caught him with a right in the gut. This punch buckled the man over some more. Donavan now hit the man with a right uppercut. The man went down and was flat on his back. To everyone's surprise, the man got right back up. He looked at Donavan and smiled. "Is that all you got boy?" he said.

"Come on over and find out," said Donavan. The two men sized each other up again. The man charged right at Donavan. Donavan tried to get away from him, but the man wrapped his arms around Donavan and held on. Then he smiled at Donavan and gave him a head butt. There was a big gash above Donavan's right eye and blood was flowing. The man still had ahold of Donavan. Donavan was maybe three inches taller than his opponent. "So that's how it's going to be," said Donavan. Donavan opened his mouth and bit down hard on the man's skull just below his hairline. The man let out a scream and let go of Donavan. As the man was backing away, Donavan threw a right and caught him right on the chin. Before the man hit the ground, Donavan caught him with a left to the jaw. The man hit the ground and didn't move. The crowd was silent. "I'll have my money now," Donavan said to Paddy.

"I don't know," said Paddy. "You bit the man."

"Look at my forehead. What did he do to me?" yelled Donavan. "Now pay up or you'll get the same. Reluctantly, Paddy gave Donavan his money. Just as Donavan put the money in a pocket, someone blew a whistle.

"Beat it. It's the coppers," someone yelled.

"Follow me," Paddy yelled to Donavan. They took off running down the alley. After a few blocks, they ducked into the back of some residential building. They made their way up to a third floor and then looked out a window into the alley. A lone cop was walking down the alley with his billy in his right hand. Then Paddy and Donavan went to the front of the building and looked out a front window. There were two more policemen out front. The cops looked around a bit, and then moved on.

"What was that all about?" asked Donavan.

"These fights are not legal in the city," said Paddy. "I don't think the law really cares much. Every once in a while, they show up and act like they're after us, but they never catch anyone. I think they put on a show for the local upstanding citizens. So young Timothy O'Clary, how would you like to be partners with me? I'll set up the fights and handle the betting. We'll split fifty fity."

"Doesn't seem quite fair," said Donavan. "I do the all the fighting and you get half."

"Well young Timothy, try and get started in this racket by yourself and see how far you get," said Paddy.

"All right, fifty fifty," said Donavan. "But I'll quit when I'm good and ready. If I ever find out that you're cheating me, I'll break both your legs."

"Look at this face," said Paddy as he grinned at Donavan. "This is the most honest face you've ever seen."

"Sure, and I'm Lord Nelson too," said Donavan.

~~~~

Paddy did a good job setting up fights. When they first started, they were having a fight almost every week. Donavan never lost a fight. He got hit some, but he never lost. Word must have gotten around that this new man was tough and couldn't be beaten because the challengers were becoming few and far between. Donavan had made some decent money and he was living in a boarding house. He became good friends with the owners and even helped them around the place.

When the war started, Donavan thought it was his duty to go. He fought in fifteen engagements during the war and was never seriously wounded. He received several decorations too. During the last year of the war, he was promoted to 1st Sergeant. He was probably the youngest 1st Sergeant in the whole Union Army. When the war ended, Donavan considered staying in the Army but decided against it. He didn't want to go down south for the Reconstruction as it was called and he didn't want to go out west and fight Indians. He went back home to Boston.

The first few months back home, Donavan couldn't find work and almost went back to fighting. One day he heard that the city was hiring several more policemen and he applied. He was hired immediately. Donavan enjoyed being a policeman. He felt like he was respected by his fellow citizens. After a couple of months on the job, he discovered that this was not so. Some of his fellow officers were abusing their positions. They were taking free things from the local shops. Some of them considered it their right. When Donavan first complained about this to his immediate supervisor, it fell on deaf ears. Donavan didn't pursue it any farther. He knew he was an honest cop and that was good enough for him.

He'd been on the job for six months when he met a beautiful young woman one day while walking his beat. He courted her and they were married a few months later. Her name was Mary Kate Dunnigan. Donavan had saved all of his army pay and still had money from his fighting days. They bought a little house and set up housekeep.

Officer Clary had gone about two blocks now and he knew that the two men were following him. Sean and Alan were laying back and following the two men. Donavan continued on until he was out of the downtown area and into a residential area. He stopped now and acted like he was tying a shoe. He stood back up and let the two men catch up to him. When they were about fifteen feet from him, Donavan told them to stop. "All right you two, just what are you doing following me around?" asked Donavan.

"What makes you think we were following you around Officer Clary?" asked one of the men.

"So you know my name do you. Don't play games with me," said Donavan. "Answer the question and give me some names."

"Just call us Victor and Sam. I'm Victor. We were wondering who those two gentlemen were that you were talking to back where the fire was," said Victor. "And what did they want."

"That would be none of your business," said Donavan. "Now move on."

"Now we're trying to be friendly," said Victor. "We can do this the easy way or the hard way." Victor pulled back his jacket exposing a revolver. "Pretty little wife you have there Officer Clary."

The words had just left Victor's mouth when Donavan's billy struck him on the left side of his head. Victor slumped to the ground. Sam had been in disbelief but before Victor was all the way on the ground, he had a pistol in his right hand and was bringing it up to fire at Donavan. Before the pistol was up to fire, Donavan swung his billy again. He swung it downward and it came down hard on Sam's right wrist. The pistol was dropped. Donavan dropped his billy and proceeded to beat on Sam. Sam's face was a bloody mess when Sean and Alan came running to stop him. "Don't beat him to death," yelled Sean. "We need to question him."

"I'll be locking these two up for attempted assault of a police officer," said Donavan.

"We'll take them off your hands," said Alan. "If they go to jail, you'll never get anything out of them and some slick lawyer might get them off anyway."

"So what will you do with them?" asked Donavan.

"It's best you don't know," answered Sean. "If you don't know, you won't be able to tell under oath if you're asked."

"I'm worried about my wife," said Donavan. "They know I have a wife and probably where I live."

"It could get ugly around here," said Sean. "If I were you, I'd make sure my wife could shoot and get her a gun. If that's out of the question, maybe she should go stay with some friends or relatives for a while. Trouble is, this bunch has eyes everywhere and even if she goes somewhere else, they could find her sooner of later. If Jeb was here he could help out."

"Who's Jeb?" asked Donavan.

"Jeb's my dog," answered Sean. "He's the biggest dog I ever did see and he can rip out a man's throat quicker than a wolf can. You got a dog or do you know anyone's that's got a dog?"

"No, but I know where I can get a dog," said Donavan. "There's always a lot of stray dogs down by the dump. I bet I could make friends with one real easy."

"I'd say you could," said Alan. "Some of them dogs would be pretty wild, but maybe you could go down there with some food. If you fed one and treated him nice, you might have a friend for life. Don't get yourself bit. Them dogs could have rabies. Stay away from any you see acting funny or slobbering. Make sure you take your pistol with you. Now you go ahead and finish your beat. We'll take care of these two."

Donavan started back on his beat. He was a little worried that someone had witnessed the altercation, but he looked around and didn't see anyone watching. Sean stayed with Victor and Sam and Alan went back and got the carriage. The driver saw the two men out cold on the ground. "What happened to them two?" he asked.

"Can't hold their liquor," said Sean. Alan and Sean loaded the two men into the carriage and then they got in. "Back to the hotel," said Sean. "Go down the alleys."

The driver did as instructed. Alan was looking for vacant buildings as they headed back to the hotel. None were spotted.

Victor and Sam were regaining consciousness as they neared the hotel. The first thing Victor saw when he opened his eyes was Sean's .44 pointed at him. "No need for words," said Sean. Victor remained silent. When Sam came to, he saw Alan's revolver pointed at him. The carriage stopped at the hotel. Sean paid the driver and they went through a backdoor. "You two open your mouth at all and I'll put a bullet through your heads," said Sean. They went to their room without going past the front desk. When they got to their room, Sean got some rope. Sam and Victor were tied and gagged. Their hands were tied behind their back and their legs were tied together. Then their feet were tied to their hands. They weren't going anywhere. "Now I've got some questions for you two," said Sean. "If you don't give us the answers we want, we'll kill you. Now, first question, who killed Michael and Betty O'Connor? If you didn't know their names, they were the pub owners that were supposedly killed in the fire. Second question, who ordered the killing? And last, who's your boss?" Now we're gonna go get something ta eat. We'll get started when we get back."

Sean and Alan went downstairs to the restaurant in the hotel and had a meal. They talked some as they ate. "See if you can find an easy way onto the roof," Sean said to Alan. "We might see if one a them boys can fly."

"What do you think we should do tomorrow if we don't get anything out of them two?" asked Alan.

"I think we should go to the downtown shops and see if we can get anyone to tell us anything," said Sean. "Maybe there'll be someone that's not afraid ta speak up. Or we can just lay back and see if anyone comes lookin' fer these two."

~~~~

When Donavan finished his beat, he went to the butcher shop and got some meat scraps. Then he went to the dump. As he neared the dump, he could see stray dogs all over the place. When he got closer, the dogs scattered and hid. Donavan knelt down and pulled out some of the meat scraps. He let out a whistle and waited. A big mongrel looking dog came out of hiding. It looked like a cross between a coon hound and a collie. The dog slowly moved toward Donavan and the meat scraps. "Come on dog, come on," said Donavan. When the dog got about fifteen feet from Donavan, it started growling and bared it's teeth. "It's all right dog. It's all right. I got something for you," said Donavan. The dog stood it's ground and kept growling. Donavan got up and backed up a few feet. The dog went to the meat scraps and wolfed them down. Donavan put some more scraps on the ground and backed a few more feet away. The dog went to the scraps and ate them quickly. Then it sat down and looked at Donavan. Donavan knelt down again and held out his hand. "Come on dog, come on. I won't hurt you. Come on," said Donavan. The dog got up and inched it's way over to Donavan. It stopped a foot short of his hand and growled again. "No need for that," said Donavan as he produced another meat scrap. This time he held it in his hand and held it out for the dog. The dog inched up to his hand and took the meat. Then it sat down again. Donavan stayed there and extended his hand. This time the dog went to his hand and sniffed it. Then he licked it all over. Donavan could tell now that the dog was a male and had been someone's pet at one time or another. The fur around it's neck was worn some where there had been a collar or a rope around it. Donavan talked to the dog as he began petting it on the head. The dog wanted more petting and went right up against him. Donavan petted him all over. "You want to go with me boy?" said Donavan. "Come on, let's go." Donavan got up and started walking. The dog went right with him. Donavan talked as they walked. "I wonder what your name used to be. I better come up with a good name," said Donavan. "I know. We'll call you Boss. I bet you were the boss at the dump. What do you say? Is Boss all right?" The dog looked up at Donavan like he knew what had been said. They were about six blocks from home when Donavan could see a couple of rough looking men ahead of him on the sidewalk. They were blocking the sidewalk and it looked like they had no intention of moving as Alan and Boss got closer. As Donavan got closer, one of them spoke.

"And where do you think you're going with that mongrel dog?" said the man.

"Move out of the way," said Donavan. They were about ten feet apart now. Boss sat down beside Donavan.

"You flatfoots, you strut around like you're Lord of the Manor," said the man. The man moved toward Donavan like he was going to get in his face. When he was almost right in front of Donavan, Boss jumped up and knocked the man to the ground. He stood on the man baring his teeth and just daring him to move. The other man took off running.

"Call off your dog copper. Call off your dog," cried the man.

"What do you think Boss? Should we make him apologize?" said Donavan. Boss continued his growl. "Boss says you should apologize for calling him a mongrel."

"All right, all right, I'm sorry I said you was a mongrel," cried the man.

"Let the man up now Boss," said Donavan. Boss stopped his growl and got off the man. The man got up and gave Donavan a defiant look. When he did, Boss started his growl again. "I'd move on if I were you," said Donavan. "It appears Boss doesn't like you, and neither do I. Now git." The man decided it would be best if he moved on. He left without another word.

Donavan was a little later than usual coming home and Mary Kate was a little worried. She was sitting on the front porch waiting for Donavan. She was very surprised when Donavan came into sight and had Boss with him. When they got closer, Boss went right over to Mary Kate and made friends. "This is Boss," said Donavan and then he kissed her. "He decided he wanted to adopt us."

"Well that's fine," said Mary Kate. "But Boss will get himself a bath before he comes into the house."

"He is kind of ripe isn't he," said Donavan. "He's been hanging around the dump."

"Well take him around to the back," said Mary Kate. "He can sit on the porch while we have supper. He'll get a bath after supper."

While they were eating supper, Donavan told Mary Kate about all that had happened during the day and why he had gotten the dog. "So you really met the famous western lawman?" asked Mary Kate.

"That's who he says he is and I believe him," said Donavan. "That man who owned the pub that burned down was his deputy out west."

"So who were those two men you had the altercation with?" asked Mary Kate.

"I have no idea," said Donavan. "But they knew about you and hinted that they could hurt you. That's why Boss is here. And whenever I'm not here, I want you to keep my extra revolver close."

"So let me get this straight. The pub owners were actually murdered and Mr. O'Rourke came all the way from out west to find out who killed his former deputy," said Mary Kate. "So now if they were murdered, why aren't the police here investigating?"

"They are not investigating because everyone just assumed they were killed in the fire," said Donavan. "No foul play was suspected. The Pinkerton Detective with O'Rourke examined the remains at the morgue and discovered they had been shot in the back of the head."

"Well why didn't he go to the police?" asked Mary Kate.

"Because he wasn't sure who could be trusted," said Donavan.

"So you're saying that there might be some corrupt men in the police department," said Mary Kate.

"That's possible," said Donavan. "Someone didn't examine the victims. Whenever there is a death, it is the responsibility of the police to find the cause of death. So we don't know for sure if they didn't want the remains examined or if they just assumed they were lost in the fire."

Boss stayed right by the back door while they were eating. When Donavan and Mary Kate came out the back door with soap and water, Boss knew what was going to happen. He let out a few whines, but didn't try to run away. After a while it seemed like he was enjoying his bath. It took a lot of water to get him rinsed because of his thick and long coat. When they were finished, Boss stood there and shook. Donavan and Mary Kate were now as wet as he was. "Why don't we go for a stroll around the neighborhood this evening," said Donavan. "That'll help Boss dry out. Maybe I'll put a short rope on him and see how he handles it." Donavan found a short rope and placed it around Boss's neck. Boss didn't mind at all. When they took off walking, Boss went right along like he had done this before. It was almost completely dark when they got back home.

"So if Boss is going to be a house dog, how are we going to handle him doing his business?" asked Mary Kate.

"I don't know," answered Donavan. "This is my first dog."

"And where will he sleep?" asked Mary Kate.

"That's another good question," said Donavan. "I'll just take him out back right before we go to bed. We'll put a blanket down for him by the back door to sleep on and see how that works."

When they got up the next morning, Boss was sitting by the back door just waiting for someone to let him out. Mary Kate let him out. Boss went to the back of the yard, did his business, and came right back to the house. Boss sat on the floor right beside Donavan as he was eating his breakfast. He never made one move like he was going to grab something off the table. "I guess we better figure out how much to feed Boss," said Donavan as he was getting ready for work. "I'll see about getting scraps from the butcher shop. I'll be off now. Remember what I said. Keep my extra revolver close. Boss you take care of Mary Kate while I'm gone." Donavan gave Mary Kate a hug and kiss. Then he petted Boss on the head and was on his way.

CHAPTER FOUR

When Sean and Alan were done eating, Sean went back to their room and Alan went looking for an easy way to get on the roof. When Sean opened the door to the room he got a whiff of something nasty. "Whew, one a you boys shit yourself?" said Sean. "Damn, what the hell you been eatin'? That'd gag a maggot off a gut wagon." Alan returned in a few minutes.

"We can get up there pretty easy," said Alan. "I found some stairs. Just go down the hall and take the stairwell on the right. The steps go to the roof."

"That's great," said Sean. "Now I hope you boys been thinkin' bout them questions. I'm takin' one a you up on the roof and if I don't get some good answers, we'll see how well you can fly. Which one a you shit his pants?" Sean checked both men. "Well Victor, you'll be goin' upstairs. You already shit yourself. Alan, untie that other fella some so he can stand over by the window. I want him to be able to see ole Victor here tryin' ta fly if he don't answer them questions."

Alan untied the ropes that were tying Sam's feet to his hands. Sean completely untied Victor and Alan held his pistol on him while he was untying him. "Well Victor, are you goin' up peaceable like?" asked Sean, "Or do I hafta carry you."

"I'm not goin' nowhere with you," said Victor. "You haven't got the guts to kill a man."

"Have it your way," said Sean as he cracked him over the head with his pistol. "I'll be takin' Victor up on the roof now. Make sure ole Sam has a good view." Sean picked up Victor and threw him over his shoulder. As he was going down the hall, he passed a young couple.

"What's wrong with him?" asked the young woman.

"Can't hold his liquor," answered Sean.

Sean got on the roof and took Victor over to the corner that was above his and Alan's room. Victor was till unconscious. Sean sat him on the edge of the roof with his legs hanging down. Then Sean shook him some to wake him up. Victor regained consciousness. He looked down. "What in the hell," said Victor as he looked down. Sean was behind him with his hands on his back.

"Now Victor, let's go over them questions," said Sean. "Who killed Michael and Betty O'Connor?"

"I don't know. I don't know," screamed Victor. "It wasn't me. I couldn't tell you if I did know. They'd kill me."

"Seems you better decide on who you want to kill you," said Sean. "Now who ordered the killing?"

"I don't know. I don't know," Victor screamed again. "Maybe I can find out for you."

"Not good enough Victor," said Sean. "Now who's your boss?"

"I can't tell you. He'll kill—," He couldn't finish. Sean gave him a good shove and he went flying. Victor screamed all the way to the ground.

Sam still had the gag in his mouth. He tried to scream when he saw Victor come flying down but couldn't. Sean came back to the room now. "Well Sam, Victor can't fly very well," said Sean. Have you been thinkin' bout them questions?" Sam nodded his head yes. Sean left the gag in his mouth and looked out the window. It was almost completely dark now. Victor's flattened body was laying there on the sidewalk and no one had spotted it yet. "Huh, maybe no one'll spot him till daylight," said Sean. Then he went over to Sam and took the gag out of his mouth. "So Sam, ya got some answers for me?" asked Sean.

"I do," cried Sam. "But I only know the answer to one of the questions. I don't know who killed them folks and I don't know who ordered it. But my boss is a man they call Cutter. Don't know his real name. They call him Cutter cause he fancies a knife."

"What does Cutter do?" asked Sean.

"He's a collector," answered Sam. "He runs the protection racket and collects from all the businesses."

"When is he due to collect again?" asked Sean.

"He'll do some tomorrow and then finish up the next day," said Sam. "He collects once a month."

"So what is it that you do for Cutter?" asked Sean.

"We just keep our eyes and ears open and see what's going on around here," said Sam.

"Well Sam, do you want to live?" asked Sean.

"I do. I do," cried Sam.

"Well Sam, I suggest you get yourself out of Boston pretty damn quick," said Sean. "If we even see you around, we'll shoot you dead on the spot. Do you understand me?"

"I do," cried Sam. "Don't kill me." Sean untied Sam. Then he handed Sam fifty dollars.

"This oughta get you started outta town," said Sean as he was handing the money to Sam. "Now git and remember what I said." Sam ran out the door. He was still running when Sean looked out the window and saw him going down the sidewalk as fast as he could. He didn't even look down at Victor's body as he was running.

"Do you really think he'll leave?" asked Alan.

"I hope not," answered Sean. "I'm hopin' he'll go round up some a his friends and they come back here after us. That'll give us a chance ta kill some more of'em. We'll take turns sleepin' tonight."

~~~~

Nothing happened during the night. Right after daylight, Sean looked out the window. There was a small crowd of people. They were all looking at Victor's body. A policeman arrived and disbursed the crowd. The policeman wasn't Donavan. Alan thought that the police might want to question some of the people at the hotel. A wagon came and took the body and the policeman talked with several of the people who were looking at the body. Sean and Sam had some breakfast at the hotel and then decided to walk downtown. The policeman was still out in front of the hotel when Sean and Sam came out the front door. The policeman walked over to them. "Excuse me gentleman. I'm Sgt. Muldoon," he began. "There was a body found on the sidewalk in front of the hotel this morning. Did either of you see or hear anything last night or early this morning?"

"I slept like a baby last night," said Sean. "Never heard a thing."

"Same for me," said Alan.

"What would your names be and why are you staying in this hotel?" asked Muldoon.

"This is Alan Cooper and I'm Sean Thornton," said Sean. "We came to Boston to visit a friend."

"And who would your friend be?" asked Muldoon.

"His name was Michael O'Connor," answered Sean.

"What do you mean was?" asked Muldoon.

"We found out that he's dead now," said Sean. "You should have recognized the name. That was his pub that burned down a while back. I'm sure you've probably been to Betty and Michael's pub."

"Sure, I knew the place, but I never went in there," said Muldoon. "I'm not a drinking man. I used to be, but it got the best of me and I quit. My Captain was there investigating the fire. Sorry about your friends."

"What is your Captain's name?" asked Alan.

"It's O'Hanly," answered Muldoon.

"Is he a good boss?" asked Sean. "I hear a lot of beat cops gripe about their superiors."

"That's probably true of everyone who has a boss," said Muldoon. "Some days you hate them. Other days you think they're great. I don't know much about O'Hanly. I haven't been with him too long. I got transferred to this precinct when I got promoted to Sergeant. That was only two weeks ago. Well, if you'll excuse me, I've got to question some more people here. Good day to you."

"Good day to you," said Sean. Sam and Sean took off heading downtown. "Well now we know who the cop was that investigated the fire," said Sean. "We'll get with him soon. Right now, I want to get my hands on Cutter."

"You think we'll get him to talk?" asked Alan.

"Hard ta say," said Sean. "He probably thinks he's one bad man. We'll find out soon enough."

They finally got downtown where most of the shops were located. The first shop they entered was a bakery. No customers were in the place when they went inside. Sean went to the counter and Alan stayed over by the door. An older gentleman was behind the counter. "What can I get for you sir?" the man asked.

"I'm just after some information," said Sean. "What do you know about the fire that took the pub?"

"Just who are you and why are you asking me these questions," said the baker.

"Those people who were lost in that fire were my best friends and one way or another, I'm gonna find out who killed them," said Sean.

"I never heard nothing and I never seen nothing," said the man. "Now would you please leave?"

"How much money does Cutter take from you every month?" asked Sean.

"I don't know what you're talking about sir. Now please leave," said the baker.

"You know exactly what I'm talkin' about," said Sean. "Maybe someday you'll get a little backbone. Let's go Alan. This old fool must be happy the way things are." Sean and Sam left. There was a young girl in the back making dough. She had heard the conversation.

"Who were those men Poppa?" she asked the baker.

"Just someone trying to cause more trouble," said the baker. "Now get back to work."

"Maybe that man was right Poppa," said the girl. "We need to get some backbone and stand up to those bad men."

"We'll end up dead like them other two if we do," said the baker.

Sean and Alan went to several more shops. No one knew anything or would say anything. Then they went into the butcher shop. There were no customers in the butcher shop and no one was behind the counter. Sean and Alan waited several minutes and still no one came to the counter. Then they heard something. Sean recognized the sounds he was hearing. Someone was being worked over in the back room. Sean had Alan watch the front door while he quietly worked his way to the back of the shop. All the way to the back behind some beef carcasses Sean could see a big man standing over an older man. The older man on the floor's face was all bloody. The standing man pulled out a long bladed dagger. "I'll have the money now or I'll go to cuttin'," said the standing man.

"Go to hell you son of a bitch," yelled the man on the floor. "You got your last dollar out of me."

"Have it your way old man," said the man with the knife.

Sean walked back to the two men. Neither one of them noticed Sean as he walked back. "You must be Cutter," said Sean. "I heard you like to play with knives." Cutter was a little startled when Sean spoke. He turned to face him.

"Who in the hell are you?" said Cutter. "Get the hell out of here or you'll get what I'm giving him."

"Why don't you make me leave you bag a shit?" said Sean.

"All right, you asked for it," said Cutter as he moved toward Sean. He was waving his knife around trying to impress Sean.

Then Sean pulled out the bowie knife. Cutter stopped dead in his tracks.

"What's a matter Cutter," said Sean. "Haven't you seen a knife this big before. The fella that used to own this knife had it shoved into the top of his skull and the tip stuck out below his chin. The undertaker had to saw his skull open to get the knife out cause he didn't think the fella should be buried with it stuck in his skull. How bout you Cutter? Would you wanna be buried with this thing stuck in yer head?"

"That's a big knife stranger," said Cutter. "Just cause you got that thing don't mean you know how to use it. I'm gonna cut you and then I'm gonna sit back and watch you bleed to death."

"All right, let's dance," said Sean. The two men sized each other up. Cutter made some slashes at Sean and Sean just laughed at him. "I think I'll start by cuttin' the buttons off yer shirt," said Sean. "Then I'll cut yer clothes off piece at a time."

"You talk pretty good mister," said Cutter. "It'll be fun watchin' you bleed.

The man who had been on the floor was standing now. He was behind Cutter and Cutter wasn't paying any attention to him. The man moved over to a table. There was a cutting block on the table. Beside the cutting block was a big meat cleaver. Cutter was keeping his attention on Sean and still not paying any attention to the other man. The man took the meat cleaver and eased over behind Cutter. He raised the cleaver and was about to strike Cutter. "No don't. I need this son of a bitch alive," yelled Sean. When Sean yelled, Cutter turned to see the man standing there with the meat cleaver and about to carve him. Before Cutter or the other man could make a move, Sean pulled his pistol and cracked Cutter over the head. Cutter slumped to the floor. As soon as he hit the floor, the other man gave Cutter a kick in the face. Alan came to the back room now.

"I'm James O'Doul and this is my shop," said James. "Just who in God's name are you two?"

"My name is Sean O'Rourke and this other gentleman is Alan Cooper," answered Sean. "We're looking into the murder of our friend. Perhaps you knew him. His name was Michael O'Connor and his wife's name was Betty."

"Oh yes, the pub owners," said James. "I knew them. They was nice folks. So you say they was murdered. I thought it was odd that no one else was hurt in that fire. And my wife said she swore she heard something that sounded like gunshots that night. Myself, I didn't hear it."

"Did you say anything to the police?" asked Alan.

"No one asked anyone around here anything," said James. "You can't trust the cops around here anyway."

"Well how about Officer Clary?" asked Sean.

"He is one of the few that's honest around here," answered James. "Now there's a new Sergeant in the precinct. Muldoon I think his name is. He hasn't been here long enough to know if he's honest or not. I think they have him sittin' at a desk most of the time. So why are you investigating the murders. They'll be after you if they find out."

"James, I'm gonna tell you somethin' and I'd appreciate it if you didn't tell a soul what I'm about to tell you," said Sean.

"I won't tell a soul. I swear it on my dear mother's grave," said James. "I'd probably be dead right now if it wasn't for you."

"James, I'm a Federal Marshal and Alan is a Pinkerton Detective," said Sean. "Michael O'Connor was my best friend and he was my deputy out west."

"So you're that Sean O'Rourke," said James. "I've heard of you. You're just what we need around here. Is there anything I can do to help you?"

"Well, first off, we need some rope to tie up ole Cutter here," said Sean. "Then I need the names of anyone you think is a crook around here. Like do you know who Cutter's boss is? Who else works with Cutter? Anything that you think might help us."

"I'll get you some rope now," said James. "I really don't know any names other than that police Captain. O'Hanly's his name. I don't think he's smart enough to run anything, but I'd say he's on the payroll to look the other way at times." James left for a minute and returned with some rope. "What are you gonna do with Cutter?" asked James.

"It's best you don't know," said Alan. "That way if you don't know, you won't be able to say anything. I'll tell you this though. He won't be bothering folks anymore."

Sean took the rope and tied and gagged Cutter. Then he went through Cutter's pockets. Cutter had over $500 in his pockets. "Well James, you take care of a this money," said Sean. "Keep what you think he's taken from you and do what you want with the rest. Hell, just keep it all. You were the only person around here that would even talk to us. Now, I need a place to stash ole Cutter till dark. You got a place?"

"There's a little shack in the alley outback," said James. "You can put him in there. I doubt if anyone would come looking for him until tomorrow."

"Well if they would come looking for him, just tell them that he got his money and then moved on," said Sean. "Now we'll tie ole Cutter so there's no way he can get loose, but maybe you could look in on him every once in a while just to make sure. Just make sure no one sees you doin't it."

"I'll be careful," said James. "Now I think I got a customer up front. I best get back to work."

James went to take care of his customer and Sean and Alan put Cutter in the shack out back. Then they visited some more shops. No one would talk to them. They decided it was time to eat so they went to a small café. The special of the day was Irish stew and they both ate their fill. After the meal, they decided they would just stroll around the area and see if they could see or hear anything. Alan thought it would be a good idea if they visited a local newspaper office. Maybe they could get an idea if it was an honest paper or not. They found one and were about to enter when they saw Officer Clary approaching them. "How are you gentlemen this fine day?" asked Donavan. "I heard something about a dead man on the sidewalk in front of a hotel. Did you hear anything about that."

"We did," answered Sean. "That was our hotel. I would say it was a suicide. No one saw or heard anything. We talked to a Sergeant Muldoon. He was there investigating."

"I don't know much about Muldoon," said Donavan. "He just got transferred here a couple of weeks ago. Seems like a good man. Hey, I got us a dog. Don't know what kind of dog he is. Probably just a big mutt, but he likes us fine and we like him. Got him over at the dump. Been calling him Boss cause I figured he was the boss at the dump. You should have seen it. Boss and me was walking home right after I got him at the dump. There was two men on the sidewalk that wanted to give me a hard time. Ole Boss knocked one of them down and stood on him growling and baring his teeth just daring him to make a wrong move. The other one took off running when ole Boss knocked his friend down."

"Sound like ya got a good dog," said Sean. "What's the Mrs. think a Boss?"

"She likes him fine," said Donavan. "They made friends right off. I think that Boss was someone's pet before. It seems like he's house broke. He let's us know when he's gotta do his business."

"That's good," said Alan. "You wouldn't want him doing his necessaries in the house."

"So is there anything going on today?" asked Donavan. "Anything I can help you with?"

"We'll let you know when we need you," said Sean. "Have you heard of the fella they call Cutter?"

"I've heard of him, but I've never met the man," answered Donavan. "I hear he's the collector for the protection racket. I'd arrest the man if I knew who he was and I could get anyone to talk."

"Well, you won't have to worry about Cutter anymore," said Alan. "He won't be around anymore."

"So I suppose you won't tell me what's going on with him," said Donavan.

"Yep, that's right. If you don't know then you can't say," said Sean.

"I suppose that's best," said Donavan. "Well, I better get back to my beat. Now you two are invited to my house for dinner tonight."

"We'll be busy tonight, but we can come another night," said Sean. "I'm sure we'll see you around tomorrow." Donavan went back to his beat and Sean and Alan went into the newspaper office. A young woman was sitting at a desk just inside the door.

"What can I do for you?" asked the woman.

"We'd like to speak to whoever runs this newspaper," said Sean.

"That would be Mr. O'Halloran," said the young woman. "And who should I say you are?"

"Concerned citizens," answered Alan. The young woman smiled and went to an office in the back. Sean and Alan watched the people who were setting type and working with the press while they waited. A few minutes later, a short stocky middle aged man came out of the office. He walked over to Sean and Alan.

"I'm John O'Halloran and I understand you are the concerned citizens," John said. "What is it I can do for you?"

"I'm not gonna waste time," said Sean. "I'll get right to the point. We're here to find out if this is an honest newspaper or if it's run by the pack a scum that run this town."

"This is my newspaper and I'll say what I want and when I want," said John. "Nobody's gonna tell me what I can print and what I can't."

"So what do you think of Tom Flannery?" asked Alan.

"He's a low life piece of shit," said John. "He's should be hung or in jail, but witnesses always come up missing or no one will ever testify against him."

"Why don't you say that in your paper?" asked Alan.

"I have, but no one cares anymore," said John. "Flannery and his bunch used to threaten me, but they don't even bother with it anymore. It's like no one cares."

"Well there's gonna be some changes around here and folks are gonna start carin'," said Sean. "We'll be back in a day or two and we'll have somethin' for ya ta print."

"You wouldn't know anything about that fella that they found dead in front of that hotel, would you?" asked John.

"We heard it was a suicide," answered Alan.

"Suicide my ass," said John. "Someone threw that son of a bitch off the roof, and good riddance. Well, if you concerned citizens will excuse me, I got work to do. I'll see you gentlemen in a couple of days."

Sean and Alan left the newspaper office and talked to a few more shops. No one would talk to them. They decided to just hang around town and just people watch for a while. They watched the people going in and out of the shops and nothing looked suspicious. After several hours, they went to the butcher shop and checked on Cutter. He was still hog tied in the shack so Sean and Alan went back to the hotel and had dinner. Alan was wondering what Sean had in mind for Cutter. "What are we going to do with Cutter?" asked Alan. "I doubt if he talks."

"There's a river around here isn't there?" asked Sean.

"Yes, the Charles River," answered Alan.

"Well I think we'll get us a horse and carriage and tonight we'll see how well ole Cutter can swim," said Sean. "I figure we'll find us a small boat. We'll find somethin' to weight him down and tie it to him. If he don't talk, overboard he goes. That won't bother you, will it Alan."

"At one time it would have, but not now," answered Alan. "I like your way of doing things. I'd say Cutter has probably killed a few folks. Save the trouble of a trial."

"All right, after dinner, you go see if you can get us a horse and carriage," said Sean. "Get one that's enclosed if you can. Should be about dark when you get back here. We'll go get Cutter when you get back."

Alan wasn't gone long. He returned with a horse and carriage. The carriage was enclosed. Alan took the reins and they went to get Cutter. Cutter was still the same way they had left him except that he had pissed his pants. When he saw Alan and Sean, he tried to talk but couldn't because he was still gagged. Sean pulled his pistol and stuck the muzzle of it on the back of Cutter's head. "All right Cutter, I'm gonna take that gag outta yer mouth," started Sean. "If you start yelling, I'll blow yer damn head off. Do you understand me?" Cutter shook his head yes as best he could. "Alan, keep watch as best you can while I ask Cutter some questions." Alan kept watch by the door of the shack and Sean started asking Cutter questions.

"All right Cutter, did you kill Michael and Betty O'Connor?" asked Sean.

"No, I did not," answered Cutter.

"Have you ever killed anyone?" asked Sean.

"I killed me a bunch of rebs during the war," answered Cutter.

"How many people have you killed in Boston?" asked Sean.

"I never killed nobody I wasn't ordered to kill," said Cutter.

"So you have killed people in Boston," said Sean.

"I have," answered Cutter.

"And who gave you the orders to kill people?" asked Sean.

"It was someone who works for Tom Flannery," answered Cutter. "Don't know his real name. They call him "The Young Ladies Man."

"Why do they call him that?" asked Sean.

"Because he runs several whorehouses," answered Cutter. "One of them specializes in young girls. And I mean young girls. There's some there that are only 12 or 13 years old. Tom Flannery likes young girls."

"You'll show us where these whorehouses are won't you Cutter?" said Sean.

"You're gonna kill me no matter what I say or do, aren't you?" said Cutter.

"Not sure yet," said Sean. "You already admitted that you killed some people in Boston. How many more folks would you kill if I let you live?"

"I wouldn't kill nobody else," cried Cutter. "I'd leave Boston. I'd go west. I'm not ready to die yet."

"I'll give you a chance to prove that," said Sean. "Alan, we're gonna get in the carriage and Cutter here is gonna show us where the whorehouses are. We'll stop at each one. We'll untie Cutter and him and me will go to the door. Cutter will ask if Ladies Man is there and tell him he needs to speak to him. You can do that, can't you Cutter?"

"I can," answered Cutter.

"Course you know that if you try to run or do anything I don't like, I'll blow yer head off," said Sean.

"I understand," said Cutter. "Now can I get some a these ropes off me?"

"Yer hands stay tied behind yer back till we get to the whorehouses," said Sean. They took all the ropes off of Cutter except the ones that tied his hands behind his back.

"They'll see that I pissed my pants and wonder why," said Cutter.

"It'll be dark," said Sean. "They won't see that."

Sean and Cutter got inside the carriage and Alan drove. Cutter gave them directions. It was very dark now, but there were a few street lights and they could see all right. After about twenty minutes, Cutter had them stop in front of a big brick building.

Cutter said at one time is was a small flour mill. It had been re-done inside and now there were several rooms for the working girls. All the big doors that had been there when it was a flour mill had been bricked over. There was a double door in the front center of the building."

"All right Cutter, now you and me'r gonna walk over there and knock on that front door," said Sean. "When someone answers, yer gonna tell'em that ya need to talk to Ladies Man. Do you understand Cutter?"

"I understand," answered Cutter.

"Remember, I will kill you if you run or do anything I don't like," said Sean.

"I won't run," said Cutter. Sean pulled out his pistol and stuck the muzzle right on the back of Cutter's head with his right hand while he untied Cutter with his left hand. Then they got out of the carriage and started for the door.

Cutter made up his mind he was going to run. He didn't figure Sean would fire and have everyone inside looking out or coming out to see what was going on. It was about fifty feet to the front door. They had gone about ten feet when Cutter started running. Sean must have expected it. He didn't want to fire his pistol and make all that noise. He pulled out the bowie knife and threw it at Cutter. He threw it in such a way that he knew the handle would strike Cutter in the back of the head. Cutter had gone about another ten feet when the knife struck him. Down he went. He wasn't knocked out, but still lost his wits for a little bit. Sean ran over and cracked him over the head with his pistol. No one stirred in the building. Alan came over and he and Sean dragged Cutter back over to the carriage and threw him inside. Sean tied his hands behind his back and gagged him again. "Take us over to that river," said Sean. "Cutter here's goin fer a swim."

Alan took them over to the river. It was really dark. There were several shacks where some very poor people must have lived, but no one could be seen anywhere. They spotted a dock and there were several small boats tied to it. Sean had Alan stay with the carriage while he looked around for something to weight down Cutter. He returned shortly with a big rock. As they were getting Cutter out of the carriage, a young boy, maybe twelve years old came out of the shadows. Sean spotted him. The boy was dressed in rags and looked like had never taken a bath in his life. "Come over here boy," Sean said to him. The boy was hesitant, but walked over to them. "Are you trustworthy?" Sean asked the boy.

"Depends on what I gotta be trustworthy about," answered the boy.

"Well, I'll give you ten dollars if you watch this carriage till we git back," said Sean. "If it's here when we git back, I'll give ya another ten dollars."

"I'll do that," said the boy. "What ya gonna do with Cutter?"

Sean was surprised when the boy asked about Cutter. "So you know Cutter do you?" asked Sean.

"I know that son of a bitch," said the boy. "He killed my Pa 2 years ago. He had a shop in town and wouldn't pay Cutter his extortion money so Cutter killed him."

"How come he didn't kill you too?" asked Alan.

"I was in the back of the shop. He never seen me, but I seen him," said Jimmy.

"Where's yer Ma boy?" asked Sean.

"She died on the ship coming here from Ireland," answered the boy.

"So how you been gettin' by all this time?" asked Sean.

"I been stealing," said the boy. "I'm pretty good at it too."

"What's yer name son?" asked Sean.

"It's Jimmy Dugan," answered the boy. "You two got names?"

"It's best you don't know our names son," said Sean.

"I bet you're in some other gang and you're trying to take over Tom Flannery's territory," said Jimmy.

"We're not in no gang son, but we are gonna get rid of all these sons a bitches," said Sean. "So you know Tom Flannery. Do you know the one they call the Young Ladies Man?"

"I know'em," said Jimmy.

"Well young Jimmy, how'd you like ta make some more money?" asked Sean.

"Sure, what do I gotta do?" asked Jimmy.

"Do you know where all the whorehouses are?" asked Sean.

"I do," answered Jimmy.

"Well I want you to keep an eye on Flannery and the Ladies Man," said Sean. "I want to know when they do everything, like when they eat and where. I wanna know when they go the whorehouses. You name it. I wanna know it. We'll come back here in 3 days. I'll make it worth your while."

"Just go to St. Mary's Church and hang out around the back. I'll meet you there," said Jimmy. "That way, you won't hafta go as far."

"Why the church?" asked Alan.

"Cause Father Darcey's been letting me sleep in the store room out back where they keep all the candles and church stuff," answered Jimmy. "Nobody but him knows I sleep there."

"That's nice a him," said Sean. "Here, I'll give you my watch so you can keep track of the times them two do things."

"Don't need yours. I got me a watch," said Jimmy. "It was my Pa's and his Pa's before him."

"Well Jimmy Dugan, we'll be takin' care a Cutter now. He won't be killin' any more folks," said Sean. "Now we'll be back shortly. I'm trustin' you Jimmy Dugan."

"I'm trustworthy for twenty dollars," said Jimmy. Alan and Sean took Cutter, the big rock, and rope over to the dock. They put Cutter in a boat. He was still unconscious. It took both of them to get the big rock into the boat. They tied the rope to the rock so it wouldn't come off and then tied the rope around Cutter's neck. They casted off and rowed out about a hundred yards. Cutter regained consciousness now and was trying to scream. He knew he was going to die. Alan steadied the boat while Sean prepared to put the rock over the side.

"Got any last words Cutter?" said Sean. Cutter nodded his head yes. Sean took the gag off of him.

"You go to hell you son of a bitch," yelled Cutter.

"You first," said Sean as he got the rock over the side of the boat. The big rock pulled Cutter right out of the boat. They didn't know how deep the river was, but it seemed liked Cutter went down pretty deep. The boat almost turned over when Cutter went over the side, but Sean and Alan got it settled down. The carriage was still there when they got back. Young Jimmy was with it. Sean handed him ten more dollars.

"Now we'll see you in three days," said Sean. "Don't go gettin' yerself caught. That bunch'll kill ya. And take some a that twenty dollars and get yerself some new clothes. Take a bath too."

"I got me some good clothes already," said Jimmy. "I wear these rags most a the time. Some folks feel sorry for me and give me a free meal sometimes cause I look like a poor street kid. I take me a bath once a month too."

"Looks like you know all the angles," said Alan. Sean and Alan headed back to their hotel.

"I'm thinkin' tomorrow we'll go back ta that newspaper," said Sean as they were moving along. "I'm gonna give him a story ta print. It should stir up some shit."

"So what have you got in mind?" asked Alan.

"I'm gonna say that a witness has come forward and there is proof that Michael and Betty were murdered," said Sean. "I'll say that the people are tired of all the corruption and some public officials are going to be indicted soon. I figure someone'll show up at the paper raisin' hell and tryin' ta find who the witness is and which public officials will be indicted. We'll be at the paper waitin'."

"What if some fancy lawyer shows up and not some thug?" asked Alan.

"We'll find out who he works for," said Sean. "If he won't cooperate, he might go swimmin' or come up missin'."

CHAPTER FIVE

T he next morning after breakfast, Sean and Alan went to the newspaper office John O'Halloran saw them when they came in the front door. "So, the concerned citizens came back," said John. "What have you got for me?"

"Does your paper have an opinion page?" asked Sean.

"Yes it does," answered John.

"Good, then what I put in the paper will be my words and not yours," started Sean. "Are you sure you'll print what I say."

"I'll need to read it first," said John. "It's my paper. I'd be the one getting sued and not you."

"Don't be worrying yerself about some dandy lawyer," said Sean. "Now give me pen and paper and I'll get started. When will this paper come out?"

"We usually finish in the morning and have it out by noon," said John.

"Good, maybe we'll get things stirred up today," said Sean. John took Sean over to a desk where he could sit and write. Sean got started. His words went as follows.

As a free born citizen of this country, I have had enough of the corruption that runs rampant in this city. Certain individuals have already been removed from our society. Where's the man they call Cutter. Has anyone seen him? Maybe he has turned state's evidence for a leaner punishment. And what happened to that poor individual who was found dead on the sidewalk in front of the hotel? He was known to consort with the bad element in town.

A witness has come forward and will testify in the murder of Michael and Betty O'Connor. Yes, they were murdered. Bullet holes were found in the back of their skulls. This was not reported by the local police or the fire department. Tom Flannery and the Young Ladies Man's days are numbered. We're coming for you. You will be indicted for murder. If the law can't get you, we will. No fancy lawyer will be able to help you.

You local beat cops better heed this warning. From now on, you will cease to take free goods from the local merchants. If you do not heed this warning, punishment will be swift and sure. You policemen of higher ranks, the days of you turning your heads and taking bribes are over. You are public servants and you will serve the public or the public will remove you.

Things are going to change in this city so be ready for it.

A Concerned Citizen

Sean looked it over and then handed it to John. His lips moved a little as he read it.

"I'll print this," said John. "I figure before three o'clock this afternoon I'll get a visit from some lawyer and maybe the Chief of Police."

"That's good," said Alan. "That's what we want."

"Yep, that's just what we want," added Sean. "Alan and me'll get somethin' ta eat and we'll be back around one." Alan and Sean left and went to a café for their lunch. As they were eating, they noticed that they were being watched by a couple of men. "You see them two across the street," Sean said.

"I see them," said Alan. "I figure they're keeping an eye on us. I guess it's about time for someone to start wondering about us. We're new in town and we've been going in and out of all these shops. I reckon someone suspects us of something."

"That's what I figure too," said Sean. "Maybe this evening we'll have us a nice chat with them two." They finished their meal and went back to the newspaper office. "Have you got a place where we can be out of sight and still hear what's goin' on?" asked Sean.

"Why don't you put on an apron and act like you work here," said John. "You'll be right in the middle of the place and you'll see and hear everything."

"Let's go to yer office," said Sean. They went to John's office. "I got some hardware that'll need ta be covered up. How big're them aprons." Sean opened his jacket and showed John his pistol in the shoulder holster and the bowie knife."

John's eyes rolled back when the saw the weapons. "Just who in the hell are you anyway?" asked John. Sean never said a word. He pulled his Federal Marshal's badge out of a pocket and showed it to John. "It's about time we got some real law around here," said John. "You got a name?"

"O'Rourke," answered Sean.

"Holy shit, you're not that lawman from out west that everyone always talks about?" asked John.

"Yes I am," answered Sean. "And Michael O'Connor was my deputy. I'm gonna find out who killed'm and I don't care how many a these pieces a shit I gotta kill ta do it. Now John, Do not tell anyone who I am and that I'm here."

"I'll not tell a soul," said John. "Now is this other fella a deputy of yours."

"Sir, I am a Pinkerton Detective," said Alan. "I have been hired to find Michael and Betty O'Connor's killer."

"I've heard of you Pinkerton's too," said John. "This is going to be one very interesting city while you two are here. I can't wait to see what happens next." Sean and Alan put on some aprons and went out on the floor acting like they were helping the real workers. The newspaper had been out now for over an hour.

~~~~

Tom Flannery had just left his house and was in a carriage headed to one of the whorehouses when one of his men saw him and ran over to his carriage. "You better read this boss," said the man. Tom had the carriage stop and he read the paper. He went into a rage.

"You get two of the boys and go over there and tear that newspaper place apart," said Tom. "I want John O'Hallaron hurt bad. Break both his legs and one of his arms. Do it now!"

"Consider it done boss," said the man.

Tom decided he would stop off at the Police Station and have a talk with Captain O'Hanly. As soon as Flannery walked into the Captain's office, the Captain knew exactly why he was there. "I just read the paper myself," said O'Hanly. "This is the first I heard about this. Want me to check it out?"

"Not just yet. Let's wait a couple hours first," said Flannery. Tom didn't say one word about his thugs going to the newspaper building. "Let me know if you hear anything."

"I will Tom," said O'Hanly. "This sounds like vigilante talk to me. We don't need that around here."

"I don't think it's vigilantes," said Tom. "Someone around here is stirring the pot and we need to find out who. His days will be numbered. Say hi to your lovely wife for me."

"I will," said O'Hanly.

Captain O'Hanly had been a good honest cop at one time. When he was a Sergeant, he was investigating the rape and murder of a young woman. After a six month investigation, he found the killer. The killer had abducted another young woman and was about to rape her when O'Hanly broke down the door of the room where the killer had taken his latest victim. O'Hanly flew into a rage and beat the man to death. O'Hanly didn't know it at the time, but the killer was the son of a prominent politician in the state. The room where the killer had taken his victim was in a building that was owned by one of the local gangs. When O'Hanly was removing the body from the room, some of the gang members saw him. They knew who the killer was. They reported what they saw to their boss. A deal was made. In exchange for their silence about O'Hanly beating the man to death, O'Hanly would turn his head when they requested it. The body was disposed of and the woman who had been abducted was paid to be silent. As time went by, Tom Flannery became the boss of the local gang and had gotten into city politics. O'Hanly was asked to look the other way a lot. Any time he questioned them, O'Hanly was told that his wife and children would be hurt. He thought about moving and going west, but when he saw some of Flannery's thugs watching his house, he changed his mind.

~~~~

About a half hour after Sean and Alan had put on their aprons and went out on the floor, three men carrying ax handles burst into the newspaper building. The first one in the door jumped up on the desk of the receptionist and kicked her out of her chair and onto the floor. She was out cold. The other two men were right behind him. After the man kicked the receptionist, he jumped off the desk and looked around for a second. He raised the ax handle back over his head and was about to hit a typesetter when Sean yelled at him. "Me first asshole. Come hit me first," yelled Sean. The man was a little surprised by this. He stood there for a second and then headed for Sean. He had the ax handle up over his head and was about to strike when Sean pulled his pistol and stuck it on the man's forehead. Not one word was said. Sean pulled the trigger and the man's head came apart. The other two men were totally at a loss as to what to do. Alan was between Sean and one of the two men. That man must have thought that he was safe from being shot by Sean. He raised his ax handle to strike Alan. Before he could strike, Alan pulled a pistol and put a hole in the man's chest. Sean noticed something. Alan was right handed. He had shot the man with the pistol in his left hand. The third man just stood there amazed, but not for long. Alan had his brass knuckles on his right hand. He ran at the third man and struck him on the jaw and the man went down hard. He did not move. Sean now noticed something on Alan's hand. "Just what in the hell did you hit him with?" asked Sean.

"I guess I never told you about these did I," said Alan. "These are what they call brass knuckles. Here, have a look." Alan took off the brass knuckles and handed them to Sean.

"Holy shit, them things'd sure put a hurt on someone," said Sean. "I gotta git me some a them."

"I'll get some for you," said Alan. "Now what are we going to do with these bodies, and what about this one's that not dead?"

"Well we'll be havin' some words with the one that's not dead. That is if he can talk. Looks like his jaw's broke," said Sean. "Them other two, well, how bout we get the police in here. This was all self defense. Them fellas come here ta hurt us and we protected ourselves."

"John, sorry bout the mess. I reckon you best get your receptionist some medical care," said Sean. "It's probably a good thing that fella's kick knocked her out. She wouldn't a wanted ta see what went on here."

John had a talk with his employees and not one of them was upset about what had just happened. They were actually glad that it happened. John had one of his men go for a doctor while the rest of them cleaned up the place. "We don't want blood and brains all over the place," said Sean. "We might be havin' some more company yet this afternoon." Sean could see that John's men were a little skiddish about the brains. They didn't mind the blood, but the brains got to one of them. He ran out back and threw up. The two dead men were taken out back.

The doctor came and examined the receptionist. She was bruised up some, but nothing was broken. Then the doctor examined the third man who hadn't been killed. His jaw was broken, but not badly. He gave the man something for the pain and told him how to care for himself. "Now who's paying for this visit?" asked the doctor when he was done. Sean handed the doctor ten dollars and the doctor left. Just as the doctor cleared the door, Officer Clary entered.

"It was reported that gunshots were heard in this area," said Donavan. "Does anyone know anything about this?" He saw Sean and Alan there and he knew they had something to do with this.

"Three fellas came in here carryin' ax handles and was gonna beat us up and tear up the place," said Sean. "We defended ourselves. Two of'em's dead and this one here's got a broke jaw. We drug them bodies out back."

"I read that article in the paper," said Donavan. "I'm sure that's why them three were here. Did they say anything when they got here?"

"They didn't say one word," said John. "One of them jumped up on my receptionist's desk and kicked her out of her chair. Then they came after us with ax handles. They were killed in self defense."

"I'll have the wagon come and pick up the bodies," said Donavan. "I'll take this one here with me to the lock up. You are pressing charges aren't you Mr. O'Halloran?"

"What do you think, you concerned citizens, should I press charges?" John asked Sean and Alan.

"Sure, press charges, attempted assault and trespassing," said Sean. "But we'd like ta know who he works for before you take him away."

"Well there's no doubt who he works for," said Donavan. "It's Flannery or one of his men. I'd sleep lightly tonight if I were you men. Now I'm off. My Captain will have me writing reports for a month about this."

"Officer Clary, I shot those two men," said John. "Do we understand each other?"

"I know more than you think Mr. O'Halloran," said Donavan. "Like I said, my Captain will have me writing reports for a month about this." Officer Clary left with his prisoner.

The owners of other shops in the area had heard the two shots. They had also read the newspaper. When they heard the shots, they just figured that John O'Halloran had gotten himself killed. Several of them were out on the sidewalks in front of their shops. They hadn't seen the two dead bodies out behind the newspaper building. They weren't surprised when Officer Clary arrived and went inside, but they were sure surprised when he came out with a man in handcuffs. Some of them walked over and looked in the windows of the newspaper building. John O'Halloran and his crew were working just like they normally were.

Sean figured that word would get to Flannery about what had happened, but he didn't think it would happen that quickly. The two men who had been watching Alan and Sean at the café were across the street from the newspaper building when everything happened. They saw Officer Clary leave with a prisoner in handcuffs. When some of the other shop owners went over to look into the windows of the newspaper building, they mixed in with them. When they saw O'Halloran hard at work, they knew something was wrong. They watched the wagon load up the two dead men and then they left to find Tom Flannery.

Tom had left the Police Station and gone to a whorehouse to talk with the Young Ladies Man. The two men found him there. Tom Flannery hated to be interrupted when he was conducting business and when the two men interrupted him, he pulled a small revolver and threatened to shoot them. "Don't shoot boss. We got things to tell you," said one of the men. "Bad things."

"All right, all right, out with it," yelled Flannery.

"Them three you sent to the newspaper office, well two of'em's dead and one's in jail," said the man. "I heard someone say they heard some shots."

"Those men weren't carrying guns," said Flannery. "O'Halloran must have shot them."

"Maybe he did and maybe he didn't boss," said the man. "There's two men we been watching down town. They been going in all the shops. We seen'em go into the newspaper building two times today. They went in late morning and then again after they got something to eat. They was in there when all this happened. Don't got no idea who them two are."

"Well we need to find out who they are," said Flannery. "They might be the ones stirring up shit. You get some more men rounded up. I want them two watched night and day. Go on now." The two men left.

"Better lay low and avoid any trouble for a while," said the Ladies Man. "Maybe you better go talk to our lawyer. We should tell that paper we're going to sue them for slander."

"That's what I was going to do," said Flannery. "I'll see you later this evening." Tom left and had his driver take him to his lawyer's office. His lawyer was with another client, but when he saw Tom Flannery entering his office, he told the client that it was urgent that he speak to him and asked him if they could meet

at a later date. The client knew who Tom Flannery was and did
not object.

~~~~

Joshua Blackburn had graduated from Harvard Law School. All
the men in his family had been lawyers and had made good livings
at it. When Joshua set up his practice in Boston, times were tough
because of the war. Clients were few and far between so he took
on every client who could pay. He discovered that some of his clients were a little shady, but they paid him well. Joshua was lucky.
He was somewhat sickly and was able to avoid going to war. He
became wealthy and got himself a beautiful wife. They had two
daughters.

Joshua was very good at what he did. There was a big murder
trial in which he was able to get his client acquitted. His client was
a known gang leader and there were several witnesses to the
crime. Tom Flannery knew the person on trial and attended the
trial. When the man was acquitted, Tom knew that this man
would be his lawyer. Joshua had heard of Tom Flannery and what
he was, but he also knew that in this country, you are considered
innocent until proven guilty. If Tom Flannery had the money, he
would work for him.

"Before Tom spoke one word, Joshua spoke. "I have read that
article in the newspaper. I'll go down there and tell them that we
are suing them for slander. I also heard that one of your men is in
jail. I'll get him out."

"Thank you Joshua. That's what I wanted to hear," said Tom.
"Let me know if you need anything." Tom smiled and left. Joshua
went to his secretary.

"I will be gone for the rest of the day," said Joshua. "If any clients come in, give them my apologies and tell them I will be back tomorrow.

Joshua got in his carriage and had his driver take him to the office of the Judge who would be presiding over Flannery's man's case when it came up. He got the Judge to go ahead and set bail. Then he went to the jail and had the man released. Officer Clary was there writing his report and he saw the man he had just arrested being released before he had even written his report. He smelled a rat.

Then Joshua went to the newspaper building. As soon as he walked into the building, Sean and Alan knew who he was. He looked the part. "Good day, I am here to see Mr. O'Halloran," said Joshua. "Is he in?"

John saw Joshua and went to greet him. Joshua extended his hand to John, but John didn't take it. "Let's go back to my office," said John. "I know what you're here for so let's get it over with." They went back to John's office. Sean and Alan came in behind them.

"Do these two gentlemen need to be here?" asked Joshua.

"Yes they do," answered John. "They are my legal representatives." Joshua extended his hand to Sean. Sean didn't take it. Joshua didn't bother extending it to Alan.

"May I ask where you two went to law school?" asked Joshua.

"Sure you can ask," answered Sean. "I'm kinda self educated. You know, kinda like Lincoln was. I went to the Sam Colt and Christian Sharps University and then the Cheyenne University."

"Oh I see. And where did you attend?" Joshua asked Alan.

"I went to the University of Hard Knocks," said Alan.

"Look, I don't know what you might be up to, but I will not be intimidated," said Joshua. "My clients are suing this newspaper for slander. We will seek damages in the amount of $10,000."

"You might as well go piss in the wind if you think you can get that kind of money out of me," said John. "Aren't you going to ask me to print some kind of retraction or something?"

"No, I'll not bother with that," said Joshua. "My clients and I will see you in court."

"Just who are your clients?" asked Sean.

"You know exactly who they are," answered Joshua. "Their names were in the article in today's paper. They are Tom Flannery and Alexander Thornton."

"So that's the Young Ladies Man's real name," said Sean. "We were wondering if he had a real name or not."

"Good day gentlemen," said Joshua and he started turning to leave.

"Just wait a minute there dandy," said Sean. "Them two clients of yers are low life scum. Why do you represent them?"

"Because they can pay me and everyone in this country is considered innocent until they are proven guilty," said Joshua.

"So you can twist laws and words to get your clients off no matter what they've done," said Alan.

"All I do is present facts," said Joshua. "A jury makes the decision."

"I don't suppose any jury in this town has ever been threatened or intimidated," said Alan.

"I wouldn't know anything about that," said Joshua. "I would never engage in anything that was illegal."

"But your clients sure would," said Sean. "So Mr. fancy lawyer, do you have a family?"

"Yes, I have a wife and two daughters," answered Joshua. "Why do you ask?"

"Do you love them?" asked Sean.

"Of course I love them," answered Joshua. "Are you trying to threaten me?"

"Do you know the man they call Cutter? He's come up missin'," said Sean. "And did you know that man they found dead in front of the hotel? I hear he was associated with Flannery's bunch. Did you know that Flannery's men came here to bust up this place and beat us up."

"I know nothing about that," said Joshua.

"Well, there was three of'em," started Sean. "Two of'em's dead and the other one's in jail with a broke jaw."

"So I'll ask you again. Are you threatening me?" asked Joshua.

"Oh we'd never do anything like that," said Sean. "We're just letting you know that things could happen. There gonna be some changes around here and the good citizens of this town will like them. Flannery and his kind are on the way out. We intend to end the corruption around here. Any Judge, lawyer, or cop on the take is gonna be found out and dealt with."

"Well good luck on your endeavors," said Joshua. He nodded his head and left.

Joshua didn't act like it when he was in the newspaper office, but he was afraid. The two men he had never seen before scared the living crap out of him. Where was Cutter? Was he off somewhere or did those men kill him? Did those two throw that other man off the roof of the hotel? Who killed Flannery's men at the newspaper building? Maybe he should divest himself of Flannery and his bunch, but he knew that wouldn't be possible. It was still his job to do the best he could do for his clients, even if they were bad men. It had to be proven in a court of law. When he went home that evening, he got a surprise. Tom Flannery was there waiting for him. He was sitting in the living room and Joshua's wife had given him a drink. Joshua asked his wife to leave them alone so they could talk business. Her name was Bonnie.

"So, how did it go at the newspaper office?" asked Tom.

"There were no problems," answered Joshua. "I told Mr. O'Halloran that his paper was being sued and that was about it."

"Did you notice any new people there?" asked Tom.

Joshua lied. "There was no one there that wasn't there the last time I had to visit them," said Joshua. "And I got your man out of jail with no problems. I noticed he was arrested for attempted assault and trespassing. What was that about?"

"Oh nothing that need concern you," said Flannery. "I'll be off now. Let me know when we're going to court."

"I will," said Joshua. "Have a pleasant evening." They shook hands and Flannery left.

As soon as he was out the door, Joshua's wife came back into the living room. "I don't like that man," she said. "I don't know why you have him as a client. You know what he is."

"I know what he's been accused of," said Joshua. "Nothing has ever been proven. He is just like you or me if we were accused of a crime. We are innocent until proven guilty."

"Well I don't like this city anymore," said Bonnie. "If things don't get better, I want us to move. You're a good lawyer. You could work anywhere. Maybe we could go to California. I hear San Francisco is a wonderful city."

"It'll be all right Bonnie," said Joshua. "I have a feeling that things will get better around here and soon."

~~~~

When Tom Flannery left Joshua's house, he went to the whore-house and met with the Ladies Man. "I want you to find out where them two pub owners were buried and dig them up," said Flannery. "If they don't have any remains, they can't prove that they were shot in the back of the head. Get on that. I want it done tonight. Have your men armed just in case."

"I'll get it done," said the Ladies Man. "And I've got a new girl for you. One of the boys'll show you what room she's in."

~~~~

Sean and Alan stayed around the newspaper office until 5pm when they closed for the day. There were no more visits from any of Flannery's people. As they left the newspaper building, they noticed that the two men who had been watching them were no-where to be seen. "Let's get somethin' ta eat," said Sean. "Mebbe them two'll show up why'll we're eatin."

"Do you think they know that we're stayin' in that hotel?" asked Alan.

"If they don't already know, they'll find out soon enough," answered Sean. They went to the same café where they had eaten lunch. They were just about done eating when both of them no-ticed the two men outside. "Well, them fellas didn't disappoint us," said Sean. "After we leave here, we'll let'em foller us a bit, and then we'll take'em. Don't kill'em unless we hafta. I'd like ta ask'em a few questions. When we get done with them, I got me hunch on somethin'. I figure Flannery'll send some a his men out to the graveyard. They'll be wantin' to dig up Michael and Betty. If they get rid a them, there won't be no evidence that they was murdered."

"You're probably right," said Alan. "Even if I testified that they were shot in the back of the head, it's only my word. A judge wouldn't accept that."

"We won't be worryin' about no judges," said Sean. "I figure some a them are crooked anyway."

Sean and Alan went walking down the sidewalk. They took their time and made sure the two men were following them. They walked about eight blocks before they ducked into an alley. Sean found a good hiding spot on one side of the alley and Alan found a spot on the other side. They both saw the two men enter the alley. When the two men didn't see Sean and Alan, they stopped for a moment. Both of them reached into their jackets and pulled out revolvers. Then they started carefully searching potential hiding spots. The two men had their revolvers in their hands, but they were carrying them low. They were getting close to Alan now. The man checking out the side of the alley where Alan was hiding thought he saw something. "Hey, I think one of'ems over here," said the man. When he spoke, the two men raised their pistols and slowly moved toward Alan's hiding spot. Sean came out of his hiding spot now. He pulled his pistol and pointed it at the two men. When Sean cocked the hammer on his pistol, the two men froze.

"Drop them pistols right now," yelled Sean. The men just stood there. "I won't say it again," said Sean. The two men turned their head a little to see Sean standing there with his pistol aimed at them. When they turned their heads, Alan came out of hiding. He had his pistol out. When Alan cocked the hammer on his pistol, the two men turned their heads back to see Alan standing there with his pistol ready. Sean had a feeling that the two men would be stupid and try something. Alan had that feeling too.

"Don't try it boys," said Alan. As soon as the words were out of Alan's mouth, Sean and Alan could see that the two men's thumbs were moving to cock the hammers on their pistols. Sean and Alan fired at almost the same instant. The two men hit the ground dead.

"Damn fools," said Sean. "I guess we won't get any information outta them two."

"What are we going to do with these bodies?" asked Alan.

"We'll just leave'em here," said Sean. "Now let's get outta this alley and back on the sidewalk. We gotta git over to that graveyard before dark."

If there was anyone near when the two shots were fired, they didn't get curious and go see what just happened. Sean and Alan were on the sidewalk now and had gone two blocks when they saw Officer Clary several blocks away and coming toward them. They stopped and let Officer Clary come to them. "Is there anything going on that I should know about?" asked Officer Clary. "I hope not. I don't want to be writing any long reports for a while."

"Well Donavan, you might be writing another report this evening," said Sean. "There's two dead men in an alley back a ways. They been followin' us most a the day. They come after us with pistols and we had ta kill'em."

"So did you give them a chance?" asked Donavan.

"Yes we did." answered Alan. "We told them to drop their guns and they wouldn't. We had no choice. Now just put it in your report that you found two dead men in an alley. No witnesses could be found. Their pistols are still there unless someone came along and took them. Now you best go take care of things. Go two blocks and it's the alley on this side of the street." Donavan just shook his head and headed for the alley. He found the two dead men. Their pistols were still there, but there was a man standing there looking at the bodies. Donavan questioned him. He was just walking home from work when he saw the two dead men.

"I don't know their names, but I know them two worked for Tom Flannery," said the man. "Maybe one day someone'll find that son of a bitch dead in an alley." Donavan let the man leave after he had the man help him get the bodies over to the side of the alley. Then Donavan went looking for help to get the bodies removed. He found the cop on the beat next to his. The other cop was closer to the Police Station so he headed back while Donavan went back to the bodies and waited.

When the wagon came to pick up the bodies, Captain O'Hanly came with it. "So Officer Clary, what in the hell happened this time?" asked the Captain.

"I was walking my beat and I found these two dead bodies in this alley," said Donavan. Donavan showed the Captain exactly where the bodies were before he moved them to the side. "There was a pistol in the hand of both of them. I took the pistols." Donavan took the two pistols out of his jacket and showed them to the Captain. O'Hanly smelled the pistols to see if they had been fired. Then he checked both of them by sight to see if they were loaded. They were both fully loaded.

"Let me see your sidearm," said O'Hanly. The Captain smelled Officer Clary's pistol and then physically checked it to see if it had been fired. It was fully loaded and had not been fired.

"There was a man standing by the bodies when I came back from sending for help," said Officer Clary. "He said he was walking home from work when he saw the bodies. He said that he didn't know their names but he knew that they worked for Tom Flannery."

"That's just what we need around here," said O'Hanly. "Some kind of gang war or something. Officer Clary, don't you think it strange that someone or more than one person shot these two and left their pistols here?"

"That is strange," answered Donavan. "I have no idea."

"Well let's get these bodies out of here," said the Captain. "I figure we'll be seeing more dead bodies shortly." The bodies were loaded and Officer Clary continued on his beat.

Sean and Alan made their way to the graveyard just before dark. They found a good spot close to Michael and Betty's graves and waited. After two hours, they decided to take turns on watch. Around 1am, Sean heard a horse and wagon in the distance. He woke Alan. The wagon came closer and closer. It stopped right beside Michael and Betty's headstones. There were three men. Two of them got out of the wagon. The two men who got out of the wagon started digging while the third man stood watch. The wagon was between Sean and Alan and the two graves. The man standing watch, stood in the wagon and looked around continually. He was armed with some kind of rifle. Sean couldn't quite make it out in the dark. The two men digging were not very enthusiastic about what they were doing. They dug for only fifteen minutes and took a break. One of them pulled a bottle out of his jacket and took a swig. He passed it to the other digger. He also took a swig. Sean and Alan were only about fifty feet from the wagon. The bottle was handed to the man standing watch in the wagon. Sean saw this as an opportunity to move closer. He and Alan moved closer. They got behind some headstones that were only about ten feet from the wagon. The man on watch took a swig and then handed the bottle back to one of the diggers. They resumed digging. Sean watched the man on watch closely. He let him look around one more time. When he turned away from where he and Alan were hiding, Sean pulled his pistol and stood up. Alan moved over behind another headstone where he could could get a better look at the diggers. As soon as Alan was ready, Sean cocked the hammer on his pistol. The instant that the man on watch heard the hammer being cocked, he raised his rifle to his shoulder and turned to face Sean. Sean or Alan didn't say a word. As soon as the man saw Sean, he tried to fire his rifle. Sean fired and the man was struck in the forehead. He was thrown backwards and out of the wagon. The two diggers were totally dumbfounded for a moment. Then they reached into their jackets for something. Alan yelled for them to raise their hands and stay still. The two men ignored him and kept trying to get something out of their jackets. Alan didn't wait. He fired and was going to fire again. As he was squeezing the trigger, he heard Sean's pistol fire. Both men were thrown backwards and hit the ground dead. "Son of a bitch, guess we won't be askin' them any questions," said Sean. "Well I'm gonna put the dirt back on the graves then we'll load up these bodies."

"Where are we taking them?" asked Alan.

"We're gonna take'em over to that whorehouse and throw'em out front," said Sean. "Then we'll head back to the hotel and get some sleep."

The dirt was put back on the graves and the dead men were loaded onto the wagon. As they made their way to the whorehouse, they never saw a living soul. They stopped the wagon right in front of the whorehouse. "I changed my mind," said Sean. "We'll just leave these bodies in the wagon. That way, they'll hafta walk over and look to see them. Course they'll know somethin's not right when they see all the blood that'll leak outta them boys over the night. Should be a bunch of it on the ground under the wagon."

Sean tied the horses to a hitching post and then he and Alan started walking back to the hotel. It was a long walk. They had gone a good ways when Sean saw someone in the shadows. He and Alan kept walking. When they got closer, Sean could see that it was Jimmy Dugan. "Just what the hell are you doin' out here this time of night?" asked Sean.

"I'm workin' for you," answered Jimmy. "I'll see you day after tomorrow. I'll have everything you need to know."

"All right, see you then," said Sean. Sean and Alan started walking again. Jimmy disappeared in the shadows.

"That boy would make a good detective some day," said Alan.

"I'd say he already is one," said Sean. "Hope he don't git careless and git caught."

"I hope so too," said Alan. "I like that boy. He's done good looking after himself after his Pa was killed. He knows how to get by."

"Yep, he's a smart kid," said Sean. "He could fall into a hog pen and come out king a the hogs."

It was after 3am when Sean and Alan got back to their hotel. They checked all around and made sure they weren't followed. They made a thorough check of all the stairwells and everything and then went to their room. Nothing had been bothered in their room so they both got some sleep.

CHAPTER SIX

T he Mayor of Boston was a man named David Cross. He was not a corrupt man. He knew that there was corruption in his city, but he figured it was always in the poor sections of town so he never worried about it. He had been Mayor for several terms now and would be seeking re-election the next year. When the Mayor read Sean's article in the paper, he wondered what the hell was going on in south Boston. He scheduled a meeting with his Deputy Mayor and the Police Chief that afternoon.

Danny Danaher was the Deputy Mayor. Mayor Cross had no idea that Danny Danaher was the head of most of the corruption in the city. Danny's political machine got Mayor Cross elected and re-elected. They wanted a man they could handle and David Cross was that man. Police Chief Munroe took bribes and knew when to have his men look the other way.

The meeting was to take place at 4pm. By this time, the Mayor had heard about the shootings at the newspaper. When the Deputy Mayor and the Police Chief entered his office, the Mayor politely told them to take a seat before he started yelling. "Just what in the God damned Hell is going on over there in South Boston?" he yelled. "Sounds to me like we're going to have some vigilantes on the loose. And who were those men who were shot at the newspaper building? Chief Munroe, your beat cops better not be helping themselves to free things from the local merchants. And if I find out that any Officers are taking bribes or looking the other way, I'll have them prosecuted. Now just who in the hell is this Young Ladies Man?"

"All of this is going on in Captain O'Hanly's precinct," said Chief Munroe. "I have never heard of this Young Ladies Man. I'll get over there and see what's going on."

"See that you do," said the Mayor. "Now what's Flannery up to this time to get that newspaper all stirred up? Whatever he's doing, there won't be any witnesses to testify against him. There never is."

"I'll meet with him tomorrow," said the Deputy Mayor. "It's hard to tell what he's up to."

"Well maybe this time we will be able to file charges against him and make them stick," said the Mayor. I want to see both of you day after tomorrow. That's all." The two men nodded their heads and left. They went to Deputy Mayor Danaher's office.

"Don't worry about ole Cross," said Danny. "He'll try to act like he's concerned for a couple of days. Then he'll forget all about this. I'll go over and see Flannery. I'll just tell him to behave himself for a few days. I'll talk to Captain O'Hanly too."

"I think I better go see O'Hanly myself," said Chief Munroe. "I need to make an appearance in the precincts every so often. I was due to go there anyway."

"Fine, I'll just see Flannery," said Danny. "See you day after tomorrow."

~~~~

Sean and Alan didn't know it, but Alexander Thornton, the Young Ladies Man, lived in the whorehouse where they had left the dead bodies in the wagon. One of Thornton's men was the first person to see the wagon and the dead bodies the next morning. The room where Thornton lived was on the top floor and in the front of the building. When his man found the wagon and dead bodies out front, he started yelling for Thornton at the top of his lungs. Thornton was awakened. He got out of his bed and went over to a window. He saw his man out there by the wagon. He could not see the bodies in the wagon. Thornton opened his window and yelled. "Just what in the hell are you yelling about?"

"You best get down here boss," said the man. "We can't be yellin' back and forth."

"All right, all right, I'll get some clothes on and be down," said Thornton. Thornton got dressed and headed downstairs. As he was walking over to the wagon, he was now able to see the blood on the ground under the wagon. "What in the hell," he said as he made his way to the wagon. He climbed up and looked in the bed of the wagon. "Holy God damned shit," said Thornton. "Just who in the hell?"

"Someone musta shot them fellas last night at the graveyard boss," said the man.

"Well no shit," said Thornton. "Get some help and get rid of these bodies. I've gotta go see Flannery. Don't let no one see you ditching them bodies. I don't care how you do it. Hell, dump them in the river."

"All right boss," said the man.

~~~~

Tom Flannery was home when Thornton arrived. He was just coming out the front door of his house when Thornton arrived. "You better have some good news," said Tom. "We're losing too many men right now."

"Well, we lost three more last night," said Thornton. "I sent three men to the graveyard last night to dig up those bodies. They were armed too. Someone shot them and left them in front of my place."

"Damn it. We have got to find out who's behind all this," said Flannery. "I bet it's those two fellas my boys were following. My boys were found dead in an alley. Those two men were seen at that newspaper too." Another carriage pulled up in front of Flannery's house. It was Deputy Mayor Danaher. Danaher got out of the carriage and walked over to the two men.

"You need to keep things quiet for a few days," said Danaher. "Our illustrious Mayor read that newspaper article and he's heard about those men getting shot there too."

"Keep quiet? Like hell," said Flannery. "Someone's killing my men. I'll make all the noise I want until I find out who's doing it. I lost four men yesterday and three more last night."

"Sounds like you pissed off the wrong person this time," said Danaher.

"I'll be pissing on him when I find him," said Flannery.

"Well don't mess up and leave any witnesses to whatever you have to do," said Danaher. "I'll be leaving now." Danaher got back in his carriage and left. Flannery and Thornton talked some more.

"Well what do we do now Tom?" asked Thornton.

"I still have men out there looking for who's doing this." said Flannery. "We'll find him or them or whoever it is. So has anyone seen Cutter yet?"

"No, I figure he's dead," said Thornton. "I'll get a new man on collections."

"Well tell him to be armed," said Flannery. "Cutter was good with a knife, but as they might say out west, don't take a knife to a gunfight."

Police Chief Munroe paid his visit to Captain O'Hanly's precinct. He told O'Hanly to take charge and not let anything get out of control. Then he went around and shook hands with some of the Officers and was on his way. O'Hanly was relieved when Munroe left. He had never liked the man and as far as he knew, Munroe was just a figure head and never did anything.

Sean and Alan didn't get up till almost 10am. They got dressed and had breakfast at the hotel. As they were eating, they noticed that two men were watching them. The two men were sitting at another table. They were having coffee and acting like they were reading newspapers. "Well what are we going to do about those two?" asked Alan.

"How bout we just go over and join them when we're done eatin'," said Sean. "I'm bout tired a playin' hide and seek."

"Fine by me," said Alan. They finished their meal and paid the waitress. Then they walked over to the table where the two men were and sat down with them just like they were invited.

"All right boys, what can we do fer you?" asked Sean.

The two men were a little surprised when Sean and Alan came over and sat down. They were not quite sure what to say. After a moment, one of them spoke. "We know that one of you is named Alan Cooper and the other one is Sean Thornton," started the man. "We've been following you. We know what room you're staying in too. We sent a man to tell the boss we'll be taking you with us so you can answer some questions."

"Who's yer boss?" asked Sean.

"You'll find out," answered the man.

"Well it's gotta be either Flannery of the Ladies Man," said Alan. "I'm betting on Flannery. And just what makes you think we're going with you?" The two men opened their jackets a little and leaned forward so Sean and Alan could see that they had pistols in shoulder holsters.

"Oh my, isn't that somethin'," said Sean. "Look Alan, these boys got guns. How bout that. Well guess what boys. We got—." Sean didn't finish. As he was about to, he saw Officer Clary enter the restaurant. "Well lookey here boys," said Sean. "Here comes Officer Clary. Officer Clary, come on over here. These two gentlemen are just dying ta meet you." Officer Clary walked over to the table.

"So, I'm Officer Clary. Now who might you be and why are you dying to meet me?" asked Officer Clary.

"We are not dying to meet you Officer Clary," said the man. "This gentleman is mistaken."

"Mistaken huh. I don't think so," said Sean. "You threatened us with guns so you must really want to meet Officer Clary."

"So you threatened these gentlemen with guns," said Officer Clary. "I'll be seeing them guns and I mean now." Officer Clary pulled his service revolver. Neither man moved. Officer Clary aimed his revolver at the man who had been doing the talking. Slowly, Donavan put his hand in the man's jacket and searched for the man's pistol. "Move the wrong way and I'll kill you," said Donavan. He found the pistol and removed it from the shoulder holster. As Donavan was putting the man's pistol in his belt, the other man made a move for his pistol. He had his hand on it when Sean's bullet hit him between the eyes. Officer Clary took his eyes off of the other man for just a moment when he saw what was happening. The moment he did, the other man made a grab for the pistol that Officer Clary had put in his belt. He had it in his hand and was almost ready to fire when Officer Clary's bullet hit him in the forehead.

The other customers in the restaurant were screaming and running out. The waitress who had waited on Sean and Alan fainted and some of the customers tripped over her when they tried to run out of the place. Finally the place quieted down. There was blood and brains all over the place. Officer Clary was standing there in total disbelief. "Are you all right Donavan?" asked Alan. Officer Clary turned away and knelt down. He threw up. Sean and Alan let him finish. Donavan got his composure back and stood. He turned and looked at the two dead men again.

"I haven't killed a man since the war," Donavan said.

"Well your sure as hell killed the hell outta him," said Sean. "You done good. That could just as well be you laying there dead."

Two men came walking into the restaurant. They took one look at the dead men on the floor and ran out of the place. Sean and Alan saw them. "You reckon that was some more a this bunch?" said Sean.

"I bet it was," said Alan. "They'll go tell the boss. Donavan, they saw you with us. They'll be wanting to find out why you were here with us."

"I didn't do anything wrong," said Donavan. "All I did was defend myself."

"Flannery won't care about that," said Alan. "When you write up your report on what happened, you'll be a good policeman and tell the truth. Who knows who else might read that report. When you say that you shot that man, Flannery or whoever won't care anything about self defense. You killed one of his men. He'll want you dead."

"I'll have to put your names in the report," said Donavan.

"That's fine," said Sean. "Go ahead and use our real names and what we are. It's about time they knew who was after them. Say on your report that you met us for the first time today when you walked into this place. Say that we told you who we were and why we're in Boston. We told you all this after the shoot out today. Hell, we'll go with you to the Police Station."

"I heard this morning that there was some shooting at the graveyard last night," said Donavan. "An officer went there to investigate but there was no one around when he got there. Do you know anything about that."

"Yes we do," said Alan. "We went there expecting some of Flannery's men to dig up Michael and Betty O'Connor and dispose of the remains so there would be no evidence of murder. Well three men showed up. They were armed and had no intention of giving up. We left the bodies in a wagon at one of the whore-houses."

"Well it's doubtful they're still there," said Donavan. "Well you two stay here if you would while I get the wagon coming for the bodies. Then we'll go to the station. Are you sure you want to go over there?"

"Yep, I think it's about time we met Captain O'Hanly," said Sean.

It wasn't long before the bodies were removed. As Donavan, Sean, and Alan were leaving, they could hear some of the restaurant employees crying. "I can't clean that up," cried a waitress. "That's a man's brains and blood all over the place. I quit."

~~~~

When they got to the Police Station, Officer Clary took Sean and Alan right to Captain O'Hanly's office. The door was open and O'Hanly was sitting at his desk. Officer Clary knocked on the door frame. O'Hanly looked up at them. "Captain, I have some men here I think you should meet," said Donavan. O'Hanly stood.

"And who am I having the pleasure of meeting?" asked O'Hanly.

Sean extended his hand to O'Hanly. "I'm Federal Marshal Sean O'Rourke," said Sean. They shook. "And this gentleman with me is Alan Cooper. He's a Pinkerton detective." Alan shook hands with O'Hanly.

O'Hanly was quiet for a moment. "You're not the famous lawman from out west that everyone hears about, are you?" asked O'Hanly.

"Yes I am," answered Sean.

"Well I'm pleased to meet such a man," said O'Hanly. "Just why would you be in Boston?"

"I'm here investigating the murders of Michael and Betty O'Connor," answered Sean. "In case you never knew their names, they were the owners of that pub that burned down a while back. Michael O'Connor was my best friend and was a former deputy of mine. Betty was his wife and also a dear friend."

"And why would you say that they were murdered?" asked O'Hanly. "They were just lost in that fire. The fire department said that they suspected no foul play."

"Well maybe them and definitely you didn't do a proper examination of the remains," said Alan.

"What do you mean?" said O'Hanly. "The bodies were all burned up."

"Yes they were, but there were small bullet holes in the backs of their skulls," said Alan. "I examined the remains myself at the morgue before I had them buried. So why didn't you examine the remains."

"I am so sorry," said O'Hanly. "I guess I didn't think it was necessary at the time. I should have. I know that now. Is there anything I can do now to make amends?'

"You can help us git this scum out of your town," said Sean.

"I'll do what I can," said O'Hanly.

"Captain, I need to tell you what happened this morning," said Officer Clary. "It'll be in my report, but I want to tell you first."

"Go ahead Officer Clary. Tell me," said O'Hanly. Officer Clary told Captain O'Hanly everything that happened at the hotel restaurant that morning."

"All right Officer Clary, you go ahead and write your report," said O'Hanly. "I want to have some private words with these two gentlemen. Donavan left the room and closed the door behind him.

"Gentlemen, I want to assure you that there was nothing I could have done that would have prevented your friends' deaths," started O'Hanly. This is not the wild west. Here we do things differently. We have laws, lawyers, and courts. That's our problem. There's too many slick lawyers and whenever we do get someone to court, the witnesses always refuse to testify or come up missing."

"That's why I'm glad we're not civilized out there yet," said Sean. "So, what else have you got to say."

"I was a good cop at one time," said O'Hanly. "I beat a man to death one time when I was investigating a rape and murder case. The man I beat to death was the son of a big politician in this state. The wrong people found out what I had done and have been holding it over my head for a lot of years. They keep an eye on my family if you know what I mean."

"I know what you mean," said Alan. "If you don't turn your head at the right time, they hurt your family."

"Well it's about time you quit worryin' about that and get some back bone," said Sean.

"It's harder than you think," said O'Hanly. "They have eyes everywhere."

"Well if you cut off the head of the snake, the snake'll die," said Sean.

"'That's true, but there's a lot of snakes in this town," said O'Hanly.

"Well help us get rid of them or stay out of the way and let us do it," said Sean.

"I'd say you're off to a good start," said O'Hanly. "I'll have a talk with the wife tonight. She needs to know what I could be getting myself into. I'll expect to see you two again in a couple of days."

"We'll see you then," said Sean. Sean and Alan left the Captain's office. They saw Donavan filling out his report and went to talk with him for a while. "Remember what we said Donavan," said Sean. "Make sure your wife keeps a weapon close. Tell her not to go anywhere without that dog a yers. I mean it now. They will be after you. Get yourself another pistol and carry it too. And have plenty of ammunition on you too." Donavan just nodded his head yes and went back to working on his report. Alan and Sean left.

Donavan finished his report and took it to his Captain. O'Hanly gave it a quick read. "You know that bunch will be after you, don't you?" said O'Hanly.

"I do," answered Officer Clary. O'Hanly reached into his desk and pulled out a small revolver. He handed it Officer Clary.

"Keep this on you too," said O'Hanly. Then he reached back into his desk and pulled out a box of bullets and handed them to Officer Clary. "Stay alert son. Don't want to lose you," said O'Hanly. "You're a good officer." Donavan thanked him and left.

Captain O'Hanly handed the report to another officer to file. He didn't know it, but the officer was on Flannery's payroll. That afternoon, Flannery found out who was killing his men. He went to the Deputy Mayor with the news. "So we've got the famous western lawman in town," said Danaher. "And I remember hearing about that Pinkerton too. He was here on a case not long ago. I never met the man personally, but I know the person who hired the agency. I'll see what I can find out. In the meantime, you need to keep things quiet for a while. Maybe I'll find out something we can use against them two. I already know that O'Rourke is from Abilene and has a wife. Maybe that Pinkerton has a wife too and we can find out where she is. Now do like I say. You've lost too many men already."

"If we get the chance, we'll kill those bastards," said Flannery.

"If you kill those two, it better look like an accident," said Danaher. "We don't need Pinkertons or Federal Marshals all over us which is what'll happen if you would kill them two. Just lay low. I'll get something worked out. Haven't I always taken care of things."

"All right, but if the chance comes, I'm taking it," said Flannery.

Flannery stormed out of Danaher's office. He had no intention of waiting on Danaher. He was going after O'Rourke and Cooper. The first person he was going to get though was Officer Clary.

~~~~

After Sean and Alan left the Police Station, they went back to their hotel and checked out. They checked into another hotel and Sean had some words with the clerk and the manager when they did. They went into the manager's office. "Now I want you fellas ta listen to me and listen well," started Sean. "I am Federal Marshal Sean O'Rourke and this other gentleman is Alan Cooper. He is a Pinkerton Detective. If you tell a living soul that we are in this hotel, that will be the last thing you ever tell anybody. Are you following me?"

"Are you threatening us Marshal?" asked the manager.

"You call it whatever you want," said Sean. "I will shoot you dead if you tell anyone we are here. If you've heard of me, then you know I'll do just that."

"What if we get threatened by someone else who might be looking for you?" asked the clerk.

"Well I reckon you'll hafta to decide on who you want to kill you," answered Sean. If I kill you, it'll be over fast. Can't say how someone else'd do it."

"That's very comforting," said the manager. "I suppose if someone does ask about you, you expect us to tell you."

"Course we do," answered Sean. "I'd be really upset if you didn't and I found out about it. You wouldn't want me to be upset would you?"

"Of course not Marshal," said the manager. "Are you through with us now?"

"Yep, go on back ta work," said Sean.

Sean and Alan moved into their new room and relaxed for a while. They went down to the restaurant in the hotel for dinner right before dark. No one seemed to be watching them so they went back up to their room. That night, they stood two hour watches.

~~~~

Jimmy Dugan was being a great detective. He found out everything Sean and Alan wanted to know. He knew where Tom Flannery lived and what his daily schedule was. He also found out everything about the Ladies Man. He would meet with Sean and Alan the next day and tell them everything. Jimmy figured he was done for the day and was working his way back to St. Mary's church. It was already dark. On his way, he ran into a couple of young boys who were also homeless and streetwise. Their names were Tommy and Andy. Jimmy thought that they might be a year or so older than him. Jimmy was eleven. Tommy and Andy were headed for one of the Ladies Man's whorehouses. "You should go with us," said Tommy. "We're going to do it."

"What do you mean do it?" asked Jimmy.

"I mean we're going to do it with one of the ladies," said Tommy.

"Who told you that?" asked Jimmy.

"These two guys who work for the Ladies Man," answered Tommy. "They said that we could do it with one of the ladies for free."

"What do you hafta do for them?" asked Jimmy.

"We just gotta run an errand sometime when they need it," said Tommy.

"And you got no idea what that errand might be, do you?" said Jimmy.

"No, but what could us boys do anyway?" said Tommy. "Come on and go with us. It'll be our first time. I bet it'd be your first time too."

"I'm not getting tied up with those people," said Jimmy. "You better think about what you're getting into."

"Right now we're thinking about getting into one of those girls," said Andy. "Suit yourself, we're going." Tommy and Andy left. Jimmy waited a bit and then decided to follow them.

When the two boys got to the whorehouse, they knocked on the front door. One of Thornton's men greeted the boys and let them in. Jimmy waited in the shadows and then moved right up to the building. He looked into every window on the first floor. The curtains were pulled on most of the windows, but most of the rooms had lanterns on and he could see through the curtains. He saw several of the girls in action with men, but he did not see

Tommy or Andy. The whorehouse had three stories. There were several trees around the building on three sides. Jimmy decided to climb the trees and see what he could see. He started on the left side. There were two trees on that side. Again he saw the girls and their clients, but he did not see Tommy and Andy. There were three trees in the front. He climbed the tree on the left first. He did not see Tommy and Andy. Then he moved to the tree in the middle. The tree in the middle was closer to the building than the other trees so Jimmy did his best to be careful. He saw the same things on the second floor and then he started looking at the third floor. He saw that the curtains of the room in the middle were partially open. He moved in the tree some so he could see better. He moved out on a limb that was maybe forty feet from the window. What he saw in the room horrified him. He almost screamed but stopped himself. He had to get out of there fast and tell what he saw. As he was getting out of the tree, he heard a voice. He had been spotted. "I know you boy," yelled the Ladies Man as he stuck his head out the window.

As soon as Jimmy hit the ground, he ran as fast as he could. He heard the door of the whorehouse open and turned to look. Two men came running out. "We see you boy," yelled one of the men. "Your ass is ours." It was fairly dark, but Jimmy knew his way around very well. He was able to evade the two men. After a few hours, Jimmy was sure it was safe and went to the church to sleep.

~~~~

On his way home that evening, Officer Clary did his best to see if he was being followed or not. After a while, he decided that it wouldn't matter anyway. They probably already knew where he lived. When Donavan got home, he kissed Mary Kate and then told her about all that had happened that day. Mary Kate could tell that Donavan was upset because he had killed a man. "Darlin', I know you are upset, but you must remember that it could have been you dead on the floor," said Mary Kate. "You are not going anywhere just yet. I'm too young to be a widow. I need you with me. Now between you and me and Boss, we'll not let anything happen to us in this house. Now kiss me again and let's have dinner." Donavan gave her a good long kiss. Boss came over and looked at Donavan with sorrowful eyes. "All right Boss, I'll give you some affection too." Donavan knelt down and gave Boss a hug and then rubbed his belly some. After dinner, Donavan read a newspaper and they talked some. They went to bed and made love and then fell asleep in each other's arms.

They had been asleep for a couple of hours when they were awakened by Boss. He always slept by the back door. They always kept the door to their bedroom open so they could hear anything in the house. Boss put his front paws on Donavan and woke him. Then Boss went into a very low growl. Donavan could hear that someone was trying to get the front door open. He woke Mary Kate. "Someone's trying to get into the house," said Donavan. "Get down beside the bed and stay there. Have your pistol ready." Mary Kate kept her pistol on the nightstand beside her bed at night. During the day, she had it on her. Now they could hear that someone was trying to open the back door too. Stay here like I said," said Donavan. "If someone comes into this room and you are sure it's not me, shoot them." Mary Kate nodded her head yes. Donavan and Boss eased out of the bedroom. "All right Boss, you take the one at the back door and I'll take the one at the front," said Donavan. Boss went into the kitchen and waited behind a cupboard. Donavan eased into the living room and hid behind the sofa.

The door in the kitchen opened first. A man eased his way inside. He had a revolver in his right hand. Boss let him get inside. Boss waited for a moment and then attacked. He got ahold of the intruder's right arm at the wrist and shook fiercely. The pistol fired once and the man let go of it. He tried to free himself from Boss's jaws, but couldn't. The front door opened now and two men entered the house. Donavan could see that they both were armed with revolvers. "Don't move or I'll kill you," said Donavan in a very low voice. The two men extended their arms like they were going to fire. Donavan didn't hesitate. He fired his pistol. One of the men fell to the floor. The other man fired his revolver and then turned to run. Before he had moved more than three feet, Boss pounced on his back and knocked him down. Donavan got out from behind the sofa now. He called Boss off of the man and then he struck the man's head with his revolver and knocked him unconscious. Donavan now wondered about the other man in the kitchen. Had he gotten away? He found some matches and lit a lantern. He moved slowly to the kitchen. The other man was laying on the floor just inside the door. There was blood all over his throat and his right arm. Then he saw the blood on Boss. Donavan got down on his knees and hugged Boss. "You're some kind of dog Boss," said Donavan. "You're some kind of dog." He hugged Boss some more and then went back to the living room. The man he had shot was dead. There was a hole in his chest. Donavan got some rope and tied up the man he had knocked out. When he was finished tying the man, he called to Mary Kate. "You can come out darlin', said Donavan. "What you see out here could be upsetting, so be ready for it." Mary Kate slowly came out of the bedroom. She cried a little for a moment and then she spoke.

"I guess they didn't get us killed, did they?" she said. "And Boss, you are sure some kind of dog. Come here and let me get this bad man's blood off of you." Mary Kate hugged Boss as she cleaned the blood off of him.

The shots had been heard all over the neighborhood. It wasn't long before some other policemen arrived. Donavan told them all that had happened. The bodies were removed and the man who had been tied was chained and taken away. He would not give his name or anything. Mary Kate and Donavan cleaned up the house as best they could.

By the time they got the house cleaned, it was time for Donavan to go back to work. When he got to the Police Station, he wrote a report on what had happened during the night. Then he met with Captain O'Hanly. The Captain seemed to be in better spirits than he had been in for some time. He shook Officer Clary's hand and thanked him for ridding the world of a couple of men who didn't need to be in it. Then Officer Clary left to walk his beat.

Captain O'Hanly was feeling better because he had had a serious talk with his wife. After a lot of years, he finally told her what he had done years earlier and why he was the way he was. She was glad that he had finally confided in her and she assured him that no one was going to mess with her. She had a shotgun in the house and knew how to use it. Captain O'Hanly felt like a new man.

~~~~

Officer Clary had been on his beat for about an hour when he heard some noises coming out of an alley. He rushed to where he thought the noises were coming from. As he entered the alley, he could see two men beating the hell out of someone. As he ran closer, he could see that the someone was just a young boy. The two men were so engrossed in what they were doing that they didn't see Officer Clary approaching. Officer Clary never said a word. He took his billy and struck the closest man to him in the head as hard as he could. The other man looked up and saw Officer Clary now. He got up and started running away. The man ran for about 50 feet and stopped. As he turned to look back, Officer Clary could see that the man had a revolver in his right hand. Officer Clary reached for his service revolver, but before he had it out to fire, the man fired. Officer Clary was struck in the left arm. The bullet knocked him sideways, but before the man could fire again, Officer Clary got off a shot. The man was struck in the forehead. He was thrown backwards and blood and brain went flying.

Officer Clary knelt down to see if the young boy was alive or not. He was beaten terribly. The boy uttered two words, "Father Darcey," and then passed out. Some other people had heard the shots and came to see what had happened. Officer Clary saw them coming and yelled for them to get a carriage or something so he could get the young boy to a hospital. Another policeman arrived and he stayed at the scene while Officer Clary and the young boy went to the hospital.

When they arrived at the hospital, a nurse saw them coming and ran inside for more help. Two men came running out with a stretcher and put the young boy on it and carried him inside. They took him into a room and told Officer Clary to wait outside.

Then someone noticed Officer Clary's wound. A nurse escorted him to another room. A doctor arrived and started working on the wound. "You are very lucky Officer," said the doctor. "The bullet passed through. You'll be good as new in no time." When the doctor finished with Officer Clary, he sent him to a waiting room. "I saw that you came in with that young boy," said the doctor. "They'll be needing to ask you some questions." Donavan nodded his head yes and then took a seat in the waiting room.

After a couple of hours, a nurse came over to talk with Donavan. "I'm nurse Bennett," she began. "Are you the boy's father?"

"No, I was walking my beat when I saw two men beating on him in an alley," said Donavan. "I have no idea who he is. The boy said "Father Darcey," and then passed out."

"Why would anyone beat a young boy like that?" asked the nurse.

"I don't know, but the two men who did it will never beat anyone again," said Donavan. A doctor came over to Donavan now.

"I'm Dr. Young. I know that you came in with the young boy," the doctor began. "Are you a relative or a friend?"

"I never saw that boy until today," said Donavan. "He said two words to me before he passed out, "Father Darcey.""

"Well I know Father Darcey," said the doctor. "He's over at St. Mary's church. Someone should go get him. This young boy might need to receive his last rights."

"Is he that bad doctor?" asked Donavan.

"It would be a divine miracle if he lives," said the doctor. "His skull is cracked in several places. His jaw is broken. Both of his arms and one of his legs is broken. Several of his ribs are broken and he has internal injuries. It would be a good time to pray."

"I'll go find Father Darcey," said Donavan. "Thank you doctor. I'll have the Father here as fast as I can."

When Officer Clary went out the door of the hospital, Captain O'Hanly was heading into the hospital. "I heard that one of my Officers got shot," said O'Hanly. "I got here as soon as I could. And how's the little boy?"

"The boy is not expected to live," said Officer Clary. "And I'm all right. The bullet went through my arm. Now I must find Father Darcey. The boy must know him or something."

"Well you just stay put. I'll have someone else find the Father," said O'Hanly. The Captain had an Officer with him. He told the Officer to go to St. Mary's church and bring back Father Darcey. "Now Officer Clary, just what happened this morning?" asked O'Hanly.

"I was just walking my beat when I heard noises coming from an alley," stared Donavan. "I saw two men beating on the young boy. I hit one in the head with my billy. The other one ran for a short distance and then turned and shot me. I returned fire and killed him. Then I got the boy to the hospital. He said "Father Darcey," and then he passed out."

"Well that man you hit in the head is dead too," said O'Hanly. "You've had a full night and day haven't you?"

"I have," said Donavan. "I bet this is related to O'Rourke and that Pinkerton somehow."

"I wouldn't know what some young boy would have to do with any of that, but nothing would surprise me now," said O'Hanly. "You go on home now. You'll need some days off to heal up. I'll take you home."

~~~~

Sean and Alan had gotten up and had their breakfast. They went to St. Mary's church and were waiting for Jimmy Dugan to show up. After a couple of hours, they were getting discouraged. "Let's wait another hour and then get some lunch," said Sean. At the same instant, they both saw a police officer approaching. "What's goin' on Officer?" asked Sean. "Did someone rob the church?"

"I need to find Father Darcey," said the Officer. "Some young boy was beaten up. He's at the hospital. The boy said "Father Darcey" before he passed out." "Well who beat up the boy?" asked Alan.

"I don't know who they were," said the Officer. "Officer Clary was on his beat when he saw two men beating up the boy. The two men are dead now, but Officer Clary was shot in the arm. The boy is not expected to live. Now please excuse me. I must find the Priest."

"We gotta get to that hospital," said Sean. "Let's move."

When Sean and Alan arrived at the hospital, Captain O'Hanly was there. He had taken Donavan home and went back to the hospital. "What are you two doing here?" asked O'Hanly.

"We heard about the young boy and Officer Clary," said Alan.

"Do you know the boy?" asked O'Hanly.

"We do," answered Alan. "His name is Jimmy Dugan. He's a homeless street kid. We met him over by the river. So how is Officer Clary?"

"He'll be fine," said O'Hanly. "He killed the two men who were beating on the boy. He shot one and got the other one with his billy. He had a full night last night too."

"How's that?" asked Sean.

"Three men broke into his house last night," answered O'Hanly. "Between him and that dog of his, two of them are dead. The other one isn't talking."

"I bet I can git that man ta talk," said Sean.

"I bet you can," replied O'Hanly. "But talk or not, we all know who he works for."

"Yes we do, and they will pay," said Sean.

CHAPTER SEVEN

F ather Darcey arrived at the hospital right after Sean and Alan. He shook hands with Captain O'Hanly and then O'Hanly introduced him to Sean and Alan. After they shook hands, Father Darcey went into the hospital and asked to see Jimmy Dugan. A nurse had him wait for a moment while she went for Dr. Young. He was there in a few minutes. He and the Father knew each other well and shook hands. "I'm here to see young Jimmy Dugan," said Father Darcey. "I hear he was badly beaten."

"He was Father," said Dr. Young. "We could use some divine intervention right now. If the boy lives, it will definitely be a miracle."

"Take me to him," said the Father. Dr. Young showed Father Darcey to Jimmy's room. Father Darcey moaned when he saw how badly Jimmy had been beaten.

"Who would do such a thing?" said Father Darcey. "Young Jimmy never hurt a soul in his life."

"It is my understanding that a police officer was on his beat and saw two men beating young Jimmy," said the doctor. "The officer was shot in the arm, but the two men who were beating on Jimmy are no longer with us."

"May they rot in Hell," said Father Darcey. "Excuse me Father. Their judgment is not up to me. Now if you'll excuse me doctor, I have work to do." The doctor left the room. Father Darcey knelt down beside Jimmy's bed and started praying. He prayed for almost an hour.

While Father Darcey was with Jimmy, Sean talked with Captian O'Hanly. "Someone wanted young Jimmy dead," said Sean. "I'll be right here with him until he recovers enough to tell us what all happened. Then there'll be some more dead men in this town. I could sure use your help."

"You will have it," said O'Hanly. "I'll be talking with my men. We'll be kicking some ass. You keep me posted on how the boy's doing. If he dies, I know who I'm going after. I was wondering. Why is it that you are so concerned with the boy?"

"Let's just say he's a friend," said Sean. Captain O'Hanly just nodded his head and left.

Sean went to talk with Dr. Young. "Doc, your people need to get another bed set up beside Jimmy," said Sean. "Me and Alan'll be stayin' here while the boy recovers. I want the best care available. Cost doesn't matter."

"I think we can do that," said the doctor. "You know it could be days before he regains consciousness if he ever does."

"I got nowhere else ta be right now," said Sean.

"All right then, I'll have them get that bed set up," said Dr. Young.

Sean went back in Jimmy's room. Alan kept an eye on things outside. Sean found himself kneeling and praying by Jimmy's bedside. Father Darcey looked over at Sean. "I never thought you'd be a praying man Marshal," said Father Darcey. "I've heard of you. I know you've had to kill a lot of men."

"I never killed nobody that wasn't tryin' ta kill me or someone else or hadn't already killed someone," said Sean.

"So, are you a Catholic?" asked the Father.

"I was raised Catholic, but there wasn't even a Catholic church where we lived in Tennessee," said Sean. "My folks were good Christians, but my Pa had trouble with that turnin' the other cheek stuff."

"I'd say you have trouble with that too," said Father Darcey. "So how is it that you know young Jimmy?"

"Father, would you take my confession now?" asked Sean.

"Of course I will my son," answered Father Darcey. Sean went over and closed the door to the room. Then he knelt down.

"Bless me Father for I have sinned," said Sean.

"When was your last confession my son," said Father Darcey.

"I can't remember," answered Sean. "It was maybe over fifteen years ago and there was no Priest to listen.

"What is your sin, my son?" asked the Father.

"It is my fault that Jimmy Dugan is here in the hospital," said Sean.

"And why is that my son?" asked the Father.

"Because he was working for me," said Sean. "He said he knew everything that went on around here, so I hired him find to out things about the local scum around here. He probably got caught doing just that and they beat him for it. And if they find out he's not dead, they'll be after him again."

"You can't know for sure why Jimmy was beaten my son," said Father Darcey. "Do you have anything else to confess?"

"No Father," answered Sean.

"Say fifty Hail Marys and twenty Our Fathers," said Father Darcey. "Now go in peace."

Sean felt a little better when he left Jimmy's room, but his anger was building. Just the very thought of anyone beating a young boy like that angered him. Some people were going to pay.

~~~~

When Captain O'Hanly got back to the Police Station, he got a big surprise. Tom Flannery was waiting in his office. "Who invited you here?" said O'Hanly.

"Kind of touchy aren't you Captain?" said Flannery.

"I don't suppose you know about some young boy being beaten almost to death, do you?" asked O'Hanly. "And one of my officers got shot."

"I don't know what you're talking about," answered Flannery.

"I bet your buddy Thornton does," said O'Hanly. "That scum works for you and if I find out either of you had anything to do with it, I'm coming after you," said O'Hanly. "Now get the hell out of my office. And another thing, I know you got rats in my force. You best tell them when I find out who they are, their days are numbered."

"I repeat, I know nothing about the beating of some young boy," said Flannery. Flannery wasn't lying. He was not aware of what happened during the night or the next morning. As he was leaving, he looked back at O'Hanly. "Nice looking wife you have," said Flannery. O'Hanly jumped up over his desk and ran right at Flannery. He grabbed him by the front of his jacket and then gave him a tremendous right to the jaw. Flannery hit the floor hard, but wasn't unconscious. He stood back up.

"You know that politician is still alive," said Flannery.

"The hell with that son of a bitch and the hell with you," said the Captain. "Now get out of here before I beat you till you can't stand."

"You'll be hearing from my lawyer," said Flannery as he was leaving.

"He can bleed too," said O'Hanly.

The Captain went back into his office and sat down. "Damn, that felt good," he said to himself. "Sergeant Muldoon, come into my office," Sgt. Muldoon reported to the Captain. "Sgt. Muldoon, we have got some rats in this precinct. You're gonna help me find them."

"May I speak freely sir?" asked Sgt. Muldoon.

"Yes, of course you may," said the Captain.

"I think I know of one already," said Muldoon. "Officer Crawford was back in the holding area talking to that man they brought in last night. You know, the one who broke into Officer Clary's house. He didn't know I saw him back there. I was going to tell you after Flannery left."

"Officer Crawford would have no reason to be talking to that man," said O'Hanly. "I suppose if I'd talk to him he'd just make up some story or something. We are basically just using Crawford as a clerk aren't we?"

"Yes, he does most of the filing for us," said Muldoon. "Maybe we can set him up or something. We haven't got Officer Clary's report on what happened this morning. Maybe we can get it from him and see if Crawford goes out of his way to read it."

"Just because he reads a report, doesn't make him guilty," said O'Hanly. "It's what he does after he reads it. I guess we can find out. I'll go over to Officer Clary's house and tell him I must have that report. I'll bring it back and you can keep an eye on Crawford."

When Officer Clary got home from the hospital, Mary Kate took one look at him and started crying. Then she stopped as quickly as she started. She went to Donavan and hugged him as best she could without hurting him. They sat down on the sofa and Donavan told her what had happened. Mary Kate cried a little more and then went to bring Donavan a cup of coffee. When she came back from the kitchen, Donavan was sound asleep. His right arm was down over the end of the sofa and was touching Boss's head. Apparently he had been petting Boss when he fell asleep. Mary Kate let him sleep.

Donavan was still asleep on the sofa when Captain O'Hanly arrived. Mary Kate let him in. "What can we do for you Captain?" asked Mary Kate.

"I need Officer Clary to write his report on what happened this morning," said O'Hanly. "I'm sorry, but it can't wait. I wasn't thinking too clearly this morning. It should have been done before I took him home." Captain O'Hanly saw Boss on the floor next to Donavan. Boss stayed where he was, but he was looking hard at the Captain.

"That's our dog Boss," said Mary Kate. "Boss, come over here and say hi to Donavan's boss." Boss got up and walked over to O'Hanly. He wagged his tail and waited for the Captain to pet him. Captain O'Hanly knelt down and looked Boss in the eyes.

"I hear you're one hell of a dog Boss," said the Captain. "I could use a dog like you over at my house." The Captain gave Boss a hug and then began petting him. Donavan opened his eyes now.

"Hey Captain, what's going on?" asked Donavan.

"Sorry to bother you, but I need your report for what happened this morning," said O'Hanly. "Normally I wouldn't worry about it, but we have a rat in the precinct. I'm trying to confirm who it is. I suppose it could be more than one."

"Well give me the forms and I'll write it up now," said Donavan. "So who do you suspect?"

"I'm not supposed to say when things like this are happening, but I would say that some of this has a lot to do with you," said O'Hanly. "Sgt. Muldoon saw Officer Crawford talking to the men who broke into your house last night. It was back in the holding area where Crawford had no business being."

"He's just a clerk isn't he?" asked Donavan.

"That's what we use him for," answered the Captain. "Somebody's got to handle paperwork."

"That means he could read every report and then go tell his friends everything," said Donavan.

"That's right," said the Captain. "We want to see if he talks to his friends after he reads your report."

"Maybe I should spice it up a bit. Maybe say that there was another man who got away," said Donavan. "That might stir things up."

"It would," said O'Hanly. "Go ahead and do that. In fact, let's have you write up two reports, the real one, and the one we'll let Crawford read." Donavan wrote the two reports and then Captain O'Hanly went back to the Police Station.

Tom Flannery left the Police Station and went straight to his lawyer's office. Joshua could see that someone had punched his jaw. "What can I do for you today Tom?" asked Joshua.

"I want charges brought against Captain O'Hanly," said Tom. "He attacked me."

"I don't suppose you provoked him did you?" asked Joshua.

"I did not," answered Tom. "He was asking me about some young boy who was beaten. I know nothing about that. As I was leaving, I mentioned that he had a lovely wife. That's when he attacked me."

"Look Tom, I'm due in court and this trial I'm on will be a long one," said Joshua. "I'll have some time in the morning. I'll talk to the Captain then and tell him you're pressing charges."

"That will be fine," said Tom. "Let me know how it goes."

"I will," said Joshua. "Just why were you at the Police Station in the first place?"

"I was going to ask the Captain if he knew anything about all the killings that have been happening," said Tom. "I never got the chance to ask him."

"All right Tom, I'll let you know how it goes with the Captain," said Joshua. "Good day to you."

Tom Flannery left his lawyer's office and went straight to Thornton's place. The Ladies Man was checking out some new girls when Flannery got there. Flannery grabbed him by the arm and took him to a room in the back. "You can check out the ladies later," started Flannery. "Just what the hell is going on around here. What's this I hear about some young boy being beaten almost to death?"

"That kid was spyin' on me last night," cried Thornton. "He got away last night, but some of my boys found him. Two more of my boys are dead too. That Officer Clary happened by."

"What'd that boy see anyway?" asked Flannery. "I suppose it was one of your frivolities."

"Hey, I don't say nothing about yours," said Thornton. "So what are we gonna do now?"

"We're going to lay low for a little while," answered Flannery. "Beating that kid and that cop getting shot has really got things stirred up. I don't think Captain O'Hanly is going to be our friend for a while. So just stay out of trouble for a while. We'll get them soon enough."

"All right boss, I'll do my best," said Thornton. "So what's Danaher doing about all this?"

"He might not know about the young boy yet or the cop getting shot, but I'm sure he'd just tell us to stay low for a while," said Flannery.

"Boss, I've a got a new one lined up for you," said Thornton. "Regular day and time."

"That will be fine," said Flannery. "Now I don't want to see you for four days."

"Gotcha boss," said Thornton. Flannery left and Thornton went back to checking out the new girls.

~~~~

When Captain O'Hanly got back to the Police Station, the first thing he did was give Officer Clary's report to Officer Crawford to be filed. Then he went in his office and resumed his normal duties. When Officer Crawford was done for the day, Sgt. Muldoon followed him. Sgt. Muldoon was in civilian clothes and was dressed like a street bum. He was good at this and Officer Crawford had no idea that he was being followed. Officer Crawford stopped at a pub and had a few words with some men who were sitting at the bar. Sgt. Muldoon ordered a glass of whiskey while he watched the men, but he only acted like he was drinking it. Sgt. Muldoon had given up liquor and spirits some time ago.

When Officer Crawford left the pub, Muldoon stayed. After a while, the men who Crawford had talked to left. Muldoon followed them. They went straight to one of the Ladies Man's whorehouses. Muldoon knew they had their rat.

The next day at the Police Station, Captain O'Hanly called Officer Crawford into his office. Sgt. Muldoon was there too. "Officer Crawford, you are terminated," said O'Hanly. "Turn in your service revolver and your badge and get out of my sight. Go and join your friends full time. If you are not out of here in three minutes, I will shoot you myself. I'll just say that you went crazy in here and I had to shoot you to defend myself. Tell Flannery and that Ladies Man that I said hi. Now get the hell out of here." Crawford never said one word. He took off his badge and laid it on the Captain's desk. Then he reached for his service revolver. O'Hanly and Muldoon both had their hands of their service revolvers when Crawford started pulling his revolver from it's holster. "Take that pistol by the butt," said O'Hanly.

Crawford did as instructed and laid the pistol on O'Hanly's desk. Crawford never said one word. He walked out of the office and went to his desk. He pulled out a few personal items and then left the Police Station.

"One down and who knows how many to go," said the Captain.

"Well maybe if there's more of them, they'll see that Crawford is gone and leave on their own," said Muldoon.

"They might," said O'Hanly. "I guess time will tell."

~~~~

For the next three days, Father Darcey came to the hospital and prayed beside Jimmy Dugan's bed for an hour, three times a day. Sean and Alan had been standing guard. They would trade off during the day. Every four hours, one of them would be in the room and the other one would be outside of the room in the hospital and would check outside of the hospital too. At night, one would sleep for three hours and the other one would roam the hospital. It had been quiet. No suspicious people were seen at all.

On the fourth day in the morning, Dr. Young came into Jimmy's room while Sean was there. "If Jimmy doesn't wake up soon, he'll die," said the doctor. "His pulse and his breathing seem strong, but he just won't wake up. He could have brain damage. I don't mean to sound unfeeling, but you must be ready for the inevitable."

"Doc, this boy is not gonna die," screamed Sean. "I won't allow it. No, I just won't allow it. Now you tell whoever it is that takes care a such things that this boy is gonna be wakin' up soon and he'll be wantin' somethin' ta eat. Go on now." The doctor shrugged his shoulders and walked out of the room. Sean watched him leave. When Sean turned back to look at Jimmy, he could see that the boy's eyes were open. Sean smiled at him.

"What's a fella gotta do ta get somethin' to eat around here," said Jimmy in a weak voice.

Sean got up and ran out of the room. "Doc, Doc, git back here. Jimmy's awake," yelled Sean. Dr. Young and most of the hospital staff heard Sean yelling and came running. Dr. Young went over and examined Jimmy. He checked his eyes and his heart and his pulse.

"You gave us a scare young man," said the doctor. "There's no good reason that you are alive."

"I'm not ready to go yet Doc," said Jimmy. "Now can I get something to eat?"

"I'll have them get you some soup," said the doctor. "I don't want you to have anything other than soup for a few days."

"That'll be fine Doc," said Jimmy. "I don't feel strong enough to chew much anyway." Dr. Young left to have them get Jimmy some soup. When he left the room Alan came in.

"Good to have you back son," said Alan. "You sure gave us a start."

"While we're here by ourselves I got somethin' that needs ta be said," said Sean. "We are so sorry that we got you involved in our business. It was wrong of us to ask you."

"I wasn't working for you when I got caught," said Jimmy.

"What do you mean son?" asked Alan. Just then a nurse came into the room with some soup. She sat in a chair beside the bed and started feeding it to him. After half the bowl was empty, Jimmy told her that he could do it himself.

"You've got two broken arms young man," said the nurse with a stern look on her face. "Now just lay there. I'll do the feeding." When Jimmy finished the soup, he asked for more. "You may not have more today young man," said the nurse. "You haven't eaten for several days. If you eat too much you'll just throw it back up. Now tomorrow if the doctor says, you will have more."

"Yes ma'am," said Jimmy. The nurse gave him a smile and left with the dishes. She left a pitcher of water and some glasses and told Sean and Alan that Jimmy could drink some water if he wanted, but not to overdo it. No more than two full glasses. Sean closed the door when the nurse left.

"Now let's pick up where we left off," said Sean. "You said you weren't working for us when you got caught."

"That's right," said Jimmy. "I already had all the stuff you wanted to know. I was going back to the church when I ran into some boys I know. They're homeless and streetwise too. Anyway, they said they were going over to the whorehouse. Some men told them they could have one of the girls for free. All they'd have to do was some favor for them later."

"How old was them boys?" asked Sean.

"Just a little older than me I'd say, maybe twelve," said Jimmy. "They wanted me to go with them, but I said I didn't want to get tied up with them people."

"So are you only eleven years old?" asked Alan.

"Yep, I'm just eleven," answered Jimmy.

"Well what happened next?" asked Alan.

"Well them boys went to the whorehouse," started Jimmy. "I decided to follow them. I wanted to see if them boys would really get to be with one of them girls. When the boys got to the whorehouse, someone let them in. I snuck up to the building after a bit and peeked in all the windows on the first floor. I seen plenty of naked women and men, but I never seen Tommy and Andy. That was their names. There's trees by the house so I climbed to see what I could see. I started on the left side. I didn't see nothing. Then I went to the front. There was three trees in the front. I climbed the one on the left and never seen Tommy or Andy. Then I climbed the tree in the middle. It was a little closer to the building. I looked on the second floor and didn't see them. Then I moved to another limb so I could see better. The room on the third floor in the middle had the curtains open some. I could see Tommy and Andy in there. They was naked and facing a wall. Their hands was tied to something. The Ladies Man was behind them. He was naked too. He was doing it to them boys."

"What, you say he was raping those boys?" said Alan.

"Yes, that's what he was doing. Tommy and Alan were screaming and crying and that Ladies Man was just laughing," said Jimmy. "He did it to Tommy for a while and then he did it to Andy. He was going back and forth to the boys. I almost screamed when I saw it. I knew I had to get out of there and tell someone. The Ladies Man spotted me as I was getting out of the tree. He yelled at me. Two men came running after me. They chased after me for a good while, but it was dark and I knew my way around. I got away from them and got back to the church. I didn't figure anyone would recognize me the next morning, but I was wrong. Them two fellas caught me in that alley and was beating on me when that cop came."

"That cop was Officer Clary," said Alan. "He got shot in the arm but them two men are now dead."

"Answer me something, will you?" asked Jimmy. "Just who are you? I know you're not some gang fellas."

"That's right. We're not in some gang," said Sean. "I'm Federal Marshal Sean O'Rourke and this is Alan Cooper. He's a Pinkerton Detective."

"I heard of you," said Jimmy. "You're that lawman from out west. Everybody's heard of you. And I've heard about them Pinkerton's too. People don't mess with you."

"Yes they do Jimmy, but some of them don't live to talk about it," said Alan. Someone knocked on the door. Alan went to see who it was. It was Captain O'Hanly.

"I see young Jimmy's back with is," said O'Hanly.

"He is, and we're goin' after the men who did this," said Sean. "We're going after them tonight. We could use a couple good men.

You got two you can spare? Better make that three. I want some-one here with Jimmy while we get it done."

"I'll have them for you," said O'Hanly.

"Have your men meet us here at the hospital at 7pm," said Sean. "I'll fill them in when they get here. We're gonna need a wagon and some good rope."

"They'll be here," said O'Hanly and then he left.

"All right Jimmy, now which whorehouse was this?" asked Sean.

"It's the one where you left the wagon and the dead men," said Jimmy. "The Ladies Man lives there. That must have been his room in the middle front on the third floor. Now every so often, that Tom Flannery goes to that whorehouse. The Ladies Man lines up real young girls for him."

"How young are they?" asked Alan.

"Eleven or twelve I'd say," answered Jimmy. "He keeps three young girls at his house too. One's a little older, maybe fifteen, but the other two are maybe thirteen or fourteen."

"How does he get away with that?" asked Alan.

"I heard he tells everyone that the girls are his daughters," said Jimmy. "I never found out how he got the girls. Maybe he bought them. That goes on more than you think."

"Where does that son of a bitch live?" asked Sean.

"His address is 423 Elm Street," answered Jimmy. "It's a big brick house with a big front porch. It has a swing on the porch."

"Well that son of a bitch is going to meet his maker tonight," said Alan. "Him and that Ladies Man won't see another sunset."

"Where's the other two whorehouses?" asked Sean.

"One's on Mill St., 522, and the other one is on 1st Street, 624," said Jimmy. "Now the Ladies Man has two men working at each house every night. Ladies Man don't go anywhere unless he's got two men with him. Flannery must feel safe cause he travels alone."

"So Jimmy, was this the first time you knew about the Ladies Man messin' with young boys?" asked Sean.

"Yes, I never even thought someone could be like that," answered Jimmy. "I was just thinking. Tommy and Andy are street boys like me. Nobody would miss them if they just disappeared. I never thought about it till now, but there's been several boys I used to see around that I just don't see any more. Do you spose he's killing those boys when he gets done with them?"

"He very well could be," said Alan. "We'd never know unless we found some dead bodies. I'll tell you this Jimmy. The Ladies Man is going to die tonight. I couldn't live with myself if I didn't take out a man who would do that."

"That's how I feel about Flannery and them young girls," added Sean. "He dies tonight. I would guess that he doesn't kill them young girls. If he starts'em out real young, he can git a lotta years out of'em."

"Jimmy, I have this back up revolver," said Alan. "I want you to have it with you. I know you have broken arms, but your hands are all right. If the situation would arise, I'm sure you could use it if you had to." Alan put the pistol under Jimmy's pillow. "Now you might need to move that pistol if they need to change your sheets. Try not to let anyone see it."

"I've never handled a gun, but I know how to use it," said Jimmy. "Nobody else is gonna hurt me anymore."

~~~~

The three policemen arrived at the hospital a little before 7pm. There was Captain O'Hanly, Sgt. Muldoon, and Officer Cline. Before Sean could say a word, O'Hanly spoke. "I'll be going," said O'Hanly. "Sgt. Muldoon is going too. Officer Cline will be staying here with the boy. He's a good man. I trust him." O'Hanly and Muldoon were not in uniform.

"That's fine, but I want to let you both know what's gonna happen tonight," said Sean. "That way if you don't have the stomach for it, you can say so before we start."

"We're going to kill them two sons a bitches, aren't we?" asked O'Hanly.

"Yes we are," answered Sean. "And anyone else who gits in our way."

"Well let's get started then," said O'Hanly.

"I aim ta hang them two," said Sean. "I'm gonna hang'em somewhere right downtown and I'm gonna put some signs on'em. Them signs are gonna tell folks just why we hung'em."

"Hanging's probably too good for them, but it sure works," said O'Hanly. "Let's go."

"Alan and me have never seen these two fellas," said Sean. "Give me a good description of'em."

"Flannery will be easy to spot," started O'Hanly. "He's got light red hair, almost blonde. His blue eyes really stand out. He's got a moustache that he curls on the ends. He's got a slender build and's around six foot one or so. He'll be wearing fancy clothes if we catch him there with his clothes on."

"Well if he's not at the whorehouse, we'll get'm at his house," said Sean. "Now what's this Ladies Man look like?"

"He's got black hair. I mean it's really black, like coal," said O'Hanly. "He's a tall skinny man. I'd say he's six foot three at least, but I bet he don't weigh 150 pounds. He's got no face hair and he's got a small scar on his left cheek."

O'Hanly and Muldoon didn't know about Flannery's little girls or Thornton's little boys. Sean told them on the way to the whorehouse. Sean and Alan could see the fire in their eyes after they were told. "I think we better kill Thornton's men too," said O'Hanly. "They know what goes on in that place. They're just as guilty as Thornton and Flannery."

"That's fine by me," said Sean.

CHAPTER EIGHT

They stopped the wagon about a hundred yards from the building. "I'm gonna go take a look see and then I'll be back with a plan," said Sean. It was completely dark now. There was no moon. The only light there was came from the lanterns in the whorehouse and a few buildings that weren't far from it. Sean eased his way up to the building. He went all around the building and peeked into all of the rooms that had lanterns lit in them. He saw plenty of men, but none of them were Flannery or the Ladies Man. No other horses or carriages were tied in front of the whorehouse, but there were a half dozen tied out back. The back door was locked. One of the carriages had a driver who apparently was waiting for someone who was inside. Sean slipped up on him. The driver was sleeping as he sat there. Sean climbed up and sat down beside him. Then he pulled out his bowie knife and put the blade of it against the man's throat. "Wake up sweetheart," said Sean.

"What in the bloody hell?" screamed the man as he woke up and felt the blade against his neck.

"Quiet down now," said Sean. "Don't make me cut ya. Now who are you waitin' for?"

"I drive for Tom Flannery," said the man.

"Do you like Flannery?" asked Sean.

"Hell no, he treats me like dirt," said the man. "But it's a job. My family's gotta eat." Sean took the blade away from the man's throat.

"What's your name?" asked Sean.

"It's Charles Cooke," answered the man.

"Well Charles Cooke, Mr. Flannery won't be needin' you anymore this evening," said Sean. "In fact, he won't be needin' you ever again. Here's $50." Sean reached into a pocket and pulled out the money and handed it to Charles. "Now you go on home now. Keep that horse and carriage or sell'em or whatever you want to do. Hope that'll help ya out some."

"It will kind sir," said Charles.

"One more thing before you go Charles," said Sean. "How long's Flannery been inside?"

"It's only been a half hour or so," answered Charles. "He usually stays at least three hours when he comes here."

"Thanks Charles. Tell the Mrs. I said hi," said Sean.

"And who should I say you are?" asked Charles.

"Just a friend," answered Sean. "Just a friend."

"Well thank you friend," said Charles. "I don't know what you're up to my friend, but be careful. Thornton's got two men working in there and they're good with knives."

"We'll be careful," said Sean. "Now you go on. You don't wanna be around here. It might get ugly." Charles waved goodbye to Sean and left in the carriage. Sean worked his way back to the other men.

"We lucked out boys," said Sean. "Flannery is here tonight. That carriage that just left was his. I had a talk with his driver.

He's been here a half hour. That driver said he's usually here for three hours or so. Now we know that Thornton's room is on the top floor in the middle front, but that don't mean he'll be in there. Flannery could be anywhere."

"So how are we going to do this?" asked O'Hanly.

"One of us needs to keep an eye on the back door," started Sean. "Three of us will go to the front door. One of us will knock and the other two will be out of sight on both sides. Captain, maybe you should do the knocking. They probably know you and might think you came to enjoy the ladies."

"They should know me, but I've never been there before," said O'Hanly. They might think I'm there for the ladies since I'm out of uniform."

"When someone opens the door, take a quick look and see if he's alone or not," said Sean. "There should be two men working in there. If one man answers the door, We'll grab him when he turns around to show you inside. If there's two, we'll worry about that if it happens."

"What will we do with him?" asked Alan.

"We'll get as much information out of him as we can," answered Sean. "If he won't talk, we'll kill'm. If he does talk, we might have 'm show us around the place before we kill'm. Muldoon, go ahead and get out back. Stay outta sight as best ya can. Ya got Flannery and Thornton's description. Don't grab nobody unless they fit the description."

Muldoon worked his way around back. The others waited a few minutes to give him plenty of time to get back there. Then the three of them went to the front door. Alan and Sean got on both sides while O'Hanly knocked on the door. O'Hanly knocked on the door, but no one answered. He waited a few minutes and then knocked a little harder. He could hear someone speaking as they approached the door. "All right, all right, don't get yourself into a tizzy," the man said. "The ladies aren't goin' nowhere." A medium build red haired man opened the door. He looked at O'Hanly and had a look of surprise on his face. "Jesus Joseph and Mary, I never expected to see you here Captain," said the man. "Not gettin' any at home?"

"Just thought I'd get me some variety," said O'Hanly.

"Well come on in Captain," said the man. "I'll show you around and you can take your pick." O'Hanly stepped inside and the man started closing the door. When it was about halfway shut, Sean grabbed one of his arms and yanked him outside. He punched the man in the jaw, but not hard enough to knock him out. He staggered, but did not fall. O'Hanly stood just inside with the door still open. Alan grabbed the man and held him from behind. He took him to the side of the door out of the light. Alan had some rope on him and he tied the man's hands behind him. Sean pulled his pistol and stuck the barrel into the man's mouth. Alan held the man, but moved to one side.

"Now don't even think about yellin'," said Sean. "This thing might just go off." The man shook his head no. "Now we're gonna ask you some questions and yer gonna answer them. Do we understand each other?" The man shook his head yes. "Now I'm gonna take this pistol outta yer mouth so you can talk." Sean took the pistol out of the man's mouth. He put the pistol back into his shoulder holster. Then Sean pulled out the bowie knife. He put the blade of it right in the man's crotch. "This thing is razor sharp," said Sean. "I can shave with it." Sean moved the knife a little and cut the man's pants. "See what I mean. It's razor sharp."

The man looked down and saw where Sean had cut his pants. The man started shaking.

"I'll tell ya whatever ya want," cried the man. "Just don't cut me down there."

"Sounds like we're gonna git along just fine," said Sean. "Now what room is Flannery in?"

"I'm not certain," cried the man. "He's usually on the second floor in the first room to the right of the stairs. Sometimes he's on the first floor in the room closest to the back door. I know he's not there today. Rodney took him upstairs today. They got a new girl for him."

"How old is this new girl?" asked Alan.

"Can't be no more than 12," answered the man. "Flannery likes'em young." Alan reached into a pocket and pulled out his brass knuckles. He put them on his right hand.

"So you know he likes little girls and you don't do anything about it," said Alan. "You know about Thornton's little boys too, don't you?"

"They're the bosses," cried the man. "You're not gonna hit me with that thing are ya?"

"Not just yet," said Alan. "Now where's Thornton?"

"He's in his room on the third floor," answered the man. "He'll be there most of the night. He's got three of'em up there now."

"You mean three little boys?" asked Sean.

"Yes, that's what I mean," answered the man.

"How does he get those boys?" asked Alan.

"Some of his boys grab'em off the street," said the man.

"So you aren't one of the boys who grab them off the street?" asked Sean.

"No, I just work here and whenever Thornton goes somewhere, me and Rodney go with him," answered the man. "He never goes nowhere alone."

O'Hanly stayed just inside the door as Sean and Alan questioned the man. He kept watch inside. He now heard someone coming down the stairs. The inside of the building was a long hall with rooms on both sides. The stairs were halfway down on the right. O'Hanly opened his jacket a little and stuck his hand close to his shoulder holster. He wanted to be ready if necessary. Finally, a man came out of the staircase. He looked and saw O'Hanly looking at him. "What in the hell are you doing here Captain?" asked the man. "And where in the hell is Will and why is that front door open?"

"Will said he needed to go out for a minute," answered O'Hanly. "He's just taking a smoke. You want me to tell him to come back in?"

"No, let'm smoke," said Rodney. "I gotta go take a dump. Tell Will I'll be back shortly."

"I'll do that," said O'Hanly. Rodney opened the back door and went to an outhouse. When Rodney went outside, O'Hanly went outside and talked to Sean and Alan. "The other man went out back to the outhouse," said O'Hanly. "I'll knock him out when he comes back in."

"That'll be good," said Sean. "Drag'm outside and have Muldoon tie'm up and gag'm."

"That fella you got outside is named Will if you're interested," said O'Hanly as he turned and went down the hall toward the back door.

"So, Will, I guess we won't be a needin' you anymore," said Sean. "Alan, you can hit'm now if ya want." Will got a very strange look on his face when he heard Sean's words. He still had that look on his face as Alan's right hand struck his left temple. Sean could hear the bones crack as the brass knuckles made contact. Will hit the ground dead. They dragged the body up against the building and then waited to hear from O'Hanly.

Muldoon watched as Rodney came out the back door and went to the outhouse. He knew that this man wasn't Flannery or Thornton. Rodney did his business and then headed back inside. O'Hanly was just inside the door and waiting. As soon as the door opened, O'Hanly cracked Rodney on the head with his service revolver. Rodney slumped to the ground. When Muldoon saw what had happened, he went over to help O'Hanly. "This is the other fella that works here," whispered O'Hanly. "The other one's out front dead. Tie this one up and gag him too." They dragged Rodney into the shadows. Muldoon tied and gagged him. "Now you stay out back here," said O'Hanly. "We got a good idea where Flannery and Thornton are and we're goin' after them. If they would happen to get away and come out here, you shoot them." Muldoon nodded his head yes. O'Hanly went back inside. He closed the door behind him and went down the hall to Sean and Alan. "Got the other one tied and gagged out back," said O'Hanly. "Let's go get them two."

"All right, let's move," said Sean. "Now we need to check all the rooms. That fella coulda lied to us. Alan you take the rooms on the right and I'll take the left. O'Hanly, you keep an eye on the stairs." Sean pulled the front door closed behind them and locked it. O'Hanly went to the staircase. Sean started down the left side and Alan down the right. There were eight rooms on the left and seven on the right. Sean could hear the bed squeaking as he got to the first door. He eased the door open. The door hinge squeaked some as opened the door. Inside was a bald fat man humping away on one of the women. Both of them looked over at Sean. "Don't mind me," said Sean. "Go on with what yer doin'. Here's five dollars. Have another'n on me." Sean laid the money on a night stand and closed the door. He stood there and listened before going to the next door. He could hear the man and woman speaking inside.

"Who the hell was that?" said the woman.

"Damned if I know," said the man. "But he's a generous sombitch. I'll be taking another turn after this'n."

When Alan opened the door of the first room on his side, he got a surprise. There were two women in bed together. They were very beautiful. They both looked over at Alan. "Would you like to join us?" one of them asked Alan.

"Thanks for the invite ladies, but I seem to be in the wrong room," answered Alan.

"It doesn't have to be the wrong room," the other woman said. "Come on now. Don't be shy."

"Very tempting ladies, but I must decline," said Alan. "Now continue with whatever you were doing." Alan closed the door and moved on to the next room. He could hear the two women giggling as he left. When Alan opened the door of the second room, a man and a woman were on the floor facing away from the door. The woman was on all fours and the man was behind her humping away. They had no idea that Alan had opened the door. Alan closed the door and moved on.

Sean could hear some very intense bed squeaking as he neared his second room. He eased the door open. The man and woman were really getting intense and making a lot of noise now. They never noticed Sean. Sean closed the door and moved on. As he neared the third room, Sean thought he heard the crack of a whip. He heard right. When he opened the door, there was a naked man tied face down on the bed. The woman wasn't naked, but had on something that was very shear and Sean could see her form underneath. She had a bull whip in her right hand. She turned and saw Sean. "Do you want to play too?" she asked Sean."

"Maybe later," said Sean as he closed the door and moved on.

Alan could hear crying as he got to his next room. He burst into the room. There was a naked woman sitting on the edge of the bed. A half dressed man was standing close to her. "Just what did you do to her?" said Alan as he walked over to the man.

"I didn't do nothin'," answered the man. The woman stopped crying. "It's just a game we play."

"A game, what sort of game?" asked Alan.

The woman spoke. "He tells me I've been bad and he needs to spank me," said the woman. "I cry a little and then he spanks me."

"Do you want him to spank you?" asked Alan.

"Course I do," answered the woman. "I like it." Alan shook his head a little and left the room. Before he got to the next door, he could hear the woman being spanked. He could hear her saying "harder, harder."

Sean was a little surprised when he got to his next room. Inside was a beautiful black woman. On top of her was a very old looking man. The old man ignored Sean and kept pumping away. "Sugar, if you want some a this, you'll hafta wait till ole Elmer gets done," she said to Sean. "He may be old, but he knows what he's a doin' and he can go a long time."

"Well good fer ole Elmer," said Sean. "Now excuse me, wrong room." Sean closed the door and moved on. The next three rooms weren't being used. When Sean got to the last room on his side, he could hear what sounded like two women and one man. He heard right. When he opened the door, there was a man in bed with two women. The man looked over at Sean.

"I'll be done in bout two hours," said the man. "You can have'em after that." Sean nodded his head and closed the door. Alan was still checking out his rooms so Sean started checking the rooms on Alan's side. The first room Sean came to had two men and one woman inside. When they Saw Sean, one of the men started to move over to where his clothes were. Sean saw a pistol belt next to the man's clothing.

"Don't be goin' fer that shooter," said Sean. "There's no reason fer you ta die tonight. Go on with what you were a doin'. I'm just at the wrong room. Sorry." Sean backed out of the room and closed the door. He stood to the right side of the door for a moment and listened.

"Who in the Sam hell was that?" one of the men asked the others.

"Hell if I know," said the other man. "Don't worry about it. Let's get back ta where we were." The next rooms that Sean and Alan checked were not in use.

"Well boys, I reckon we'll do this again on the second floor," said Sean. "Now Alan, if Flannery is in one a yer rooms, don't kill'm. Knock his ass out. I want him alive when we hang'm. Be quick too. He might have a pistol close by."

"I'll get'm," said Alan. "Let's move."

As soon as the three of them stepped out of the stairwell on the second floor, they could hear crying. It was coming from one of the rooms at the end of the hall on the right side. O'Hanly stayed at the stairwell while Sean and Alan eased toward the end of the hall. As they got closer, they could tell which room it was.

The crying was getting louder now. A young girl was saying "no, quit, you're hurting me." It sounded like she tried to scream once, but her scream was stopped. Sean eased the door open. Hate filled his eyes when the door opened. Flannery was on top of a little girl and pumping away. He had a smile on his face and his left hand was over the girl's mouth. Before Flannery realized that the door was even open, Sean rushed over and punched Flannery on the side of his face. The punch knocked him clear out of the bed and onto the floor. The little girl had no idea what was happening and started screaming. Alan got ahold of her. He put a hand over her mouth, but talked to her nicely and tried to calm her down. "You're all right now darlin'," said Alan. "This man won't hurt you anymore. He won't hurt anyone ever again after this night." The young girl grabbed ahold of Alan and hugged him like she would never let him go. Alan pulled a sheet off the bed and wrapped her naked body. Sean stood over Flannery and made sure he was unconscious. "Can you do something for me darlin'?" Alan asked the girl. She nodded her head yes. "That's good. Now I want you to stay in this room. There's another bad man in this building that we need to get. You stay right here in this room. Lock the door behind us. Don't open that door for anyone except me or Sean here. My name is Alan. What's your name?"

"It's Mary, Mary Campbell," answered the girl.

"Well Mary Campbell, you do like I say now," said Alan. "We'll be back for you when this is over." Mary nodded her head yes. Alan and Sean dragged Flannery out of the room. They heard Mary lock the door behind them.

"Let's take'm down ta one a those empty rooms downstairs," said Sean. "We'll tie'm up good and then go git Thornton." They carried Flannery downstairs. A customer was coming out of one of the rooms.

"What's wrong with him?" the customer asked Sean.

"Can't hold his liquor," answered Sean. The man shrugged his shoulders and went out the back door.

They put Flannery in the closest empty room. Then they got some more rope. They tied his hands behind his back and then tied his hands to his feet. Then they put a big gag in his mouth. "Captain, you stay here with him while Alan and me go git Thornton," said Sean. "Lock the door behind us."

Sean and Alan eased their way up the stairs to the third floor. When they cleared the stairwell, they could hear some crying. It was coming from the room at the end of the hall. It was Thornton's room. They eased their way to the door. They could hear Thornton talking as they got closer. "I bet you boys never thought this was gonna happen, did ya?" said Thornton. "Now squeal."

Alan had heard enough. He slammed himself into the door and forced it open. Thornton was standing there naked with a horrified look on his face when he saw Alan coming at him. Alan didn't have on his brass knuckles, but he hit Thornton so hard on the chin that it picked him clear up off the floor and knocked him a few feet backwards. He hit the floor unconscious. There were three naked very young boys in the room. They were facing a wall with their hands tied to a bar that went across the whole wall of the room. The boys crying stopped when they saw Thornton hit the floor. Sean pulled his knife and cut the boys loose. "You boys get your clothes back on and get out of here," said Alan. "Go home or wherever you got to go."

"Mr., what are gonna do with that son of a bitch?" asked one of the boys. "He needs ta die for what he done ta us."

"He is gonna die," said Sean. "We're gonna hang'm and we're gonna pin a sign on'm sayin' why we hung'm.

"Can I watch Mr.?" asked the boy.

"I spect you got the right," said Sean. "But I don't think you should watch. You'll be able ta see'm after it's done. We aim ta hang'm right downtown fer everone ta see. He'll be dead boy. Don't you worry bout that."

"Hey Mr., are you that man that knows Jimmy Dugan?" asked the boy.

"Yep, I know Jimmy," answered Sean. "Are you a friend a his?"

"I know'm," said the boy. "Sometimes he shares some food with me."

"So yer a street boy too, huh," said Sean.

"Yep, I was at the orphanage, but I ran off," said the boy. "Sometimes them Sisters can be nasty. I heard Jimmy was in the hospital. How's he doin'?"

"He got hurt pretty bad, but he's doin' good now," said Sean. "It'll take'm a long time ta heal."

"He got beat up by some a the same scum that grabbed us, didn't he?" said the boy.

"Yep, and he's the one that told us where this scum was," said Sean.   "What's   yer   name   boy?"
"It's Johny, Johny Pierson," answered the boy.

"Well Johny, I'll tell Jimmy you was askin' bout him," said Sean.

"Don't tell'm what happened to us," said Johny. "Nobody needs ta know that."

"Well Jimmy already knows that stuff was happenin' here," said Sean. "It's gonna be hard fer you ta git over it, but it wasn't yer fault. Ya done nothin' wrong. You boys need ta stick together and make sure nothin' like this happens again. Now you boys finish dressin' and go. Wait a minute." Sean looked around the room. He started going through everything. He found what he was looking for. There was a bunch of money in a drawer on a night stand by the bed. Sean counted it out. There was $900. "Well boys, you can have this money," said Sean as he handed each of the boys $300. "Don't be foolish with it. If you flash it around, someone'll be wantin' ta take it from ya. Some folks kill fer that kind a money. You boys know what I'm sayin'?"

"We know," said Johny. "We'll be careful." The boys finished dressing and left. Alan tied Thornton's hands behind his back and gagged him. Then he found a pitcher of water and threw it on Thornton's face. Thornton regained consciousness. Sean grabbed him and stood him up.

"Let's go sweetheart. You got a date with the hangman," said Sean. Thornton tried to speak but couldn't because of the gag. "What's that yer sayin'?" said Sean. "You don't wanna hang. Well maybe later, if you tell us what we want ta know, we won't hang ya." They left Thornton naked and made him walk downstairs to the first floor. They went to the room where they had Flannery. O'Hanly let them in. Flannery was conscious now. "You all stay here," said Sean. "I need ta look around a bit. I won't be long." Sean left the room and went back up to Thornton's room. Up there was what he wanted. There was a desk in a corner of the room and there was plenty of pens and ink. Sean took out the bowie knife and cut out two pieces of sheet about a foot and a half by two feet. On the sheets, he made the signs that he was going to pin on Flannery and Thornton. It took longer than he thought it would. When he finished, he took the signs and shook them so the ink would dry quicker. When he was sure the ink was dry, he folded up the signs and put them in a pocket. When he got to the first floor, he went to the room where ole Elmer was with the black woman. Sean knocked on the door and then walked in without waiting for an answer. Elmer had just finished and was getting dressed.

"You can have some a this now honey," the woman said to Sean.

"Thanks for the offer ma'am. But what I need is some pins," said Sean. "You got any hat pins or any kind of pins at all?"

"There's some pins in that top drawer on that stand in the corner," said the woman. "What you gonna do with pins? You're not doin' funny stuff, are ya?"

"No ma'am. Just gotta pin up somethin'," said Sean. Sean reached into the drawer and found some pins. He put them in a jacket pocket and then faced the woman and smiled. "Many thanks," said Sean and then he laid a $5.00 bill on the stand. The woman got up from the bed and went to Sean. Sean was amazed at her shape. It was beautiful. She went to Sean and kissed him on the cheek.

"You can get pins from me anytime," said the woman. Sean smiled at her and left. He went back to the room where they had Flannery and Thornton.

"I guess we can go get it done boys," said Sean as he entered the room.

"I want to go talk to that young girl again," said Alan. "I want to reassure her that we're coming back for her."

"Go ahead," said Sean. "Captain, you go ahead and git the wagon and Muldoon and that other fella. I'll stay here with these two." O'Hanly left and Sean stayed in the room. He made Thornton sit on the floor next to Flannery.

Alan went to the second floor and knocked on the door of Mary's room. "Mary, it's me Alan," said Alan. "Let me in please." Mary got up from the bed and let Alan in. As soon as he closed the door, Mary wrapped her arms around him and started crying. "Don't cry Mary. Things will be all right now," said Alan. "I won't let anything bad happen to you again."

"Promise me Alan. Promise me," cried Mary.

"I promise," said Alan. "Now I need for you to be brave for a while longer. I have to leave again and take care of these bad men. I need you to stay right here again till I get back. I will be back. I promise."

"I'll stay here till you come for me," said Mary. Alan gave her a kiss on the cheek and left. When he got downstairs, O'Hanly had the wagon out front and Muldoon was there with the other man who worked for Thornton. Sean untied Flannery's legs and walked him and Thornton out to the wagon. Their gags were not removed. They put Flannery and Thornton in the wagon first and then loaded the dead man. The man from out back was loaded last. Then Alan, Sean, and O'Hanly got on the wagon. O'Hanly drove the wagon. Sean got in the wagon bed and pulled out his bowie knife. He went to the man from out back and cut his throat down to the bone.

"That's to show you that we're serious," said Sean. Flannery and Thornton looked horrified as they watched the blood flow from the man's neck. Sean then tied Flannery and Thornton's legs so they couldn't try to jump out of the wagon. "Well Captain, let's get downtown and find us a good strong tree or somethin' ta hang these two from. O'Hanly worked the reins and the wagon moved.

They had only gone a short distance when Sean had O'Hanly stop the wagon. "Boys, I think one'r two of us should stay at the whorehouse," said Sean. "Could happen that some of Thornton or Flannery's boys'd stop by and need to see'em. Could be they'd come ta git them young boys'r that young girl. They might get a little crazy if they'd show up and nobody'd be there. I wouldn't want them takin' that young girl."

"I'll stay," said Alan. "I can handle it by myself."

"Are you sure?" asked Sean. "It could get ugly if some a their boys show up."

"It could, but I bet them boys'd be lost if they knew we cut off the head of the snake," said Alan.

"All right, you stay," said Sean. "We'll get things done and come back for you. If we hear shootin' before we git too far, we'll high tail it back." Alan got down off the wagon and went back to the whorehouse. Sean and the others headed downtown.

When they were almost downtown they kept looking for a good tree to do the job. Nothing seemed to suit Sean. They were downtown now and right in front of the newspaper building. In front of the building were two huge flagpoles. One was for the U.S. flag and the other one was for the state flag. The state flagpole was a little shorter than the U.S. flagpole. Sean eyeballed the flagpoles slowly. "I think we found what we were lookin' for," said Sean. "We'll just hafta decide which one a these fellas gits top billing."

"Oh, I think Flannery should get top billing," said O'Hanly. "This Ladies Man isn't much more than a murdering pimp."

"Fine by me," said Sean. "I'll get these ropes ready." Sean got two ropes and got in the wagon bed so Flannery and Thornton could watch as he made the hangman's nooses. He made them very slow and meticulously. He had a grin on his face as he worked. Thornton kept trying to speak, but couldn't because of the gag. When the nooses were ready, Sean got out of the wagon and tied the ropes onto the ropes on the flagpoles that were used to raise and lower the flags. He used all of his weight to make sure that the flagpole ropes were strong enough to hold a man's dead weight. They were. "All right Flannery, you're first," said Sean. Sean and Muldoon took Flannery out of the wagon and stood him by the big flagpole. Sean placed the rope around his neck and pulled it tight. "I got one question before I hang you," said Sean. "Who's yer boss?" Then Sean took the gag from Flannery's mouth.

"Go to hell you son of a bitch," yelled Flannery.

"You first," said Sean as he yanked on the rope and pulled Flannery about ten feet off the ground. He tied off the rope and watched as Flannery kicked and squirmed. Thornton was trying to scream but couldn't. "Your turn now," said Sean as he and Muldoon pulled Thornton out of the wagon. They took him over and stood him by the flagpole. Thornton's knees kept buckling so Muldoon had to hold him upright while Sean placed the noose around his neck. "Same question fer you now," said Sean. "Who's yer boss?" Sean took the gag from Thornton's mouth.

"It's Danaher," yelled Thornton. "Danny Danaher." Sean started yanking on the rope. "But you said you wouldn't hang us if we told you who our boss was."

"I lied," said Sean as he yanked on the rope and pulled Thornton about ten feet off the ground. Then he tied off the rope and stepped back to watch Thornton kick and squirm.

"What are we gonna do with these other two?" asked Muldoon.

"We'll just put them on the ground by their bosses," said Sean. He and Muldoon pulled the two dead bodies from the wagon and over by the flagpoles. "Now I got somethin' else to do," said Sean. "Captain, take the wagon over next to them we hung. Either one first. It don't matter. I need to stand up on the wagon and pin somethin' on them two."

O'Hanly drove the wagon over next to Flannery. Sean stood on the wagon and pulled the pieces of sheet that he had cut from his pocket. He unfolded one of them a little so he could make sure he had the right one. He did. He unfolded it the rest of the way and then took some pins out of his jacket pocket. He pinned the top of his sign to Flannery's waist and let it hang down to cover his naked privates. The sign said as follows.

I am Tom Flannery

Thief
Murderer
Arsonist
Extortionist
Child Molester

Then O'Hanly moved the wagon over to Thornton. Sean took his sign and pinned it to Thornton just as he did to Flannery. The sign said as follows.

I am Alexander Thornton
Some call me The Ladies Man

Thief
Pimp
Murderer
Extortionist
Child Molester

They all stood there for a moment and looked at the hanged men. "Does anybody feel any remorse?" asked Sean.

"I think I should," answered O'Hanly. "But I don't. I feel good. How bout you Muldoon?"

"When I think about them young boys and that little girl, I want to hang them all over again," said Muldoon. "Now we need to figure out how to get Danaher."

"Who is this Danaher?" asked Sean.

"He's our Deputy Mayor," answered O'Hanly.

"We'll git him too," said Sean. "One way or another, we'll get him. Now we best git back to that whorehouse. Hope nothin' happened."

"I hope nobody watched what we did tonight," said O'Hanly.

"If anyone was watchin', they sure didn't run out here ta stop us," said Sean. "Hell, they'd a probly wanted ta help us. It was pretty dark too. I doubt they'd recognize us. Now let's move."

CHAPTER NINE

Back at the whorehouse, Alan was on the first floor. The front and back doors were locked. He thought about going back upstairs and talking to Mary Campbell, but decided against it. It might distract him. He got himself a chair and sat down just inside the front door. He also had a good view of the back door. He had been sitting there for about a half hour when he heard someone coming down the stairs. He stayed in his chair and opened his jacket so he could get to his revolver quickly if necessary. A middle aged man came out of the stairwell and looked around and saw Alan sitting there. "I'll be leaving now," said the man to Alan. "You can lock up behind me." Alan got up and headed to the back door. He opened the door for the man. The man stopped halfway out the door and looked at Alan. "Where's Will and Rodney?" asked the man.

"They were dead tired so I told them I'd spell them for a bit while they took a nap," said Alan.

"Oh," said the man. "See you again in a couple of weeks."

"Goodnight," said Alan. "See you then." Alan watched the man as he got in his buggy and left. Then he closed and locked the door. He went back to his chair and sat down. A couple more customers left shortly after he sat back down. There we no words spoken. Alan just locked the door behind them after they left. One of the working girls came out of her room and stared at Alan for a while. Then she walked over to him.

"You're new here, aren't you?" she asked. "You're kinda good looking. How about a free one?"

"No thank you ma'am. I'm working," said Alan. "But I thank you for the offer."

"Maybe another time," she said as she turned and went back to her room. "My name's Mabel if you get the urge."

"Goodnight Mabel," said Alan. Mabel smiled and went back into her room. Alan could tell that she didn't lock her door. Then he thought for a moment. "None of the doors were locked when we were checking the rooms. Maybe that's their policy," thought Alan. "Maybe they keep their doors unlocked so if anything would happen, the men could get into the rooms without breaking the door down. That would make sense."

Another hour went by. Alan started pacing in the hallway. He was near the back door when he heard knocking on the front door. He moved slowly to the front door. He waited and listened. Whoever was outside knocking on the door was getting impatient now. They started beating on the door. Alan could hear that two men were outside. "Just where in the hell is Will now?" said one of the men.

"He could be in the outhouse," said the other man.

"Well then Rodney should be answering the damn door," said the man. "I might just kick his ass."

"Well quit your bitchin' and go out back and see if he's in the damn outhouse," said the other man. Alan could hear the man walking away. There was no knocking for a while. Then Alan could hear the man coming back from out back.

"He's not in the damn outhouse Phil. Where in the hell could them two be?" said the other man.

"Well George, maybe them two decided to take a turn with some of the girls," said Phil. "Sometimes the boss don't care if there's not too many customers. We'll just keep trying. Sooner or later one of em'll answer the damn door."

About every two minutes George or Phil would bang on the door. Some customers stuck their heads out the doors of their rooms to see what was happening. Finally, Alan decided to answer the door. Before he opened the door, he put his brass knuckles on his left hand. He made sure his jacket was unbuttoned and held his right hand inside the jacket close to his shoulder holster. Then he opened the door. "What can I do for you gentleman?" asked Alan.

The two men were surprised seeing Alan standing there. "Who in the hell're you and where in the hell is Will and Rodney?"

"First off, Will and Rodney were just dead so I'm keeping watch while they lay down a bit," started Alan. "Second off, I'm someone you don't want to mess with."

"The hell you say," said Phil. "Hey, I seen you before. I seen you at the newspaper building that one day." Phil was reaching for something as he was talking. Alan didn't hesitate. He pulled his revolver and shot Phil point blank in the chest. As Phil was falling backwards, he fell against George. George had just taken a revolver from his pants pocket. When Phil fell backwards into him, the pistol was knocked from his hand. When the pistol hit the ground, it went off. The bullet struck Alan in his right upper arm. Alan dropped his pistol as the bullet struck him. George bent down and was attempting pick up his pistol when Alan kicked him in the face with his right foot. George was knocked backwards.

Alan didn't hesitate. He ignored his pistol and went after George with the brass knuckles. He struck George twice on the right side of his head. George didn't move.

The shots made several people come running to see what had happened. Most of the women and customers took one look at the two dead men and Alan's bloody arm and ran back to their rooms. Mabel had been one of the first ones to see what had happened. She took a look at the dead men. "Well, can't do nothin' for them two," she said. "Come on honey, I'll patch you up some and then you best get to a doctor soon as you can." Alan didn't say a word. He retrieved his pistol and the other men's pistols and went with Mabel. Mabel had him sit on the edge of her bed. She helped him take off his jacket and shirt. "You're lucky honey," she said when she got a good look at the wound. "Bullet went straight through. Didn't hit bone. You'll be good as new in no time."

Alan watched her as she cleaned and dressed his wound. He was impressed. "You'd make a good nurse," said Alan. "You do good work."

"I was a good nurse," said Mabel. "I figured I should help out during the war since my husband was doing his share. He got himself killed at Petersburg."

"I'm sorry for your loss," said Alan. "You could still be a nurse you know."

"I know I could but I really don't mind doing this," said Mabel. "I'll keep doing this as long as I can stand it and then maybe go back to nursing or something."

"Maybe you could run your own place someday," said Alan. "Then you could just be the boss."

"I've thought about that, but it could never happen in this town," said Mabel. "The bunch that runs this town don't let no competition even get started. The last bunch that tried to get started ended up in the Charles River."

"Well, maybe things'll change," said Alan. "We can hope."

"So why are you talking to me like this?" asked Mabel. "You're not one of them, are you?"

"No Mabel, I'm not," said Alan. "For now, we'll just let it go at that."

"All right, we'll let it go," said Mabel. "How bout a shot of some good bourbon? You look like you could use some."

"That would be nice," said Alan. Mabel went to a closet and pulled out a bottle. She found two glasses and poured them both a drink.

"You're a gentleman," said Mabel. "Your Mrs. is a lucky woman. Here's to your health."

"And here's to yours," said Alan. They both took a sip of their bourbon.

Sean and the others heard the two shots in the distance. O'Hanly cracked the reins and got the horses moving as fast as they could go. He took the wagon right up to the front door. They saw the two dead men out front and knew that something had happened. "Muldoon, you go out back," said Sean. "Captain, you stay here. I'm goin' in." Sean waited a moment for Muldoon to get out back. Then he pulled his pistol and went inside. He noticed right away that the front door was unlocked. He stood for a moment and stared down the hall. A room on the left had its door open. He eased down the hall toward the open door. As he got closer he could hear a man and a woman talking. He recognized the man's voice. He peered inside the room. Alan was sitting there on the edge of a bed with a beautiful half naked lady. They were drinking whiskey and talking. Sean could see that Alan had been wounded. He put his pistol back in its holster and walked in. "How bout introducing me to your friend?" said Sean as he entered the room. Both of them were a little startled when Sean started talking. They hadn't seen him walk in.

"Well Sean, this is Mabel. Mabel, this is Sean," said Alan. Sean took Mabel's hand and kissed it.

"I see you're a gentleman too," said Mabel. "Just my luck, you're both spoken for."

"Yes we are," said Sean. "So how's Alan's wound?"

"Bullet went right through," said Mabel. "I cleaned him up good. Should still get to a doctor though. So do you boys have last names?"

"Course we do," answered Sean. "Mine's O'Rourke and his is Cooper."

"O'Rourke, Sean O'Rourke. I know who you are," said Mabel. "Your that lawman from out west aren't you?"

"Yes I am," answered Sean. "And Alan here is a Pinkerton. Now lovely lady, we'd appreciate it if you wouldn't tell a soul we were here. They know we're in town, but they don't know everything we're doin'. Can you do that for us?"

"I can," answered Mabel. "Are you here to help clean up this city?"

"We are," answered Alan.

"What about places like this?" asked Mabel.

"Mabel, as far as I'm concerned, there is nothing wrong with the oldest profession," said Sean. "My wife Maggie and I have working girls at the two saloons we own. We just want to make sure there are no underage girls or girls working against their will around here."

"Well that damn Flannery likes his little girls and that Ladies Man liked his little boys," said Mabel.

"Well, there's gonna be some changes made," said Sean. "I guarantee it. So Mabel, how bout you lookin' after things for a while till we can get back. We gotta be goin'. There's a little girl upstairs who's been through hell and is scared ta death. We gotta get her home."

"What about Thornton and his men?" asked Mabel.

"They shouldn't be botherin' you for a while," said Sean. "Alan, leave Mabel them extra pistols I see you got now. You know how to use one don't you?"

"I sure do," answered Mabel.

"Good, now we're gonna git that young girl and git her and Alan here to the hospital," said Sean. "You got them pistols now. Don't take no crap off nobody. If some more a Flannery's men show up and give you a hard time, shoot'em. Just say it was self defense."

"What about them two dead men out front?" asked Mabel.

"I guess we'll drag'em out back fer now," said Sean. Sean went back outside and he and O'Hanly dragged the bodies out back.

"This one fella here used to be a cop," said O'Hanly as they dragged the first body out back. "That was Officer George Crawford. We found out he worked for this bunch and I fired him. Told him to go work for this bunch. Looks like he did."

"Well he won't be doin' much work now," said Sean. They got the other body and took it out back. Then Sean, O'Hanly, and Muldoon went back to the front.

Alan went upstairs to get Mary Campbell. When Alan knocked on the door and told her it was him, she ran to the door and opened it. She hugged Alan again like she would never let him go. "We're leaving this place now Mary," said Alan. "I'll wrap you in a blanket and we'll take your clothes with us. You and I will be going to the hospital." Mary didn't say a word. She let Alan wrap her in the blanket and then grabbed ahold of him again. Alan picked her up and carried her as gently as he would a newborn baby. He grabbed her clothing and then went downstairs.

Mary didn't say one word on the way to the hospital. In fact, none of them spoke until they had the hospital in sight. "Do you suppose they got a doctor there this time a night?" asked Sean.

"I don't know," said O'Hanly. "But I know they have nurses on duty around the clock. We'll find someone." O'Hanly stopped the wagon in front of the hospital.

"You and Muldoon go on home now," said Sean. "We'll be here a good while. It'll be interestin' ta see what happens around daylight when folks see them bodies hangin' downtown."

"It surely will," said O'Hanly. "I guess I better act surprised or something. I wonder who I'll hear from first. Will it be the Mayor, the Police Chief, or maybe Danaher?"

"I bet ole Danaher will high tail it outta town as soon as he hears that his boys got hung," said Sean. Maybe that Police Chief will too."

"I guess we'll see," said O'Hanly. "I'll see you men later. Stay safe. Never know what might happen yet."

"Same to you Captain," said Sean.

~~~~

When Sean and Alan entered the hospital, there was not one person in sight. Then a nurse came down a hall and introduced herself. "I'm the duty nurse tonight, Betty Norman, can I help you folks?" said Betty.

"You can Betty," said Sean. "This young girl has been raped and the man holding her has been shot. Her name is Mary and his name is Alan."

"Oh my, follow me," said Betty. She took them to an examining room. "Lay the child on the bed over there. And Alan will be in the room right next door." Alan laid Mary on the bed, but when he tried to get up and leave, she wouldn't let go of him."

"Don't leave me Alan. Please don't leave me," cried Mary.

"I'll be staying right here," said Alan. Mary loosened her grip on Alan some but did not let go.

"I guess this will be all right," said Betty. "Now Mary, we must unwrap you so we can check you for injuries. Alan, we need you to remove your jacket and shirt." Sean helped Alan remove his jacket and shirt. Mary let the nurse unwrap her. Mary had some bruising on her body where Flannery had handled her roughly and her private area was injured. "There, that didn't hurt," said Betty. "Now I can tell the doctor what to expect." Then she looked at Alan's wound. "Whoever cleaned you up did a very good job," said Betty. "The doctor will just clean it a little more and dress it. I'd say you'll be fine in no time. Now excuse me, I'll be back shortly with the doctor."

Alan tried to get Mary to talk some after the nurse left. "We have got to get you home when we're done here," said Alan. "I bet your folks are missing you."

"My Ma and Pa died a long time ago," said Mary. "It was Typhus or something. I live at the orphanage."

"I'm sorry to hear about your folks," said Alan. "I bet they've been missing you at the orphanage."

"I don't know," said Mary. "Kids run away from there all the time. I don't know if they miss them or not."

"Do you know Johny Pierson?" asked Alan.

"I do," answered Mary. "He ran away from there a while back."

"We know Johny," said Alan. "Do you know Jimmy Dugan?"

"I know him too," answered Mary. "He's a nice boy. He shares things when he can. I like him."

"Johny said that the Sisters at the orphanage are mean sometimes," said Alan. "Is that true?"

"I think they're a lot meaner to the boys than they are to the girls," said Mary.

"So the Sisters can be mean sometimes," said Sean. "What have they got to be mean about?"

"Oh, they get mean if you don't do your chores right or if they think you don't pray hard enough and things like that," answered Mary.

"I'll be havin' a talk with them Sisters when we get you outta here," said Sean. "I won't be puttin' up with no mean Sisters. I had me a mean teacher one time. My Pa run'm outta town." The doctor arrived just as Sean finished talking.

"Hello, I'm Dr. Clayton," he said as he entered the room. "And your're Mary. Well Mary, let's have a look at you." The Dr. examined Mary thoroughly to make sure there were no broken bones or internal injuries. Then he cleaned up her privates. "Has this been reported to the police?" the Dr. asked Sean and Alan.

"We are the police," answered Sean.

"Good, now Alan, let me take a look at your arm," said the Dr. "Whoever patched you up did a very good job. Tell them we need nurses here. I'll hire them on the spot. Now I'll just do a little more cleaning and dress the wound and you can be on your way."

"What about Mary? Will she be able to leave?" asked Alan.

"I think she should stay for a couple of days for observation," said the Dr. "You know, just to make sure everything is all right."

"Well I have a request then Doc," said Alan. "And I won't take no for an answer."

"What is your request?" asked the Dr.

"There's a young boy here, Jimmy Dugan," started Alan. "He and Mary are friends. I want them put in the same room."

"I think we can do that," said the Dr. "And Jimmy is doing very well. I checked on him today. It will take a very long time for him to heal, but he will. Now if you'll excuse me, I'll get an orderly and we'll get this young lady moved." The Dr. left.

"So what do you think Mary?" asked Alan. "Will being in the same room as Jimmy be all right?"

"I like Jimmy," said Mary. "But I'll want you to stay with me too."

"Mary darlin', I would love to stay with you, but Sean and I have more bad men to take care of," said Alan. "I will visit you while you're in here and I'll visit you every day after you get back to the orphanage."

Jimmy was asleep when they moved Mary into his room, but he woke up. "Hey, what's going on?" said Jimmy as he woke.

"Jimmy, Mary Campbell will be in your room while she's here," said the orderly. "There are some other gentlemen here too. Jimmy looked over and saw Alan and Sean. "Hey, did you get those guys?" Jimmy asked Sean and Alan.

"We got them," answered Alan. "They won't hurt anyone ever again."

"That's good. Now why is Mary in the hospital?" asked Jimmy.

"Flannery had her," answered Alan. "May he rot in hell." Jimmy looked over at Mary and smiled. She smiled back at him.

"You two know each other," said Alan. "Everything will be all right now. Sean and I need to get some rest. We'll be going back to our hotel to get some sleep. We'll be back. Don't you worry about that Mary." Alan went over to Mary and gave her a kiss on the cheek. She cried a little at first, but quit when Jimmy started talking to her when Sean and Alan cleared the door.

Sean and Alan walked back to the hotel. They talked some as they walked. "That young girls gettin' attached ta you Alan," said Sean. "You can see that can't you?"

"I can and I don't mind. I'm getting attached to her too," said Alan. "I like that Jimmy Dugan too."

"So are you thinkin' about adoptin' them two?" asked Sean.

"I've been kicking it around some in my mind," said Alan. "They're good kids. I need to do a whole lot of thinking on this. I know Elizabeth wanted children, but wasn't blessed with them. Like I said, I have a lot of thinking to do before I would even talk to Elizabeth about this. But right now, we've still got things to do around here. We need to get Danaher and the Police Chief. There's two more whorehouses that are owned by that bunch. We need to check them out."

"You're a good man Alan," said Sean. "Those kids couldn't ask for a better Pa if that's what gets decided. And we do have more to do around here. We'll get some sleep and see what all happens tomorrow when the town folks see Flannery and Thornton hangin' from them flagpoles."

John O'Halloran was the first person to see Flannery and Thornton hanging from the flagpoles in front of the newspaper building. He didn't live very far from the building. He was walking to work a little before daylight as he always did and was sipping on a cup of coffee. He was thinking about a story he was going to write for the day's edition and not really paying any attention to where he was going. He almost tripped over one of the dead bodies on the ground by the flagpoles. Then he looked up. "Holy shit!!! Jesus, Joseph, and Mary. What in the hell?" he said. Then John read the signs that were pinned to the bodies. "I'd say someone was busy last night," he said to himself. John was a sketch artist too. He ran into the newspaper building and returned with paper and pencil and started sketching the scene. One of his employees showed up when he was almost done with the drawing.

"Holy shit," he said. "We have got to get a picture of this. I told you a while back that we needed a new camera."

"Well you know that photographer guy who runs that shop down the street," said John. "Go wake him up and get him here. I'm sure he'll want to get a picture of this." The man left and John finished his drawing. When he was about to go into the newspaper building, people started showing up. It wasn't but a few minutes until there was a huge crowd. They were all standing there staring at the bodies hanging from the flagpoles. John waited a while before going to his office. He wanted to hear what the people in the crowd were saying to each other. No one in the crowd had anything good to say about the dead men. Most of the comments were, "them sons a bitches got what they deserved," or "good riddance," or "it's about time someone hung them bastards."

Officer Clary's wound wasn't that bad and although it had not been very long since he was wounded, he requested to go back to work. He had healed well and had no pain in his arm. Captain

O'Hanly let him return to work, but he was supposed to be honest and let the Captain know if walking his beat caused him any pain. Officer Clary assured him that he would let them know if there were any problems. He was walking his beat and headed downtown when he noticed the huge crowd gathering. When he got closer, he could see the two dead men hanging from the flagpoles. "I bet I know who's responsible for this," Donavan said to himself. When he got closer, he could see that it was Flannery and Thornton hanging there. "I wish they'd have let me help them," he said to himself.

Officer Clary left and went back to the Police Station to report what he had seen. Captain O'Hanly was in his office sipping some coffee. Officer Clary knocked on his office door and entered. "Captain, someone strung up Flannery and Thornton last night," started Donavan. "They're hanging on the flagpoles in front of the newspaper building. There's two more dead men on the ground there too."

"You don't say," said the Captain. "Saved the city some taxpayer money. Well, better get the meat wagon over there and get the bodies. I suppose there's a big crowd there too."

"Yes, and that fella that has the photography shop is taking pictures," said Officer Clary.

"I bet O'Halloran'll have that picture and a good story in today's paper," said O'Hanly. "Maybe it'll scare some of them others that worked for them out of town."

"That would be nice, but it could make things worse," said Officer Clary. "Those people might just go around killing anyone they thought had something to do with this. Some other new bunch might try to get started in town. Just because the head of the snakes got cut off, doesn't mean that more snakes won't show up."

"Well we've got to discourage them," said O'Hanly. "How would you feel about working tonight? I'll understand if you don't want to since you're on duty today."

"What have you got going on Captain?" asked Officer Clary.

"You can't breathe a word of this to anyone," said O'Hanly. "We're going to raid a couple of whorehouses tonight. We know that Thornton runs the houses around here. One of them was raided last night. We're getting the other two tonight."

"I bet Marshal O'Rourke was in on that raid last night," said Donavan. "I bet I know who hung them fellas last night too."

"You go ahead and think what you want," said O'Hanly. "If you don't know for sure, you won't have to lie in a court of law. Speaking of courts, maybe what happened last night will straighten out some of those crooked judges we have in this city. So, are you available tonight?"

"I wouldn't miss it," said Donavan. "Will Marshal O'Rourke be in on this?"

"I hope to talk with him this morning," said O'Hanly. "Now let's get those bodies taken away. I imagine most folks have seen them by now."

When the meat wagon arrived to get the bodies, the crowd was still fairly big. Captain O'Hanly nicely asked the crowd to disburse. Most of the people left, but a few stayed till the bodies were loaded. James O'Doul from the butcher shop stayed. "Hey O'Hanly, have you got any idea who we can thank for this?" James asked.

"No, but I suppose I should find out and thank them myself," said O'Hanly. "Now go back to your shop please." James just smiled at O'Hanly and walked back to his shop. Then O'Hanly went into the newspaper building. "Where's John?" asked O'Hanly as he walked in.

"He's working on today's edition," answered the receptionist. "He was the first person to see those bodies hanging there today."

"Well would you please tell him that I need to speak with him," said O'Hanly. The receptionist got up and went to John's office. She was back in a moment.

"He said for you to go on back to his office," said the receptionist. O'Hanly went to John's office.

"Hey John, have you got your story written yet?" asked O'Hanly. They shook hands.

"I have most of it done. Is there anything you want me to add?" asked John.

"Well I want you to say stuff like maybe the other scum in this town better get out or this could happen to them too," said the Captain. "You know, kind of give them a good warning."

"I know what you mean," said John. "I've already done that. So can I ask you off the record if you know who did this."

"You can ask on or off the record if you want, but the answer will be no comment," said O'Hanly. "Now please excuse me. I think I'll be very busy today."

~~~~

Sean and Alan slept in a bit. They had breakfast at their hotel. The restaurant was fairly busy and everyone was talking about the men hanging from the flagpoles. When a waitress brought them some coffee, Alan asked her what everyone was talking about. "You mean you haven't heard?" asked the waitress.

"No we haven't," answered Alan. "We just got up."

"Well this morning there was two men hanging from the flagpoles in front of the newspaper building," said the waitress. "One of them was that Councilman Tom Flannery and the other one was the one they call the Ladies Man. He runs some houses of ill repute. There were two other dead men there too. No one said who they were, but they probably worked for them two."

"So young lady, what do you think about this?" asked Sean.

"I heard that them two were some really bad men," answered the waitress. "If they were as bad as what they say, then they got what they deserved."

"How about innocent until proven guilty and all that legal stuff?" asked Alan.

"I've heard that some of the judges in this town are not honest," said the girl. "I've heard that about lawyers too. If that's true, maybe they should be hanging from flagpoles too."

"I like this girl," said Sean.

"I like her too," said Alan.

Alan and Sean finished their breakfast and headed to the Police Station. Captain O'Hanly was back in his office. He saw Sean and Alan and told them to come into his office. "Mornin' Captain, I bet they've been screamin' in yer ears all mornin'," said Sean. "Who's been yellin' the most?"

"I haven't heard from any of those higher ups yet," said the Captain. "Officer Clary was on duty this morning and come back here to tell me what was downtown. We got the bodies removed and I talked to John at the newspaper."

"I bet John'll have one hell of a story today," said Sean.

"He will. He was the first one to see them hanging here," said O'Hanly. "He got pictures too. He's putting stuff in the story that we hope will scare off some more of the scum around here."

"I hope it does scare'em," said Sean. "Now I want to get Danaher and that Police Chief today if we can."

"I got me a hunch about them two," said the Captain. "I bet they got the word early this morning and have high tailed it out of town. What say we go find out?"

"Let's go," said Sean.

CHAPTER TEN

C aptain O'Hanly got a buggy and the three of them headed for the Municipal building. They went to Chief Munroe's office first. He wasn't there. O'Hanly asked a clerk if they had seen him today.

"He hasn't been in yet today," answered the clerk.

"How about the Deputy Mayor? Have you seen him today?" asked O'Hanly.

"He has to go past me to get to his office," answered the clerk. "And I haven't seen him either. He didn't give me anything that says he would be somewhere else or anything."

"Is our Mayor in?" asked O'Hanly.

"Yes he is," answered the clerk. "He's all worked up about what happened over by the newspaper building. He's wondering where Chief Munroe is too."

"We'll be seeing the Mayor," said O'Hanly.

"I'll go tell him you're here," said the clerk.

"Don't bother," said O'Hanly. "He's going to see us whether he would want to or not." The three of them headed to the Mayor's office.

Mayor Cross was sitting at his desk cursing to himself. He looked up when he saw O'Hanly, Sean, and Alan enter his office. "Oh, Captain O'Hanly, maybe you can tell me what the hell is going on around here," said the Mayor. "No one can seem to find my Police Chief."

"Well Mayor, I'd say that Chief Munroe and your Deputy Mayor have left town," said O'Hanly.

"Just why in the hell would they leave town?" asked Mayor Cross.

"Because Mr. Mayor, we have discovered that your Deputy Mayor is the head man behind most of the corruption in this city and Munroe is on his payroll," said O'Hanly.

"The hell you say," said the Mayor. "You got any proof of those accusations."

"No we don't, but we're working on it," said O'Hanly.

"Who the hell are these other two?" asked the Mayor.

"I'd watch my mouth if I was you Mayor," said Sean. "I might just put my fist in it."

"Are you threatening me Mr." said the Mayor.

"I don't make threats you fool," said Sean. "That's a promise. Now I'm Federal Marshal Sean O'Rourke and this other gentleman is Alan Cooper. He's a Pinkerton."

"You're that cowboy lawman or something like that from out west," said the Mayor. "I've heard of you. I can assure you that the way you handle things out west is not how we handle them here."

"You know Mayor, it's a shame you can't be locked up for being stupid, cause you'd never git outta jail," said Sean. "Now we're gonna clean up this town and yer gonna stay outta our way. Hell, when we git done, the folks of this city might think you're some kinda hero fer cleanin' up their city and such. Hell you'll probly get re-elected. Or maybe they'll see how stupid you were for having the biggest crook in town as yer Deputy Mayor. Maybe you couldn't get a job sweepin' the street."

"O'Hanly, do you want to keep your job?" asked Mayor Cross.

"Don't threaten me Mayor," said O'Hanly. "I'll lock you up for threatening me. Now we're going to do just what this gentleman said. You stay out of our way. You say one word of this visit to a living soul and I'll lock you up for obstructing justice. And if we find out during our investigations that you are tied in criminally to this bunch, there won't be a rock you can hide under. Now excuse us. We have work to do." The three of them left the Mayor's office. As soon as they were out of sight, the Mayor reached into his desk and pulled out a bottle of whiskey. He poured himself a tall drink.

The three of them got in the buggy and left. "I know where Munroe lives," said O'Hanly. "Let's go there first. I'm not sure where Danaher lives, but if we find Munroe, he knows."

~~~~

When they got to Chief Munroe's house, they could see a woman out back hanging up some laundry. O'Hanly recognized her and the three of them headed out back. The woman wasn't a beauty but she wasn't ugly either. She recognized O'Hanly as they approached her. "Well Captain O'Hanly, if you've come for the Chief, he isn't here. He got up early this morning. He said he had a lot going on. Is there something I can help you with?"

"No, no, Mrs. Munroe. If you see the Chief tell him we're looking for him," said O'Hanly. "Oh, I almost forgot. We need to see the Deputy Mayor. Can you tell me where he lives?"

"Sure, it's just two blocks over," answered Mrs. Munroe. "It's 134 Sycamore. It's a huge brick house and there's a white picket fence in the front. Who's your friends?"

"Mrs. Munroe, these two gentlemen are Federal Marshal Sean O'Rourke and Alan Cooper," answered O'Hanly. "Alan is Pinkerton detective."

"Pleased to meet you ma'am," said Sean as he tipped his hat.

"Same for me Mrs. Munroe," said Alan as he tipped his hat too.

"I've heard of you Mr. O'Rourke," said Mrs. Munroe. "You're that famous lawman from out west. What brings you to our city?"

"I'm not permitted to say ma'am," answered Sean.

"Sound serious," said Mrs. Munroe. "Well good luck with whatever you're doing."

"Thank you ma'am," said Sean. "And good day to you."

They got back in the buggy and headed for Danaher's house. No one was home at Danaher's house or at least no one would answer the door. Sean went around back and forced the back door open. He went to the front door and opened it for O'Hanly and Alan. "Let's have a look around and see what we can see," said Sean. The three of them split up and explored the house. Alan found a room that looked like it was an office. There was a safe in a closet in that room. The safe door was open and the safe was empty. Sean went into a bedroom and looked around. Most of the clothing had been removed from the closet. Sean went through a couple of chests of drawers. There were some women's combs and brushes and hat pins. O'Hanly went into the kitchen and looked around. There was plenty of dry goods and canned goods in the pantry. Then he noticed something on the floor. It was a bank deposit slip. Danaher had deposited $10,000 two weeks ago. They checked out every room and met by the front door.

"Well men, he's gone," said O'Hanly. "I did find a bank slip. Let's go pay that bank a visit." They loaded up and headed for the bank. "I want the bank President right now," said O'Hanly to one of the tellers. The man left and returned with a short, bald, middle aged man.

"I'm Art Watkins, the bank President," he said. "What can I do for you?"

"I want to see Danny Danaher's accounts," said O'Hanly.

"I can't do that," said Art. "Those accounts are private."

"Tell ya what," said Sean. "Either we see the accounts, or your wife visits you in the hospital."

"You can't bully me sir," said Art. Sean grabbed him by the front of his jacket and picked him up off the floor.

"Now Art, the accounts or I start breaking bones," said Sean.

"My lawyer will hear about this," said Art. Art left for a few minutes and returned with some paper work. "Mr. Danaher closed his accounts early this morning. Now get what you want and please leave."

"See Art, that wasn't hard at all," said Sean. "Now if you feel compelled to talk to your lawyer, go right ahead. Tell him Federal Marshal Sean O'Rourke says hi." O'Hanly looked over the accounts and saw what he wanted to see. He nodded his head and the three of them left the bank. They could hear Art talking to himself as they were leaving.

"Can't be him, can't be him," he said over and over.

They got in the buggy and headed back to the Police Station. "Danaher had a lot of money in that bank," said O'Hanly. "For the last two years he was depositing at least $10,000 a month. There were some withdrawals, but when he closed the accounts, he got over $150,000."

"Probly had a bunch a money in that safe a his too," said Sean. "Should a seen this comin'. We should a expected him to run and watched the train station. Hard ta tell where he went. Hell, he might be headed to Canada. So what do we do next?"

"We're going to raid them other two whorehouses tonight," said O'Hanly. "Wanna come along?"

"Love too," said Alan. "We need to make sure there's no children in those places. We should check on Mabel too and make sure none of Thornton or Flannery's men bothered her."

"Yeh, and we need to see if them dead bodies are still out back," said Sean. "And I wanna send a telegram ta Maggie today. I miss that woman a lot."

"I miss Elizabeth too," said Alan. "I got an idea too. We need to find out if the telegrapher is honest or not. How about we send a fake telegram and see what happens. I'm pretty good at following people without being seen. Maybe we'll find us another one of that bunch."

Captain O'Hanly went back to his office and Sean and Alan headed to a telegraph office. When they got close, they decided on their plan. Sean would go inside and send a telegram to a fake address and use his real name. Alan would lay back and watch the telegrapher and see if he did anything. Sean went inside and sent the following telegram.

Judge Alfred Turner
Washington D.C.

Judge<<stop>>almost   done   here<<stop>>will   return
within week

Federal Marshal Sean O'Rourke
Boston

Sean left the telegraph office and walked down the sidewalk
like he was just going about his business. Alan watched the telegrapher. As soon as Sean was a couple of blocks away, the
telegrapher got up and handed a copy of Sean's telegram to another man. The man put on a jacket and left the office. Alan
followed him. Sean could see that Alan was moving so he turned
and followed him. He stayed back a good ways so the man Alan
was following couldn't see him.

Alan followed the man for eight blocks. When the man approached the courthouse, he went inside. Alan followed. The man
went down a hall and disappeared into another hall. Alan followed. At the end of the hall was a door. A sign above the door
said "Judge's Chambers." Sean had seen Alan go into the courthouse and went inside. He snooped around until he found Alan.
"Seems our boy went right to a judge," said Alan. "Let's let that
fella leave and then we'll have some words with this judge. We can
git the telegrapher and him later."

Sean and Alan went into another office in the court house
and talked to a woman in the Treasurer's office. Sean let Alan do
the talking. He asked the woman about taxes and a few other
things. It was only a couple of minutes until the man they had
followed left the Judge's Chambers. They waited a moment. Alan
told the woman that he needed to be somewhere else and then he
and Alan went right to the Judge's Chambers. The Judge was at

his desk when Sean and Alan entered his office without knocking. "Gentlemen, you are not allowed here in my chambers," said the Judge. "Remove yourself or I will have you removed."

"Just sit there and shut your mouth for a minute Judge," said Sean. "I am Federal Marshal Sean O'Rourke and this gentleman is Alan Cooper. He's a Pinkerton. Now why would you need to read my telegram?"

"I'm sure I don't know what you're talking about," said the Judge. Then the Judge stood up and started yelling for help. "Help, I need a—." He didn't get out any more words. Sean pulled his pistol and stuck the muzzle of it right in the Judge's mouth.

"Now sit yerself back down Judge and keep your mouth shut," said Sean. "We know who your boss is. Danaher and Chief Munroe have skipped town." Sean took his pistol out of the Judge's mouth. "Now you will be leaving town too, but first you're gonna tell us who the other crooked Judges are in town."

"I have no idea what you're talking about," said the Judge.

"You are a terrible liar," said Sean. "Now we can do this the easy way or we can do it the hard way."

"What do you mean by that?" asked the Judge. Sean pulled out his bowie knife and stuck the tip of it into the Judge's right nostril. He cut the Judge just a little to make sure the Judge knew how sharp the knife was. When the Judge saw blood dripping on his desk, his tune changed. "All right, all right," he cried. "There's two of us. There's Judge Conley and myself."

"What's yer name?" asked Sean.

"It's Malone," answered the Judge.

"Well Judge Malone, you and Judge Conley better be on the first train out of town tomorrow," said Sean. "If you are not, we will kill you and your bodies will never be found. You will be watched. We have people everywhere. I'm sure you know by now that Flannery and Thornton are no longer with us. A lot of their men are gone too. Now consider yourself lucky that we are not killing you right off. Now I'll put my knife away and we'll be leaving. Remember, you are being watched. One wrong move and it's good bye Judge." Sean and Alan left the Judge's Chambers and headed for the telegraph office. They talked as they walked.

"So do you figure we scared that Judge enough?" asked Alan.

"I think we did," answered Sean. "We will find out when the first train leaves in the morning. We'll keep an eye out or we'll git someone else to watch. Maybe we can get Muldoon or Donavan. They probably know that other Judge too."

"They probably do," said Alan. "Now what are we going to do with them two at the telegraph office?"

"First off, we'll find out who the boss is and have some words with him," said Sean. "Then we're gonna escort them two fellas ta jail. They might get a few bumps and bruises along the way."

When they entered the telegraph office, there were three people inside. The telegrapher was there and the man who had given Sean's telegram to the Judge was there. The third person was a young woman. She was at a desk in the front of the office. Sean went to her. "How do Miss," said Sean. "Who's the boss in this place?"

"That's him over there with his back turned to you," she answered. "That's Mr. Baker. He's the supervisor." Mr. Baker wasn't paying any attention and had no idea Sean and Alan were there. The telegrapher had his back to them and was busy taking a message. Sean started for Mr. Baker. Baker finally turned and saw Sean. The moment he saw Sean, he tried to run. Sean ran after him and knocked him to the floor. The telegrapher saw Sean now and tried to run. Alan caught him and threw him to the floor. The young woman was terrified and let out a scream.

"It's all right Miss," said Sean. "We're the law and these two are under arrest."

"If you take them, there won't be anyone here to work the key," said the woman.

"Well you just stay here and wait for another operator to come to work," said Alan. "Tell him to tell his supervisors that these two got arrested. You can tell him that if him or any others work for this crooked bunch in town they'll be getting arrested too."

"I know where the next operator lives," said the woman. "Would it be all right if I went and got him?"

"That would be fine Miss," said Alan. "Now we'll be taking these two to jail. Have you got a piece a rope or something we can use to tie these fellas?"

"I can find something," answered the woman. She went to a closet and came back with a short piece of rope. "Will this do?"

"Sure and thank you Miss," said Alan. The rope was about six foot long. It was about the size of a clothesline rope, but it would do the job. They tied the two men's hands behind their back and headed for the Police Station.

Sean taunted the two men a little as they walked. "You two are some no good sons a bitches," said Sean. "We oughta just beat ya ta death and throw your bodies into the river."

"We only done what we was told," cried one of the men. "When the Judge tells us to do something, we do it."

"So you broke the law even though you knew you was doin' wrong," said Sean.

"We woulda been fired if we didn't," said the man.

"Well that's probly true," said Sean. "But you broke the law. You probly lost yer jobs already. Mebbe some lawyer can help ya out, but yer goin' ta jail. Them people you were workin' for had my best friend killed. Maybe the ones you work for didn't actually do the killing, but it was still the same bunch." They didn't talk anymore until they got to the Police Station. They went inside and went to a desk Sergeant. "These two are gittin' locked up fer stealin' private property," said Sean to the Sgt. "Don't know their names." The two men gave their names to the Sgt. and then he escorted them to a jail cell. Sean and Alan went over to Capt. O'Hanly's office. Sean told the Captain about the telegrapher, the other man, and their meeting with the Judge.

"This is good," said O'Hanly. "I'll get a good man to watch the train station in the morning and make sure them two Judges leave. Now why don't we meet here about an hour before dark."

"All right, we'll be here," said Sean. "Now I think me and Alan'll git somethin' ta eat and go visit Jimmy and Mary over at the hospital."

Sean and Alan had a meal at a café and then went to the hospital. Mary was glad to see them. When they went into the room, Mary got out of bed and ran to Alan and hugged him. He gave her a kiss on the cheek and carried her back to bed. The Alan went over to Jimmy's bed. He took Jimmy's hand and shook it as best he could without causing Jimmy any pain. "How you doing Jimmy?" asked Alan. "Are they treating you right?"

"Yep, got good food and good company," answered Jimmy. Sean went over and gave Mary a kiss on the cheek. Then he shook Jimmy's hand easily. They had just finished the handshake when Father Darcey walked in.

"You two are lookin' pretty good," said the Father. "The Lord must be workin' hard helpin' you Jimmy. You're comin' along fine."

"They take good care of me," said Jimmy.

"And how bout you Mary Campbell?" asked the Father. "Are you doing well?"

"Yes Father, I'm well. I got Jimmy here with me and now Alan's here," said Mary.

"I think she's takin' a fancy to you Alan," said the Father.

"And I've takin' a fancy to her too," said Alan. "Father, while you're here. I'd like to ask you some questions if you don't mind."

"Of course I wouldn't mind," said the Father. "Now what would you be wantin' to know?"

"Well we've heard that some of the Sisters at the orphanage can be mean sometimes," said Alan. "Is that true?"

"I'm not in charge of the orphanage but I do visit there regularly," said the Father. "No one has ever complained to me and I've not seen any inappropriate behavior by the Sisters while I was there. Could be that the children are afraid to say anything. Jimmy, have you heard anything?"

"I have Father," answered Jimmy. "I know several of the boys who have run away from there. They say that the Sisters, especially the Mother Superior is real mean sometimes."

"What does she have to be mean about?" asked the Father.

"Well, if the chores aren't done right or fast enough or they don't pray hard enough," said Jimmy. "You know, stuff like that."

"Well what does she do to punish the people?" asked Father Darcey.

"She uses switches on them," answered Jimmy. "Johny Pierson told me that one time she switched him so bad he couldn't sit down for over a week."

"So Mary, does this stuff happen?" asked the Father.

"Yes, but mostly to the boys," answered Mary. "I only ever saw one girl get switched the whole time I've been there."

"Well I'll be having a talk with Mother Superior and the others," said Father Darcey.

"I believe I'll have some words with them too before we leave," said Sean. "I won't tolerate someone beatin' children. Now mind ya, I'm not against a good paddlin' when it's needin', but sounds like the good Sisters are overdoin' it."

CHAPTER ELEVEN

They all met at the Police Station an hour before dark as planned. They had two buggies and a wagon. Captain O'Hanly and two other Officers who could be trusted were in the wagon. Officer Clary and Sgt. Muldoon were in a buggy and Sean and Alan were in the other buggy. They had plenty of rope with them. The first place they went to was the whorehouse where they had captured Flannery and Thornton. Muldoon and Clary went around back to watch the back door. When they got out back, they found that the two dead bodies were still there. One of the bodies had been chewed on by some animal, probably a stray dog. Clary thought he saw a dog running away as they approached the bodies. O'Hanly stationed a man on each side of the place in case someone tried to exit out a first floor window. Sean, Alan, and O'Hanly, went to the front door.

Sean knocked on the door. No one answered. Sean waited a few minutes and knocked again. Still no one answered. They were about to break the door down when it slowly opened. When the door was almost wide open, they could see two dead men laying on the floor. There was a good bit of blood too. As they started to enter, Mabel stepped out from behind the door. She was half naked and had blood all over her right side. She held a pistol in her right hand. "Hey boys, you missed all the fun," she said. "These two sons a bitches thought they was gonna run the place after they found out about Thornton and Flannery. We had some words. They're dead. I'm not."

"Let's git you ta bed and take a look see at your wound," said Sean. Then Sean picked her up and carried her to her bed.

"What's a girl gotta do to get a man like you or Alan?" asked Mabel. "I'm kinda getting used to being treated like a lady. I like it."

"You are a lady Mabel. Don't let nobody tell you yer not," said Sean. "Now you relax and let me have a look at you." Mabel had a shawl wrapped around her. When Sean moved it out of the way, he could see that she had been shot twice. "Christ a mighty Mabel," said Sean. "You been shot twice, but they both just grazed ya some. Skinned yer ribs some. We'll be gettin' you to the hospital ta make sure ya got no broken ribs."

"Will you carry me there?" asked Mabel.

"I would if I had to," said Sean. "But we got some buggies. Now the bleedins' stopped. You lay here for a spell while we have a look around."

"There shouldn't be anyone here except the girls," said Mabel. "After the shooting, all the customers took off."

"So are there any young girls here that don't wanna be here?" asked Sean.

"No, I went around myself and talked to all the girls," said Mabel. "There' nobody here who don't wanna be here."

"Well we'll take a look anyway and make sure there's none a Thornton's men hidin' out," said Sean. Now you stay put."

"I will," said Mabel. "I'll wait right here for you to come back to my bed."

"Ya got a way with words Mabel," said Sean. "There's a good man out there somewhere for ya. You'll find'm."

Sean left Mabel's room. The others had already started checking out the other rooms. When they were confident that none of Thornton's men were there, Sean went back to Mabel's room. The other men removed the bodies from the hallway. After those bodies were loaded on the wagon, they took the wagon out back to get the other two dead bodies. "So are you gonna carry me out to the buggy?" asked Mabel.

"Let's get some clothes on you first," said Sean. "Have ya got somethin' that fits loose and ya won't worry bout gettin' blood on it?"

"There's a big robe over in the closet," said Mabel. "That'll do fine." Sean got the robe from the closet.

"Now you git out a that bed and let's git this robe on ya," said Sean. Mabel slowly got out of bed and stood there waiting for Sean to put the robe on her. He gently helped her put it on and then picked her up.

"Did you like what you saw when you looked at me?" asked Mabel.

"I'm not dead Mabel. Course I did," said Sean. "Yer a fine figure of a woman. Now quit tryin' to seduce me and let's git you in that buggy."

"I don't think I could seduce you," said Mabel. "That woman of yours has got a strong hold on you."

"Yes she does," said Sean. "Now one of us needs to take Mabel to the hospital. Captain, how bout one a yer men takin' her?"

"You mean you're not taking me Sean?" asked Mabel.

"No darlin', I got work to do yet," said Sean. "You'll be in good hands. Alan and me'll be at the hospital tomorrow visitin' some people. We'll see ya then if yer still there. Now is there another girl who can be in charge while yer gone?"

"Sure, you probably met her," said Mabel. "She's the Negro woman. She'll take charge."

Captain O'Hanly had Officer Martin take Mabel to the hospital. Officer Martin was a good honest Police Officer. He was in his late twenty's and was a widower. His wife and baby had both died during child birth a year and a half ago. He was not a church going man and he enjoyed a beer once in a while, but he did not abuse it. He was a tall handsome man and Sean could see that Mabel noticed that right off. As soon as the buggy started moving, Mabel slid over next to Officer Martin and held onto his arm. He looked at her and smiled. She returned the smile.

Sean went down the hall to the black woman's room. He knocked on the door and waited. "Come on in sugar," she said. Sean entered the room. "Need some more pins?"

"No darlin'. Mabel got herself shot and we're takin' her to the hospital," said Sean. "She said you'd be in charge while she was gone. Is that all right?"

"Yep, I can watch things," she said. "Is Mabel gonna be all right?"

"Bullets just grazed her right side. Maybe skinned some ribs," said Sean. "She'll be all right." Then Sean handed her the two pistols that Mabel had. "Now anybody comes here and gives you any shit, you just shoot'em. Can you do that?"

"I can," she answered. "Now don't be goin' out there and getting yourself killed. I'm gonna have my way with you yet." Sean gave her a smile and left.

When they got to the next whorehouse, Officer Clary went around back to watch the back door. Muldoon took one side of the house and the other officer took the other. Sean, Alan, and O'Hanly went to the front door. This whorehouse was not big like the other one. It was just a big two story house. From the outside, It looked like there were maybe four working rooms downstairs and six upstairs. Sean knocked on the front door and waited. There was no answer. He waited a few minutes and knocked again. Sean had a strange feeling come over him right then. Then he yelled out, "Git down. Git down now." As the three of them were hitting the ground, the front door exploded. Someone on the other side of the door had cut loose with a shotgun. There was one blast and then another right behind it.

Sean and Alan had both drawn their pistols as they were hitting the ground. Immediately after the second blast, both of them cut loose with their pistols. O'Hanly had his pistol out now and started firing too. Sean fired four shots. Alan fired five, and O'Hanly emptied his service revolver. When Officer Clary heard the shotgun blasts, his first thought was to run around to the front door. Then he decided to stay put and have his service revolver ready. When the shooting out front stopped, it got very quiet for a moment. Then a man came running out the back door. He was carrying a double barreled shotgun. Officer Clary was only twenty feet from him and in plain sight but the man didn't see him. "Stop right there," yelled Officer Clary. His pistol was aimed right at the man. The man saw Officer Clary now but didn't stop. He tried to cock the hammers on the shotgun but before he did, Officer Clary's bullet struck him in the forehead. He was knocked backwards and hit the ground dead. The back of his head was gone.

Sean quickly fully loaded his pistol. Alan and O'Hanly reloaded too. Sean moved toward what was left of the front door. He knocked a lot of the splinters out of the way and slowly entered the house. Just inside, dead on the floor, and shot to pieces was one man. Officer Clary entered the house through the back door. He yelled out so they would know it was him so he wouldn't get shot by mistake. Captain O'Hanly had Muldoon and the other officer stay outside while the rest of them would check out the rooms. They got several surprises when they checked the rooms. There were no customers at all in the place. Not one of the working girls could speak English. There were ten girls there and they were all very beautiful. Six of them were Oriental, but none of the men could tell if they were Chinese, Japanese, or something else. One of the girls might have been Polynesian. They could only guess. The other girls were all white, but none of them recognized the languages they spoke.

"Jesus H. Christ, I never seen nothin' like this before," said Sean. "Just where and how in the hell did them sons a bitches git these girls. Just what are we gonna do with'em? We can't leave'em here like the other place. I bet they charged a good bit fer these girls too. They're beautiful and no one knows what they're sayin'. Some men'd like that I 'spect. Damn, this is really gettin' me pissed. I wanna hang them two all over again."

"I'm thinking that one of these girls might be German," said Officer Muldoon. "There was an old German woman that lived not far from us when I was a boy. I remember a word she used a lot. It was bitte. One of those girls keeps saying "bitte, bitte."

"Well finding someone who can speak German shouldn't be too hard," said Captain O'Hanly. "Let's load up these bodies and get over to that other whorehouse. Muldoon, you stay here and keep an eye out. Try your best to show the girls they don't need to be afraid now."

"I'll do my best Captain," said Muldoon. The other officer stayed with Muldoon. Sean, Alan, O'Hanly, and Officer Clary loaded up the dead bodies and headed for the other whorehouse.

The last whorehouse was a huge building. It had been a warehouse or something. It still looked like an old warehouse. It had doors on the front, the back, and both sides. Sean took the front door. Alan covered the back door, and O'Hanly and Officer Clary covered the sides. Sean eased up to the front door and then gave it some hard knocks. He had a pistol in his right hand. A few seconds after he knocked, he heard a deep raspy voice. He thought it was a woman's voice, but he wasn't sure. He stood to the side of the door and listened. "Come on in honey," said the voice. "We been spectin' you. Don't you worry that cute ass a yours. You're not gonna get shot." Sean kept his pistol ready and cautiously entered the house. He got somewhat of a surprise. Just inside the door and sitting in a very nice chair was a very beautiful woman. Whatever she was wearing was completely shear and Sean could see every bit of her shape. Sean walked over to her and when he was just a few feet from her, she stood up. Sean found himself looking up at her. "Damn, she must be over six and a half feet tall," Sean said to himself. He couldn't take his eyes off her. Her long dark hair partially covered her breasts, but they were so big that they couldn't be covered. Sean's eyes followed the contours of her body. They stopped at her waist. Her waist was so small that Sean thought that if she bent over too hard she could break in half. Her hour glass figure was at least two hours. The woman just stood there while Sean looked her over. When his eyes got back up to her face, she spoke. "I hope you liked what you saw," she said. "I'm Big Tall Sally and this is my place. "There's none a Flannery's boys here. Never have been. Like I said, this is my place. I just give that scum a big cut so they'd leave us alone." Sean still didn't speak. "You gotta be O'Rourke, the famous lawman from out west. Now what can I do for you?"

"Well Sally, nice ta meet ya and I must say that I have never met or seen a woman that can compare to you," said Sean.

"I hope you meant that as a compliment," said Sally.

"I surely did Sally. I surely did," said Sean. "Now would you mind if we have us a look see? We wanna make sure you don't have no young girls or anyone here against their will."

"Help yourself," said Sally. "None a my girls don't wanna be here." Sean went back outside and told the others what Sally had said. They went back inside and checked out all the rooms. Sally had told the truth. All of the girls seemed happy to be there. They were also glad that Flannery and his bunch were gone. That meant more money for them. Sally had a quite a selection of girls. There must have been twenty of them. They were all attractive and there was an Oriental girl who could speak English, Chinese, and Japanese. Another woman was from Norway and could speak English, German, and French. After everything was checked out, all of the men went back to Sally.

"I don't get it," said Sean to Sally. "How come Flannery and his bunch left you alone?"

"It wasn't always that way," answered Sally. "They killed my men off back when they first was gettin' started. After that, they took thirty percent from me. I had good girls and good customers so I raised my rates. They was gonna start takin' forty percent from me next year. I'm glad you come ta town. I wasn't gonna give that scum that much. I'd hire someone ta kill them before I'd pay that much."

"So I guess business'll be good for you now," said O'Hanly. "I bet you can get some more girls to work for you. We got ten soiled doves at another house with no where to go. Their bosses are dead. Not one of them can speak Englsih. Maybe them two girls a yours could pay them a visit. Maybe they'll wanna work for you or maybe they just wanna go back home, wherever that might be."

"I heard that they had a house where none of the girls could speak English," said Sally. "I bet some of the men liked that. They could say whatever they wanted and the girls could too. Sure, I'll have them girls go over there. So what are you boys gonna do now that Flannery and that Ladies Man is dead? You'll probably be going back out west won't ya O'Rourke?"

"Not sure what we'll do next," said Sean. "We gotta get the main boss yet. He's skipped town."

"So Flannery wasn't the big boss huh," said Sally. "Just who in the hell was the boss?"

"It was our illustrious Deputy Mayor," answered O'Hanly.

"Danaher, never woulda guessed that," said Sally. "He used ta visit some of the girls once in a while. No, never woulda thought that. What'll ya do with him if you ever catch'm?

"He'll hang," said Sean. "Even if I have ta shoot'm first, he'll hang."

"That's good to hear," said Sally. "So, famous lawman, could I interest you in taking a turn?"

"Sally, any man with a pulse would want to take a turn with you, but you're a big woman Sally. I bet you could hurt me," said Sean.

"I wouldn't hurt you at all," said Sally. "I can be nice and gentle. I can be so gentle you'd never want to be with another woman."

"I do appreciate the offer, but I already have the most beautiful woman in the world for my wife," said Sean. "And I miss her somethin' awful. Seein' you today's gettin' me worked up. We gotta get done here and get home."

"You're wife's a lucky woman," said Sally. "Tell you what. I got lots of friends in this town. I'll see if anyone knows anything about Danaher's whereabouts. Would there be any reward?

Sean had never thought about a reward, but Danaher was responsible for the death of his best friend and his wife. Then there was all the crimes he committed besides that. If posting a reward would help catch the man, why the hell not. He would like to kill Danaher himself, but as long as Danaher got dead and he could see the body, that would do. He could still hang his dead body. Between Sean and Alan, they had already created a lot of corpses in Boston. He had more money that he could ever spend in several lifetimes and maybe the city would put up some money too. He thought for a moment. "Yes Sally, there will be a reward for Danaher and it will be for dead or alive," said Sean. "How does $10,000 sound?"

"Hell, I might just track the son of bitch down myself." said Sally. "I bet for that kind a money someone'll get him. His own friends might turn him in for that much money."

CHAPTER TWELVE

S ean and all of them spent the next week scouring the city. They followed every lead they got, but Danaher was nowhere to be found. At the end of that week, Chief Munroe was found, or his body was found. Some young boys found his body down by the river. It was under a big oak tree. His service revolver was still in his right hand and it appeared that he had shot himself in the right temple. The powder burns indicated that he had been shot at close range, but Sean and Alan were not convinced that he had committed suicide. Alan figured that Danaher, or some of Danaher's associates did it to keep him from talking.

Sean and Alan had enough of Boston. They both missed their wives and were ready to leave. They had done all they could and now the rest was up to Boston. With a lot of prodding and pushing, they convinced the Mayor to add more to Danaher's bounty. $5000 was all they could get but $15,000 was a lot of money. A lot of people would sell their mother for a lot less than that.

The Mayor was under a lot of criticism for everything that had been going on in the city. He kept talking about resigning. Capt. O'Hanly told him to take it like a man and learn from his mistakes. O'Hanly must have given him some backbone because he didn't resign. He actually went out and made several public speeches and informed the city that from now on things would be different. Corruption would not be tolerated in the city and for those people who thought he was just a stooge, they would find out differently. One of the first things he did was make Capt. O'Hanly the new Chief of Police. He figured that if O'Hanly and his men rid the city of Danaher and his troop, he was the man for the job. The first thing O'Hanly did was make Sgt. Muldoon Capt. Muldoon and Officer Clary Sgt. Clary. O'Hanly went to every precinct and fired any man who had not performed as expected or was just putting in time, and promoted every man who deserved it and would take charge. "We're servants of the public and by God we're gonna serve the public," O'Hanly would say everyday when he came to work. More Officers were hired too. Anyone who was suspected of having associated with any of Danaher's clan was told to straighten up or get out of town. They would not be told a second time. Several men were seen being escorted to the train station by Officers. Some of them had a few bumps and bruises on them. Also, no words were spoken and no orders were given, but Chief of Police O'Hanly did not want the brothels bothered. He had met again with the ladies from the three places they had raided and assured them they would not be bothered unless crimes other than the oldest profession had been committed there. O'Hanly knew that there were many more brothels in the city. They would be raided from time to time to make sure none of Danaher's clan was around and to make sure no minors were there.

Sean and Alan would leave Boston in two more days. They sent a telegram to Cincinnati informing the women they would be returning. They would spend two more days following leads. Of course Sean and Alan had visited Jimmy Dugan every day at the hospital. He still had a long way to go before he could even think about leaving the hospital, but he was healing well. Mary Campbell stayed at the hospital for three days and then went to the orphanage. When she went back to the orphanage, Sean and Alan took her.

When they entered the orphanage, they were greeted by a very young looking nun. "Hello, I'm Sister Ann," she said. "I see you have brought our Mary back to us."

"Yes we have. I'm Sean O'Rourke and this other gentleman is Alan Cooper," started Sean. "Mary's been through quite an ordeal. Is the Mother Superior around?"

"She's in her office now with one of the children," said Sister Ann. As Sister Ann finished her words, The sound of a boy screaming in pain and a switch hitting him could be heard.

"I reckon we know what's goin' on in there," said Sean. "You don't do that to the children do you Sister?"

"No, Sister Agnus, the Mother Superior handles all disciplinary action," answered the Sister.

"Do you agree with what she does?" asked Alan.

"I do not," answered Sister Ann, "but the Mother Superior is in total charge and I have no say in those matters." Sean wanted to ask Sister Ann few more questions, but the Mother Superior had finished in her office and came out to see who Sister Ann was conversing with. She introduced herself and Sean introduced himself and Alan.

Sean had a hard time keeping himself composed. He and Alan were extremely upset having just heard the Mother Superior beating one of the boys. Sean took a deep breath and then explained all that had happened to Mary. Then he had some words with the Sister about her treatment of some of the children. He didn't give her a chance to speak once he started on that subject. Sean had taken a buggy whip with him and the Mother Superior's eyes stayed glued to it while Sean spoke. "Look Sister whatever your name is, there's nothing wrong with a good paddlin' once in a while if it's needed," Sean started. "But from what I hear, you are abusing some of these children. Just who in the hell do you think you are anyway? Beating kids because you don't think they pray hard enough or whatever stupid ass reason you have is just not gonna make it." The Mother superior tried to get in a few words, but Sean cut her off. "Shut the hell up bitch," yelled Sean. "I'm leaving Boston shortly and if I get word from anyone that you're unjustly beatin' on any of these kids, I'll come back here and whip you with a buggy whip so hard that you won't be able to sit down for a year." Then Sean cracked the whip.

The Mother Superior stood her ground and went over and got in Sean's face. "Look you heathen, I'm here doing the Lord's work," she began. "These children need disciplined and I'll hand it out whenever I think it's necessary. Now you remove yourself before I call the Police."

"Bitch, I am the Police," said Sean. Mary and Alan had been standing next to Sean the whole conversation. "Mary, go find the other kids around here and bring them right here. They might get to see this bitch get a whippin'."

"You wouldn't dare," said the Mother Superior. Sean didn't say a word. He just looked at her and smiled.

Mary Campbell returned shortly with fifteen children. One of them was the boy who had just been whipped. She introduced them all to Sean and Alan. "So, how many of you have been beaten by the Mother here?" Sean asked them. There were ten boys and five girls. All of the boys and one of the girls raised their hands. "Why did she say you were being punished?" Sean asked them.

"For not praying hard enough," they all answered in unison.

"So how many of you would like to see the Mother here get a whippin'?" Sean asked them. They all raised their hands. Even the ones who had not been beaten raised their hands. "It's unanimous Sister. You're gonna get a few whacks. Before I get started, I want you young ladies to cover your eyes and face away. The girls complied. Now I want you young boys to lower your pants so Alan and I can see how bad the good Mother here has been beating on you." The boys were hesitant at first, but they dropped their pants. Every one of them had scars on the backs of their legs and their backsides. Sean and Alan were horrified when they saw all the scars. "All right boys' pullem' back up," If the Mother Superior had been a man, Sean would have beaten her till she couldn't stand. A whippin' would have to do for now. Sean reached out and grabbed Sister Agnus. He took her to a pew and laid her across his lap. He pulled up her robe and gave her four good whacks across her backside. The girls had uncovered their eyes and witnessed the Mother Superior getting her just reward. Sean knew that it hurt, but the Sister never made a sound. Sean let her up when he was done. She tried to slap him but he stopped her. "Aren't you sposed to turn the other cheek?" said Sean. She gave Sean a look of disgust and stormed off. As she was leaving, Sean yelled at her. "If I hear that you did anything at all to these kids for what I done here, I'll come back and make you wish you hadn't. Oh, and pardon me for my language." Sister Ann stood there with a smile on her face. "You best not let your boss see you smilin'," said Sean. "She'll get you sent off to who knows where. Now Mary, Alan and me gotta be goin'. You know we love you girl. Now do the best you can here and maybe good things will happen for you. Sister Ann, if your boss lays one hand on any of the kids, I expect you to get ahold of the new Chief of Police. He'll take care of it." Sister Ann nodded her head yes. Sean and Alan hugged Mary and were on their way. Mary had tears in her eyes as they left.

That evening after they had finished dinner at the hotel, Sean started questioning Alan about Mary and Jimmy. "Well, are you gonna adopt them kids?" asked Sean. "They sure are attached to you."

"I know they are and it's the same for me," said Alan. "When we've been back home for a couple of days, I'll set down with Elizabeth give her the whole story. I think she'll want them two after I get done telling her everything."

"Well, you'd make a damn good Pa," said Sean. "You might want to think about trying to be home more if you two do adopt them kids."

"I know," said Alan. "I'll want to be with them as much as I can. I don't need to work anyway. You'll be thinking this way too when your baby shows up."

"Yes I will," said Sean. "I certainly will."

~~~~

The next day when they were visiting Jimmy at the hospital, they got a visit from Father Darcey. He came into Jimmy's room after Sean and Alan were already there. "I think we should have a talk," said the Father to Sean. "Some things have been brought to my attention."

"How bout you and I take a walk around the block and talk," said Sean. Father Darcey nodded yes and he and Alan left.

Father Darcey spoke first as they were walking. "Now Sean, I can't condone someone whipping a Mother Superior," he started, "but from what I was told by Sister Ann and the children, it was well deserved. Sister Agnus told me her story first and then I talked with all of the children and Sister Ann. The boys showed me their scars. If it was up to Sister Agnus, you would be crucified or something worse. She has no idea that she did anything wrong."

"Not very Christian of her, huh Father," said Sean.

"No, not very Christian," said Father Darcey. "I wish I had known all of this was happening at the orphanage. I would have put a stop to it."

"So what will happen now?" asked Sean.

"Sister Agnus will no longer be in charge of the orphanage," started the Father. "She will be transferred within the week. Sister Ann will be in charge."

"She seems like a good person," said Sean. "She'll do well."

"Yes she will," said the Father. "Now is there any chance that Alan is going to adopt Mary or Jimmy or both of them? I can see that he dearly loves those two."

"Yes he does Father," said Sean. "When he gets back home, he's going to have long talk with his wife and see what she says. She's a fine woman. I think she would agree to adopt both of them."

"Lord be praised," said the Father. "Lord be praised."

"Now don't let this slip out yet Father," said Sean. "I'd hate it if things didn't work out."

"I won't say a word and I'm sure it will work out," said the Father. "Now let's get back. I want a few words with Jimmy and then I've got to work on Sister Agnus's transfer."

~~~~

When they got back to the hospital, Sean got a pleasant surprise. Mabel and Officer Martin, soon to be Sgt. Martin, were there to greet them. Father Darcey went on to Jimmy's room while Sean stayed with Mabel and Officer Martin. "You're looking good Mabel," said Sean. "How's them ribs feel? Are you a little sore?"

"They are a little sore, but I'm doing good," started Mabel. "I know you and Alan come here every day to visit Jimmy Dugan. I know you two are leaving soon and I wanted to see you one more time and thank you for all you have done. William and I both want to thank you."

"No need, you're a good woman Mabel," said Sean. "I'm sure William knows that. Looks like you two are an item now. That's good."

"Yes, it is good," said Mabel. "I'll be working at the hospital as soon as I heal up and William and I will see how things work out."

"They'll work out Mabel," said Sean. "Bill's a good man. Yep, things'll work out." Sean grabbed Mabel and gave her a hug, but not too hard, and then shook William's hand.

~~~~

Back in Cincinnati, Maggie and Elizabeth had received the telegram telling them when Sean and Alan would be returning. They were so excited. Maggie had been feeling a lot better as her morning sickness had subsided. When Maggie told Jeb that Sean would be home soon, he seemed to know exactly what she had said. He squirmed and danced around like new puppy. They would be counting down the hours.

CHAPTER THIRTEEN

Danny Danaher was born in England in 1820. His real name was Alfred Nelson. His father Charles, was a career officer in the Army. Somehow, he was related to Lord Nelson, but not close enough to pull any weight. Charles had joined the army when he was seventeen and fought as a Private at the battle of Waterloo when he was eighteen. He fought so hard and well at the battle that the Duke of Wellington himself gave him a battlefield commission. In the last hours of the battle, Charles took charge of his unit because all of the Officers and NCO's had been killed. The Duke of Wellington had witnessed him in action and had him commissioned as soon as the battle was over. Charles decided then and there that he would make his life in the Army. Charles was on a leave in 1819 when he met Alfred's mother, Mary O'Malley. They had a whirlwind romance and were married right before his leave was over. Upon returning to duty, he was shipped to India for three years. Alfred was born nine months later. Mary wasn't permitted to go as Charles was a junior officer.

When Charles did return to England, he wasn't there for long. He was sent to Natal with some other officers to see how things were going there. The Zulu leader, Shaka, was now allowing Europeans on

Zulu land. Charles made friends with Shaka, and Shaka gave him a Zulu short spear and a shield as a gift. Unrest was brewing between Shaka and his brothers and other tribes. Charles and the others were able to leave Natal before Shaka was assassinated by his brothers. Shaka's successor also wanted to slaughter all the Europeans who had come to Natal. When Charles returned to England, he gave the spear and the shield to Alfred. Alfred would always remember them as the only things he got from his father other than a hard time. Alfred was only nine years old, but Charles treated him as though he was an army recruit. Everything was strict discipline. Anything out of line was cause for severe punishment.

In 1832, Charles was diagnosed as having consumption. It got worse and worse and after two years, he was forced to leave the army. He had heard that consumption, although not curable, was not as severe in America. The climate was better than in England and the disease did not advance as rapidly. The arrangements were made and the family sailed for America. Charles got worse and died five days before the ship docked in America.

Mary was devastated. She didn't have much money, no prospects, and a fourteen year old son to care for. New York City was not a warm welcoming place. Mary found the cheapest boarding house around and then went looking for any kind of work she could find. While she was out looking for work, Alfred roamed the streets. Alfred was small for his age, but he was very smart. Several times when he was roaming the streets, he found himself in neighborhoods that he should have avoided. He got himself beat up more than once in the beginning, but later on, he was able to talk his way out of bad situations.

A month went by and Mary found no work. The money was gone and they were about to get evicted from the boarding house.

Mary was out looking for work one day and just broke down and was crying uncontrollably as she stood on a street corner. A middle aged well dressed man approached her and handed her a handkerchief. When she finally finished crying, she thanked the man and handed him back the handkerchief. "May I be of any service to you my dear?" the man asked.

"What do you mean kind sir?" Mary asked.

"I can see that you are very upset about something and I would be happy to help you any way I can," the man said. "My name is Thomas Danaher, and you are?"

"I am Mrs. Charles Nelson," answered Mary. "And I appreciate your concern."

"Is Mr. Nelson near? I can get him for you if that would help," said Thomas.

Mary started crying all over again. Before she knew it, she was sobbing on Thomas's shoulder. "I'm sorry. I didn't mean to get your coat all wet," cried Mary. "It's just that my husband died a little over a month ago. We were coming here from England. My husband had consumption and we were coming to America because we heard the climate here is more favorable than it is in England. He died five days before the ship docked here."

"I'm so sorry Mrs. Nelson," said Thomas. "Maybe there is a way I can help you. I am in need of someone to take care of my house and things."

"You mean like being a maid or a servant or something?" asked Mary.

"I'm not sure what the proper term is, but my wife died five years ago and the woman who has been taking care of things is very old and wants to spend her last days with her family," said Thomas. "Can you cook and clean and such?"

"I am a good cook and I can clean with the best of them," said Mary. "I will do whatever is necessary to clothe and feed my son and I."

"So you have a son. How old is he?" asked Thomas.

"Alfred is fourteen. He's small for his age, but he is very smart," answered Mary. "His father was a career army officer and was very strict with him."

"He'll be a man soon," said Thomas. "So, Mary Nelson, what say you come with me and I'll show you my house. It's not far from here."

Mary was impressed with Thomas's house. It was huge. Most people would say it was a mansion. The inside of the house was immaculate. "When may I start?" asked Mary.

"You may start as soon as you and your son get moved in," answered Thomas.

"Moved in? You mean we'll be living here in your house?" asked Mary.

"Of course, there's plenty of room," answered Thomas. "You and your son will have your own rooms. This house has been empty too long. My last woman has been gone now for two months. She was with us for ten years."

"I hope I meet your expectations," said Mary. "Alfred can help me around the house too."

"Has Alfred had much schooling?" asked Thomas. "The public school is not far from here and there are also some private schools too."

"Alfred has been schooled properly. He is a very smart boy," said Mary. "I would like to see him attend college some day if that were possible."

"Well after you get settled in, we'll take him over to the public school and get him enrolled," said Thomas. "We'll see how he does."

"May I ask how you earn your living?" asked Mary. "I don't mean to be nosey. It's just that we have just met. We are strangers. I do feel awkward about this."

"I am a business man. I own several businesses and I am a partner in others," said Thomas. "Once we see that things are working out, I'll take you around and show you some of my businesses. Maybe Alfred would like that too. Now why don't you take another look around the place and then go get your son." Mary gave herself another quick tour of the house and then went to find Alfred.

Alfred was sitting in front of the boarding house. All of their belongings were with him. He saw Mary approaching and spoke. "That nasty old bitch threw us out mother," started Alfred. "She wouldn't even wait till you got back."

"Please watch your language," said Mary. "We have a new place to stay and I have a job too."

"What is it mother?" asked Alfred.

"I met a nice man today," said Mary. "He needs a live in person to take care of his household."

"What about me and are you sure that's all he's interested in?" asked Alfred.

"Alfred, I'll not have you thinking that way," said Mary. "Mr. Danaher seems like a very nice gentleman. He has a big house and we will both have our own room."

"Well what does he do for a living?" asked Alfred.

"He's a business man and I would say from the looks of his house, he does very well," said Mary. "Now let's get going. His house is not far away."

They only had one trunk for all of their belongings. Alfred drug it along while Mary carried Alfred's Zulu shield and spear. They got some strange looks from people as they went down the sidewalk. Thomas saw them struggling as he was looking out a front window and went out to help. "I should have gone to help you," said Thomas. "I must not have been thinking about your luggage."

"Alfred may be small but he's strong," said Mary. "Alfred, this is Thomas Danaher. Thomas, this is my son Alfred."

"I am pleased to make your acquaintance," said Alfred as he extended his hand to Thomas. They shook hands.

"A good firm handshake," said Thomas. "A man should have a good firm handshake. I'm pleased to meet you too. Now what on earth is your mother doing with that spear and shield? It looks African to me."

"It is sir," started Alfred. "Shaka Zulu himself gave the spear and shield to my father."

"Now that's something. I never knew those Africans got along with any outsiders," said Thomas.

"Shaka did, but after he was killed by his brothers, his successor wanted to kill all of the Europeans down there," said Alfred. "My father and the others got out before that happened."

"So did you get along well with your father?" asked Thomas.

"No, actually we didn't get along at all," started Alfred. "He was always gone and when he was around, he treated me like an army recruit. This spear and shield are the only things he gave me that wasn't a hard time."

"I'm sorry to hear that," said Thomas. "I hope we can get along."

"I hope so too," said Alfred.

"Well let's get your luggage inside and get you both into your rooms," said Thomas. "Mary, once you get settled, you can check the kitchen and see if we have anything for dinner tonight. I have been dining out almost every meal since my woman left. She always took care of the kitchen."

After Mary had her room ready, she helped Alfred get his room ready. Then she went to the kitchen. There was nothing in the house except some flour and oats. She reported to Thomas.

"Thomas, I'm sorry to report that the cupboard is bare," said Mary. "I can do some shopping if there's time. Your wood supply is very low too."

"Well we'll dine out this evening and tomorrow morning I'll give you some money and you can go marketing," said Thomas. "I'll get us a new supply of wood too. Now why don't we meet in the living room in an hour and we'll go to dinner."

"Do we need to dress for dinner?" asked Mary.

"No, what you two are wearing is fine," said Thomas. "We won't be going to a high class place this evening. We'll be walking too. The place we're going isn't far."

As they walked to the café, Thomas pointed out places of interest. Thomas carried a cane, but Alfred could see that it was only for looks as Thomas walked perfectly and had no need for a cane. The café wasn't a place where rich folks went to eat, but it wasn't a dump either. The food was excellent and Thomas and Mary had wine with their meals. Thomas asked Alfred if he would like some wine, but he declined. He wanted tea instead. He hadn't had any tea since they left England. They didn't talk much as they ate. Thomas did ask Alfred if he wanted to attend school or not.

"I will go to college one day sir," said Alfred. "I believe knowledge is power and the more a person knows, the better off they will be."

"You sound wise for a young man," said Thomas. "But a person needs other knowledge that doesn't come from books. And please don't call me sir. It is not necessary. My name is Thomas."

"All right Thomas, and I know about other knowledge," said Alfred. "I've already learned some of it on the streets of New York. Sometimes I was able to use my brains and not my brawn to get me out of trouble. I don't have much brawn anyway."

"Maybe one day I'll show you a few things," said Thomas. "So if we're done here, let's head home." Thomas paid the bill, left a tip, and they left. It was dark as they walked down the sidewalk, but there was almost a full moon. They had gone about a block when two men came out of the shadows behind them. Mary almost screamed but Thomas told her to remain calm.

"We'll have your wallet mister, and the woman's jewelry," said one of them. Thomas turned around to face them.

"You gentlemen, and I use that term lightly, had better just move on," said Thomas. Alfred and Mary turned around now to watch. Mary was surprised when she saw the two would be robbers. They were fairly young, maybe early twenties, and were dressed fairly well. Mary assumed that they would look like the poor rag tag bums she had seen in London and on the streets of New York when she had ventured into the slums when she had been looking for work. The one who had done the talking was a fair sized man, over six feet tall. He had jet black hair and probably weighed over two hundred pounds. He was also clean shaven. The other man was smaller, maybe five foot eight or so, and had blonde hair. He was on the thin side and it looked like he was trying to grow a moustache.

"Purty woman you got there Mr.," the bigger man said. "Wouldn't want nothin' ta happen to her would ya?" The one who had been doing the talking now pulled out a big knife. The other man produced a billy club.

Thomas never said a word. He took his cane in his left hand and gave the top of it a yank with his right hand. A long shiny blade glowed in the moonlight. Before the two men reacted, Thomas struck the one with the knife on the top of his head with the bottom part of the cane. At the same instant, he swung the blade at the man's hand that was holding the knife. The man screamed. The knife fell from his hand and two of his fingers with it. Then Thomas gave the man a kick in the chest and knocked him down. He stepped over him and went after the man with the billy club. The man took one swing at Thomas with the billy and missed. The man was now leaning forward and off balance. Thomas swung the blade again and put a gash on the right side of the man's face. The man let out a scream and took off at a dead run. Thomas watched him for a moment and then went back over to the man who was down. He stood over him and spoke. "If I were you I'd find another way to make a living," said Thomas. "Now pick up your knife and your fingers and get the hell out of here. If I ever see you again, I will run you through." The man was in terrible pain, but he did as instructed. Thomas watched him until he was out of sight.

Mary and Alfred just stood there and stared at Thomas for a while. Thomas stared back at them but didn't speak. After a minute or so Mary spoke. "I hope things like that don't happen around here on a regular basis. Do you use that cane of yours very often?"

"Mary, I do not use my cane unless I feel that the situation warrants it," said Thomas. "I believe those two fools would have hurt us badly if they could have. I did not enjoy hurting them, but they got exactly what they deserved."

"I'm not condemning your action, although I was very surprised by it," said Mary. "I'm glad your protected us. I just hope that you don't have to protect very often."

"I hope that too," said Thomas. "Now let's be on our way." Thomas took out a handkerchief, wiped the blood off of the blade, and put the cane back together. Then they started for home. Alfred stared at the cane the whole time they walked, but he never said a word.

~~~~

The next morning, Mary fixed some oats for breakfast and then she and Thomas went marketing. Thomas wanted to go with her to show her the best places to shop and he also wanted to be with her in case the two would be robbers might still be in the area. Thomas took his cane with him.

Alfred stayed home. He wanted to explore Thomas's library. There was a room in the house that Thomas sometimes used as an office. One wall of the room was completely filled with books. More than half of them were some type of law book, but the others were just about everything else. There were history books, poetry books, Shakespeare, novels, and books on different kinds of religion. On another wall was a copy of Thomas's law degree.

He had received his law degree from Harvard. Alfred read the degree and wondered why Thomas wasn't a practicing lawyer.

When Mary and Thomas arrived back at the house, they were in a very nice buggy. Thomas had hired the buggy when Mary told him how much stuff they needed. It was too much for them both to carry. Alfred saw them arrive and went out to help them carry everything inside.

After everything was put away, Thomas and Alfred went over to the public school. Mary stayed home to organize the kitchen. The headmaster at the school interviewed Alfred and was impressed with his knowledge. He escorted Alfred to his classroom. Alfred was introduced and then the headmaster went back to his office. Thomas left and went back home.

Alfred found out very quickly who the bully was in his class. Right away this bigger boy started making fun of Alfred's British accent and shot spit wads at him most of the first day. Alfred figured he would be in a fight right after school, but when school let out, the bully had disappeared. That evening at dinner, Mary and Thomas quizzed him about his first day at school.

"I knew most of what we went over in class today," said Alfred. "I found out who the bully is in my class too. I thought for sure I'd be in a fight after school, but he must have had something else to do. I never saw him after class let out."

"Is he much bigger than you?" asked Thomas.

"Yes, he's a lot bigger than me," answered Alfred. "But I'm not afraid of him."

"It's good that you're not afraid," said Thomas. "You need to make sure he knows you're not afraid. Don't let him bully you. I'll show you some things after dinner."

"I'll not have my son getting into fights all the time," said Mary.

"He won't once the other boys learn that he won't be pushed around," said Thomas. "I'll just show him a few things so he can defend himself better."

~~~~

That evening after dinner, Thomas took Alfred into the library for some self defense instruction. "One thing you need to always remember is that there's no such thing as a fair fight," started Thomas. "If someone wants to fight you, they want to hurt you. You have to hurt them first if possible. Use your feet, knees, elbows, and teeth if you have to. And when you use your fists, make sure you hit hard and in a good spot. Don't just flail away with your arms. Put your whole body into a punch and exhale when you throw it. That way if you were to get hit in the gut, it wouldn't knock the wind out of you." Thomas showed him how to throw a proper punch and Alfred threw some practice punches. "All right now son, I'll be the big boy and I've got you cornered," started Thomas. "Show me what you got."

Thomas made out like he was raring back to throw a punch at Alfred with his right hand. As soon as he rared back, Alfred moved in close and stomped Thomas on his right foot, but not too hard. When Thomas bent down some to grab his foot, Alfred threw a punch into his gut. When Thomas double over from the punch in the gut, Alfred brought up his right knee like he was going to knee Thomas in the face. Thomas acted like he had been kneed in the face and started falling backwards. As he was falling backwards, Alfred then acted like he was kicking Thomas in his privates. "All right, all right," said Thomas. "I think that's enough for a first lesson. You seem to be very resourceful. I think you'll be all right. There's one more thing I think we should discuss today. A lot of the time, bullies don't work alone. If there's more than one of them, you need to shame the bully into facing you alone. If you can't do that, you could get yourself hurt bad. Get yourself away as fast as you can. If you can't get away, grab anything that you could use as a weapon, rocks, boards, bottles, anything. Do you understand?"

"I do," answered Alfred. "Maybe some day you'll show me how to handle that cane of yours."

Thomas smiled. "Maybe one day down the road if it becomes necessary," said Thomas. "Now maybe you have some studying to do for school tomorrow."

"I do have some, but I've got a question for you," said Alfred. "I know that you have a law degree from Harvard. Why aren't you a practicing attorney?"

"I did practice law for several years after law school," answered Thomas. "I found out that I was a better businessman than I was a lawyer. Now being a lawyer does come in handy. If something come up that needs sorted out legally, I can handle it myself and not have to hire a lawyer."

"So when can I find out about your businesses?" asked Alfred.

"Maybe this weekend I'll show you some of them," said Thomas. "I know your mother would like to see them too."

~~~~

The next day at school, the bully didn't waste any time before picking on Alfred. Alfred was pretty much ignoring him until Ox, that's what the kids called him, referred to Alfred as a son of a bitch. Alfred wasn't going to let anyone insult his mother. About an hour before class let out, the teacher was called to the office for something. Of course she told the kids to behave while she was gone for a few minutes. Alfred's desk was toward the front of the classroom. Ox's desk was at the very back of the classroom. As soon as the teacher was out the door, Alfred got up and walked back to Ox's desk. He stood there staring at him. "What do you want you son of a bitch?" said Ox. "I'm gonna stomp your ass soon as school's over today. Git ready." Ox stayed seated at his desk. His large Arithmetic book was laying there on top of his desk. Before Ox could react, Alfred grabbed the book with both hands and smacked Ox on the side of his head as hard as he could. Ox was knocked out of his seat and onto the floor. Alfred walked back up to his desk and sat down. Most of the other kids were not sure how to react to what had just happened, but some of them let out a few cheers. Ox had gotten to his feet now and was about to start after Alfred when the teacher came back into the classroom. She saw Ox standing there and she noticed that the side of his face had a large red mark on it.

"What happened to you Frances?" asked the teacher. "Why are you not sitting at your desk?

Now Frances Turner was Ox's real name. No one called him Frances except the teacher. Even his mother called him Ox. "I think he fell asleep and fell onto the floor," said Alfred.

"Well whatever, take your seat Frances," said the teacher. Ox did as instructed. The whole class could see the hate shooting from his eyes. There was going to be a fight after school.

Most of the school fights took place on an empty lot about a block from the school. By the time the fight was ready to start, about half the school was there to watch. They formed a circle around the two boys and started yelling at them to get started. Ox was about a head taller than Alfred and outweighed him by more than twenty five pounds. They were about fifteen feet apart. "It's time for you ta bleed you bastard," shouted Ox as he took off running right at Alfred.

Alfred squatted down and as Ox was almost on him, he jumped straight up as high as he could. Ox was about to wrap his arms around Alfred when Alfred's kick caught him in the face. The blood went flying and Ox fell backwards. He lay on his back with blood pouring from his nose. Before he could get back up, Alfred came over and stomped him in the gut with his right foot. Ox sat up holding his gut. Alfred bent down and hit Ox on the chin with a powerful right. Ox went back down and didn't move. He was unconscious. All of the kids just stood there for a while in total disbelief. The fight hadn't lasted a full minute. They had never seen anything like this before. The fight hadn't even been over for a minute, when someone shouted. "Hey, you kids, what's going on over there?" Some adult had happened by and saw the gathering. When the kids heard that, they all got the hell out of there. That is, all except Ox. The person that had yelled at the kids stood there while the kids took off. After they had gone, he saw one kid lying there on the ground. He went over for a look. The man recognized the boy right away. The boy was his son. The man was on his way home from a tavern. "So you finally got what you been givin' out for a change," said the man. "It's about time." He knelt down and shook Ox. Ox finally came to. He looked up at his father. He didn't speak. "Finally got yours didn't ya boy," said his father. "I've told ya and told ya that sooner'r later someone'll kick your ass. Looks like they done a good job." Ox got to his feet but still didn't talk. "C'mon boy, let's git home," said the father. "Your ma'll clean ya up some. I bet yer nose's broke. Sure looks like it." They slowly headed home.

At the dinner table that evening, Alfred didn't say one word about the fight. Mary asked him how school was today and he just said it was fine. Thomas knew better. He had heard through the grapevine about a fight after school. After dinner, while Mary was cleaning up in the kitchen, Thomas had Alfred meet him in the library. "So you must have done all right today," said Thomas. "There's not a mark on you. Was the other boy hurt bad?"

"It was a short fight," started Alfred. "He come at me and I jumped up as high as I could when he was about to grab me. I kicked him in the face and he fell backwards and went all the way down. Then I stomped him in the gut and when he sat up grabbing his gut, I gave him a good right to the chin. He was knocked out. That was it. Some adult happened by and all of us scattered. All except Ox."

"So that was his name," said Thomas. "I know that name. That boy's got two older brothers and his father is a hard drinker. I'd keep my eyes open for them brothers just in case they want to get even. So what made you think about jumping up like that and kicking him?"

"I don't know," answered Alfred. "It just came to me at the time. It sure worked."

"Well I doubt it'd work again, but you never know," said Thomas. "Well you should get any studying done that you have. Remember, watch out for those brothers."

"I don't know what they look like," said Alfred.

"I'm pretty sure they'll tell you who they are when the time comes," said Thomas. "Now I'll see you tomorrow."

~~~~

The next day at school, Alfred found out that he had made lots of new friends. It seems that Ox had been giving just about everybody else a hard time. Everyone was glad he got his just rewards. Ox wasn't at school that day either. In fact, he never came back to school at all.

The very next week, Alfred began noticing that two older looking boys had been watching him as he got to school in the morning and as he left when school was out. They were even bigger than Ox. On Friday as he was walking home, he looked back and saw the two boys following him. After about a block, the two boys started walking a little faster. One of them yelled out. "Ox was our brother. We're gonna hurt you bad."

Alfred took off at a dead run. Ox's brothers were in hot pursuit. Alfred was small, but he was fast. His lead increased in no time. He turned a corner and a general store was ahead of him. There was a barrel in front of the store that had ax handles in it. The brothers hadn't rounded the corner yet. Alfred grabbed an ax handle from the barrel and hid behind the barrel. When the brother's rounded the corner and were just past the front of the store, Alfred sprang from behind the barrel. The brothers must have seen or heard Alfred because they stopped and started to turn around. They were side by side. Before they were completely turned around, Alfred struck. He raised the ax handle above his head with both hands and brought it down as hard as he could on the boy on his right. It just missed his head and struck the top of his left shoulder. The boy went down and went down hard. The other boy was completely turned around now but was totally amazed. He just stood there looking at his brother. Before the brother moved at all, Alfred took the ax handle and struck the boy on his right leg below the knee. Down he went. Alfred stood over them. It was like he was daring them to get up. A voice now came from the front of the store. "See here boys. What's going on out here?" Alfred recognized the voice. It was Thomas. Alfred turned and looked at Thomas. Thomas smiled. "I bet these two are Ox's brothers," said Thomas.

"They are," said Alfred. Then Alfred turned and looked down at the brothers. "Look you two, I never did anything to wrong you and your brother got what he asked for," started Alfred. "Now I'm going to ask you real nice like to just leave me alone. Well, are you going to leave me alone?"

"You probly broke my leg and mebbe his shoulder," one of the boys said. "You expect us to just let that go?"

"Well just what were you two going to do to me?" said Alfred. "It could have been me laying there instead of you two. Now you two pick yourself up and get out of here. Please?" The brothers never said a word. They helped each other up and limped off. Alfred watched them for a good while and then turned back to Thomas.

"So what were you doing at this store?" asked Alfred.

"I own this store," said Thomas. "It's one of my businesses. Now let's walk on home. Take the ax handle with you."

Nothing was mentioned about Alfred's latest encounter at the dinner table that evening. "Tomorrow is Saturday. How about I take the both of you and show you my businesses," said Thomas.

"That would be nice," said Mary. "I've been curious about them."

"How about you Alfred?" asked Thomas. "Would you be interested in seeing my businesses?"

"I would," answered Alfred. "Maybe I could work in one of them for you."

"Maybe you could. I'm always looking for good people," said Thomas.

~~~~

The next morning after breakfast, Thomas showed Mary and Alfred his businesses. Besides the general store, he owned a butcher shop, a bakery, a livery stable and blacksmith shop, a tavern, and he was part owner of a bank. Mary and Alfred were impressed. "Just how can you take care of so many businesses?" asked Alfred. "It must have taken a lot of money to get started too."

"It did take a lot of money to get started," answered Thomas. "It took a lot of time too. All of this didn't happen overnight. Now I have good trustworthy people working for me. I pay them well and treat them well. Alfred, remember this. If you want people to work for you and remain loyal, you must pay them well and treat them well. People who work for you are not your property or slaves. They're people just like you and they have families that they must care for."

"I understand what you're saying," said Alfred. "I would treat someone the way I'd want to be treated."

"That's good. Now what say we go have us some lunch," said Thomas. "I'm getting hungry." They went to the café where they had eaten their first night at Thomas's house. That evening after dinner, Thomas announced that he and Alfred were going out for some man to man time. Mary thought it was a good thing to do since Alfred didn't have a father now.

A buggy picked them up right before dark. They had gone about a block when Thomas spoke. "Now Alfred, what we're doing this evening must be kept in the strictest confidence," said Thomas. "Do you understand."

"I do," answered Alfred. "So where and what are we doing?"

"I'll be showing you my other businesses," answered Thomas. "Your mother must not find out about them. Not just yet anyway."

"So why the secrecy?" asked Alfred. "Is what you're doing against the law?"

"Let's just say that some people don't agree with what I do," said Thomas.

"Must have to do with whiskey, gambling, or prostitution," said Alfred. "I see nothing wrong with any of those."

"Well some people can't handle their whiskey and some people love to gamble, but can't handle it when they lose," said Thomas. "Prostitution is considered the oldest profession. Men will always want sex and I just provide them a service. There's less problems with it. Now sometimes a gent might think he's in love with one of the girls, but it doesn't take much to persuade them otherwise." The buggy stopped in front of a big brick building. They got out and went to the front door. Thomas knocked on the door. A young and very attractive woman answered the door.

"Good evening Mr. Danaher," she said. "It's always nice to see you. Do you need to see Mr. Brown this evening?"

"Thank you Cynthia, I would like to see him and this young man is Alfred Nelson," said Thomas. "His mother is my new housekeeper."

"Good evening Alfred," said Cynthia. "I'm pleased to make your acquaintance." She gave Alfred a smile and then went to get Mr. Brown. He was there in a few minutes.

He went to Thomas and shook his hand. "Good to see you this evening Thomas," said Mr. Brown. "Would you like to see the books or something?"

"That won't be necessary Sam," said Thomas. "This young gentlemen is Alfred Nelson. His mother is my new housekeeper. I'm just showing him my businesses."

"Would you like for me to show him around or do you want to do it?" asked Sam.

"I'll do it Sam. You go on back to whatever you were doing," said Thomas.

"All right, if you need me for anything, just let me know," said Sam.

Sam left and before they started looking around, Thomas explained some things about the place to Alfred. "Now what we have here is a first class place," started Thomas. "All of the girls are beautiful and want to be here. They are of legal age and I have a doctor on hand to make sure that my girls do not get or pass around any of the diseases asscociated with sex. We charge more for our services too. Our clients come from the upper class. Many of them are married. Do you have any questions?"

"I was wondering Thomas, do you indulge yourself?" asked Alfred.

"I do not," answered Thomas. "I never wanted another woman but my wife. I have not wanted another woman since she died. Maybe one day I'll meet another woman I'd want to spend the rest of my life with. Now come on, I'll introduce you to the girls who aren't busy right now.

The place was bigger on the inside than it looked from the outside. There were fifteen working girls there and Alfred got to meet ten of them. Alfred was extremely impressed. Not only were the girls very beautiful, but the rooms and the whole inside of the place was tastefully decorated. Alfred was excited with every girl he met, but there was one it particular he really liked. Her name was Laura. Laura was a little older than the other girls, but she was drop dead gorgeous. Thomas could see that Alfred's pants were about to rip. "So Laura, do you have any clients scheduled soon?" asked Thomas.

"Not for another hour," answered Laura. "Do you have something in mind?"

"How would you feel about taking care of Alfred here on his first time?" asked Thomas. "It would be your first time, wouldn't it Alfred?"

"Yes, I'm a virgin," answered Alfred. "And I won't mind if Laura doesn't mind."

"I won't mind at all," said Laura. "I'll show how to do things right."

About an hour later, Thomas and Alfred were in the buggy again and headed to another one of Thomas's businesses. They talked some as they moved along. "Well, how was it? Was it as good as you expected?" asked Thomas.

"It was wonderful," answered Alfred. "I'd like to do it all the time. Laura was an amazing teacher. Someday when I get married, I hope my wife knows everything she knows. She taught me a lot. I hope that someday the women will think that I'm a great lover."

"It's good that you want women to think that about you," said Thomas. "Most men just want to get their own pleasure and to heck with the woman. You be good to the women and they'll be good to you. Don't forget that."

"I won't," answered Alfred. "Now I noticed there were some other men in there besides Mr. Brown. Are they employees too?"

"Yes they are," answered Thomas. "They are there in case there might be any trouble."

"What kind of trouble?" asked Alfred.

"Well when you have a place like that, somebody is always wanting to take over or extort money from you," said Thomas. "My men are well armed can handle themselves in a fight."

"Do you ever have that kind of trouble?" asked Alfred.

"We haven't for a good while," answered Thomas. "I have very good people on the outside too. They keep their ears open and watch out for any new threats that could come along."

"So have you ever had to kill someone that was threatening your businesses?" asked Alfred.

"I have and I don't regret it," answered Thomas. "They were evil men and got what they deserved."

"Was there any trouble with the law?" asked Alfred.

"No, the law and I are good friends," said Thomas. "The men in question were scum and not missed by anyone except maybe their mothers."

"I think I'll enjoy working for you one day," said Alfred. "So how many other places do you have?"

"I have two more houses," answered Thomas. "There are fifteen girls in both of them too."

"Do you ever have girls that want to leave?" asked Alfred.

"Of course we do," answered Thomas. "Not many women want to do that forever. Some really like it and want to do it as long as they can, but realize they also need to be desirable. Not everyone keeps their looks as long as they'd like. Others want to get married some day and have families."

"Would someone really want to marry a whore?" asked Alfred.

"Let's get something straight right now young man," started Thomas. "Do not use that term around me or my girls. I do not like it. It sounds dirty and ugly. There's nothing dirty or ugly about sex. It's a beautiful thing."

"So what should I call them?" asked Alfred.

"They have names," said Thomas. "Call them by their name." The buggy stopped at the next place. Alfred met all of the girls this time. They didn't expect to be busy till later. Thomas let Alfred have another turn with a girl of his choice if the girl was willing. She was. Her name was Karen and she was a dark haired beauty. Alfred thought she might only be a year or two older than him, but she told him she was twenty two.

Thomas thought Alfred had seen enough for the night and they went home. Mary was still awake and waiting for them. "So how was your evening?" Mary asked them when they entered the house.

"It was good mother," answered Alfred. "I can't wait to start working for Thomas."

"Well get cleaned up and get to bed," said Mary. "I'd like for us to go to church in the morning if you don't mind."

"I won't mind," said Alfred. "Thomas, would you go with us?"

They hadn't attended church since they had been to New York. Mary didn't know if Thomas was a Catholic or a Protestant or nothing at all for that matter. "I'll go with you. I was raised Catholic, but I haven't been to Mass for years," said Thomas. "Are you Catholic?"

"I was raised Catholic, but when I married, the few times we attended church, we went to a Protestant church," answered Mary. "We were married in a Protestant church. I never thought about it before, but since we never married in a Catholic church, our marriage wasn't recognized by the Catholics."

"Well that's a lot of humbug," said Thomas. "You were husband and wife. It doesn't matter who did the ceremony. You lived together and had Alfred here. He was not born out of wedlock. So we can go to whatever church you'd like."

CHAPTER FOURTEEN

Alfred and Thomas got to be very good friends. Thomas was also growing fonder and fonder of Mary. Two years after Mary accepted the position at Thomas's house. He asked for her hand in marriage. He did it very formally too. As Alfred was the senior man in her family, he first asked Alfred if he could court his mother. This happened after they were in his house for a year. The next year he asked Alfred for his mother's hand in marriage. Alfred said if it was all right with him if it was all right with Mary.

They had a huge wedding and then went on a month long honeymoon. Alfred had a growth spurt in the two years in New York and was now a fair sized young man. He stood five foot ten and weighed maybe one hundred seventy pounds. He was a good looking young man too.

Thomas had allowed Alfred to work at all of his businesses. Thomas was hoping that one day Alfred could take over for him. Alfred was like the son he never had and he dearly loved him. Alfred got to be a very good meat cutter and he was also becoming a shrewd businessman. He was paid a decent wage when he worked, but he didn't use all of his money on the working girls. Alfred found out that there were young girls out there his own age who wanted to expand their carnal knowledge. He had learned from the working girls about a woman's fertile times and such and he used this knowledge to keep from fathering any unwanted children. He also liked working at the bank. He had not known how money worked, but he learned quickly. Working at the tavern was also enjoyable. Thomas's tavern was not one of those run down slum type places. It was a nice place and higher class men went there. Alfred enjoyed watching them get drunk.

One evening at the tavern, Alfred was sure he saw the bartender pocket some money that was not his. He saw him do it several times. He was pouring drinks and then pocketing the money instead of putting it in the cash box. He did it at least four times that evening. Alfred decided he would wait till Thomas returned from his honeymoon before confronting the bartender. He also decided he would have some type of proof for Thomas.

Two days later, before the tavern opened and before the bartender or any of the help arrived, Alfred went there. Thomas trusted Alfred completely and had given him a complete set of keys for all of the businesses. So he had a key for the back door of the tavern, the cashbox, the office in back, and the safe. Every day when the tavern closed, the cash box was placed in the safe. The next morning, the money was placed in a bank bag and the date marked on it. Thomas would count it at his convenience and make deposits at the bank when he thought it necessary. There was some loose change in a container in the safe also and every morning, the bartender put some of it into the cashbox to start the day. Alfred's plan was to count all of the loose change in the container. When the bartender arrived, he would ask him how much loose change he took out to start the day. Alfred would tell him that he was asking so he would know about how much to get if it ever happened that he would be behind the bar or helping out. It was Saturday and business would be good most of the day. He had pen and paper and acted like he was doing something for his studies. When a drink was sold, he would mark it down. He knew the prices of everything, so he marked down if it was beer, whiskey, rum, or wine.

Thomas had two bartenders working for him and they both worked on the weekends. Maybe Alfred would see if both of them were skimming. The tavern opened early and the first bartender was by himself till noon when the other one arrived. Sometimes they also had a woman help wait on tables when they were very busy.

The bartender that Alfred had seen skimming was the one who came in first that day. Alfred kept a close watch on him and did not see any skimming that morning. Later in the day, the place got very busy. It was hard for Alfred to keep track, but he did his best. The first bartender was skimming on about every fourth drink. The place was crowded and no one probably saw the man pocketing money that wasn't his. That is no one except Alfred. If the other bartender was skimming, Alfred didn't spot him. Alfred stayed the whole day.

The tavern was open on Sunday, but didn't open early. Alfred got there before opening and counted the money in the cash box. By Alfred's count, the skimming bartender had poured eighty drinks. If he skimmed every fourth drink, he should be short the value of the skimmed drinks. He was short, and right to the penny. Apparently, the other bartender wasn't dishonest. Alfred did the same thing the next Saturday and the results were the same. He couldn't wait to tell Thomas.

~~~~

When they arrived back home, Alfred could tell just by look-ing at his mother and Thomas, that they were very much in love with each other. He was happy for them. That evening after din-ner, Alfred asked Thomas to join him in the library. Alfred told his mother they would be discussing some man things and to please not interrupt them. Thomas's curiosity was going now. "So you must have something important to tell me," said Thomas. "Couldn't it have waited. This is your mother's and mine's first day together in this house as husband and wife."

"I know it is and I am sorry, but I feel you should know what I found out while you were gone," said Alfred.

"It must be important," said Thomas. "Please tell me."

"I found out that one of your bartenders has been skimming from you," started Alfred. "I spotted him pocketing money one day instead of putting it in the cash box. Then I came up with a plan and I have proof of his dishonesty. Two Saturdays ago, he poured eighty drinks and skimmed every fourth one. He did it again the next Saturday."

"Is that so?" said Thomas. "I'll not have anyone steal from me. You're about to learn something about me Alfred. I do not tolerate things like this. I pay people well and treat them fairly. If someone wrongs me, they incur my wrath. I have a terrible tem-per when it comes to things like this. If someone does me wrong whether physically or business wise, I get even. I hold a grudge as long as it takes."

"So what will you do to him?" asked Alfred.

"It's best you don't know," answered Thomas. "That way if you were to be asked, you can tell the truth. You don't know."

Two days later, the bartender never showed up for work. He never showed up for the rest of the week either. Thomas hired a new man. About two weeks later, word got around that he had left town. He had a sick mother he had to visit. Strange thing though, when he left, he had a broken left arm, two black eyes, and maybe some broken ribs.

Alfred had always thought he would attend college one day, but the more he worked with Thomas, he realized that it would be a waste of his time. He loved the banking business and Thomas's partner was very fond of Alfred too. After Alfred was finished with school, he would have his own office at the bank. That's where the money was and that's where he wanted to be.

Alfred also decided that he would start reading all of Thomas's law books. It would be helpful to understand the law and how it worked. He and Thomas spent a lot of time discussing cases and things. One day while they were in the library, Thomas started calling Alfred, Danny. Alfred let it pass one time and then asked Thomas why he was calling him Danny. "I'm sorry," answered Thomas. "I didn't realize I was doing that. My wife always liked the name Danny and said when we had a son we would name him Danny. We were not blessed with children."

"Well, you've been good to my mother and me," said Alfred. "You can call me whatever you like. I won't mind."

"Your name is Alfred. I'll call you Alfred," said Thomas.

After two more years of school, Alfred decided that there was nothing more he could learn, so he quit. His mother and Thomas talked with the Superintendent and he agreed that there was nothing more he could learn at the school. Alfred was the brightest student who had ever attended his school.

Alfred was about to turn seventeen. Thomas and his partner were not worried about his abilities at the bank and decided to go ahead and give him his own office. Their main concern was he was so young and customers would not want to deal with such a young man. Their worry did not last long. Customers were weary of Alfred at first, but he had such a way with words and knew what he was talking about. He was in charge of small loans and business was booming. Word got around about Alfred and the bank's business increased greatly. After a year, he was promoted. A year later, he was promoted again.

Alfred was becoming quite the ladies man too. He was very good looking and well mannered. The women were attracted to him. A lot of them were married women. A lot of older business-men had young wives and liked to show them off. At times, the young wives went with them when they had business at the bank. Alfred was very discreet and never got caught, but one man had his suspicions and challenged Alfred to a duel. Of course Alfred and the man's wife denied any wrong doing. The man would not back off, so Alfred agreed to a duel. Alfred had never handled a firearm in his life. Thomas had showed him a few moves with his sword cane. Since Alfred was the one challenged, he had the choice of weapons. A time was arranged for the men to discuss the choice of weapons. They met at Thomas's tavern on a Sunday morning.

Alfred was already there when the other man arrived. He was a fit looking man, probably in his late forties. His hair was gray and he had huge muttonchops. Alfred guessed that he was just under six feet tall and weighed around one hundred ninety pounds. "I see you came, you little dandy," the man said. "I thought you might leave the country or something."

"No, I'm here and I've decided on weapons," Alfred began. "I have a short Zulu spear and shield that my father gave me. It was given to him by Shaka Zulu. You may use a spear or a sword with a shield."

"Who the hell is Shaka Zulu and I'll not have you throwing spears at me?" said the man.

"Shaka Zulu was a famous Zulu chief in Africa. The spear is not a throwing spear. It's for stabbing and slashing," answered Alfred.

"All right, I'll use my old cavalry saber," said the man. "I'll cut you right in two with it. To hell with a shield."

"As you wish sir," said Alfred. "How about a week from today, next Sunday. You pick the place."

A place was decided upon. "You can bring a second if you want," said the man. "I'll be bringing one."

"What's a second?" asked Alfred.

"You stupid pup. A second is a person who makes sure we do everything properly," answered the man.

"I understand," said Alfred. "Bring plenty of bandages with you too. You're going to need them." The man laughed and then left the tavern.

That evening, Alfred told Thomas all about his upcoming duel and asked if he would be his second. "Of course I will be your second," said Thomas. "And I'll tell you right now, I will not go unarmed. I've been to a few duels in my life and not all the participants are gentlemen. Now just what is this duel about?"

"A woman," answered Alfred.

"I suppose she's the man's wife," said Thomas.

"Yes she is," answered Alfred.

"Alfred, I hope you learn something from this," started Thomas. "There a lots of women out there. You're a good looking man and they are attracted to you. You should not have to be with another man's wife."

"I know that," said Alfred. "But she came after me. I couldn't help myself."

"Well, just remember that it could get you killed one day," said Thomas. "So what is your choice of weapons?"

"I'll be using my Zulu shield and spear," answered Alfred. "And my opponent will be using a cavalry saber."

"Do you know how to handle that thing?" asked Thomas. "And is that shield good enough to take blows from a saber?"

"I'll be all right. My father showed me a few things," said Alfred. "And the shield will hold up if I take him out quickly, which I will. The fool says he won't use a shield."

~~~~

The day of the duel came. It was to be in a big warehouse owned by a friend of the challenger. He and his second were already there when Alfred and Thomas arrived. The challenger went right to them and introduced himself and his second. "I am Samuel Blackwell and my second is William Lords," he said.

"I am Alfred Nelson and my second is Thomas Danaher," said Alfred.

"Oh, a Mick, huh," said Samuel.

"Sir, I didn't come here to be insulted," said Thomas. "I'll expect an apology from you when this duel is finished, if you're still with us."

"Don't hold your breath Mick," said Samuel. "So that's a Zulu spear, huh. This'll be the easiest fight I was ever in." Alfred just looked at him and smiled.

Thomas was giving Samuels second a good look over. He had a cane with him and his jacket seemed to have bulge under it on the man's left side. Thomas wondered if the bulge might be a pistol. He couldn't tell if the cane was a sword cane or not. He had brought his cane and had two small pistols in his jacket pockets.

The two combatants stripped down to their waists. Samuel did a few stretching moves and said he was ready. Alfred just said let's get started and so they did. Samuel came at Alfred hacking away with his saber. Alfred had the spear in his right hand and he held the shield with his left. The shield was blocking the blows well. He stood there acting helpless as Samuel hacked away. He could have stabbed Samuel in the gut several times but didn't. He backed away like he might start running away. Samuel thought he was running and started after him. Alfred stopped, side stepped Samuel, and when he was directly to Alfred's left, Alfred gave him a hard shove with the shield. Samuel was knocked to the ground. Before he could get up, Alfred was standing over him. The tip of the spear was at his throat. "How about two out of three or have you had enough?" said Alfred.

Samuel was full of rage. He never suspected that this dandy could get the best of him. "Let me up and I'll carve you up," said Samuel.

"As you wish sir," said Alfred. Alfred moved and let Samuel get up.

"This is not how a duel goes gentleman," said Thomas. "You have lost Samuel. Alfred could have killed you any time. The duel is over."

"We're not dueling anymore Mick," shouted Samuel. "Now we're just fighting and I'm going to kill this pup." Alfred just shook his head.

The two men stood about ten feet apart sizing each other up. This time Alfred charged. Samuel sidestepped him and hacked with the sword as he passed. The shield blocked the blows, but Alfred had used the spear and cut Samuel across his belly about a half inch deep as he went by. The blood flowed freely. "You've killed me boy," yelled Samuel.

"You're not dying. You're going to need a lot of stitching though," said Alfred. "I take it we're done here."

"Yes, I've had enough," said Samuel. Samuel took his shirt and wrapped it around himself to slow the blood.

Alfred walked over to Thomas. His back was turned from Samuel and his second. When he was almost to Thomas, he saw Thomas quickly reach into a pocket and pull out a pistol. "I wouldn't do that if I were you," yelled Thomas. The pistol was aimed at Samuel's second. The bulge under his jacket was a pistol. It was in his hand, and he was raising it to fire. The man did not move. "Now toss that pistol over here," said Thomas. "And make sure it's not cocked. Do it now." The pistol was not cocked. He tossed it over toward Thomas. "I'll have that apology now sir."

"I'm sorry I called you a Mick," said Samuel. "I have a request for my opponent."

"What is it?" asked Alfred.

"Would you please stay away from my wife?" asked Samuel.

"Your wife means nothing to me sir," said Alfred. "I'll not see her ever again, but you should know this. Your wife came after me. She is young and has a big appetite. You should do your best to feed that appetite. Now I suggest you get yourself cleaned and stitched up as soon as possible."

Samuels second helped him to the buggy. Thomas took the man's pistol, fired the single shot into the floor and then threw it back to the man. He and Alfred stood there and watched them leave. Thomas wanted to make sure the man didn't try to reload and take a shot at them. He did not. Alfred got his shirt and jacket back on and they headed home. "We won't discuss this with your mother," said Thomas as they headed home.

~ ~ ~ ~

The next several years went by quickly. Thomas spent most of his time with Mary and let Alfred take care of the businesses. Mary kept hoping that Alfred would marry and settle down, but Alfred was enjoying bachelorhood too much. Then the war with Mexico came.

CHAPTER FIFTEEN

F or some reason, Alfred thought he should go fight in the war with Mexico. Mary and Alfred were against the war. They thought it was just some political move for western expansion. Alfred was determined to go. Thomas used his influence and got Alfred a Commission. He would be in the Quartermaster Corps.

Alfred soon became bored in the Quartermaster Corps. He thought most of the Officers were thieves and cowards. He wanted to get into the fight and prove himself. It took over a year, but he finally got himself into the infantry. He did well and his men liked him. He always felt bad when some of his men were killed, but he told himself that this was war and that's what happens in war. By the time the war ended, he was a Captain. He had been wounded a couple of times, but not seriously. He was waiting to be shipped home when he received a letter from home. His mother was gravely ill and not expected to live much longer. They were not sure of her illness, but her condition worsened daily.

Before Alfred got home, she died. It had taken him a month to get home after he had received the letter. She died three days after the letter was dated. When he arrived home, he found Thomas to be a shell of a man. He was totally withdrawn. He looked ill and the house was a mess. He had been ignoring his businesses too. Alfred did his best to take care of Thomas, but it was no use. Thomas died two weeks after Alfred got home.

Alfred was the sole beneficiary in Thomas's will so he inherited everything. Two days after Thomas's funeral, Alfred went back to work. He hired a new housekeeper first thing. Then he went to the businesses. The bank was in good shape and doing fine. But Alfred could tell by the books from the other businesses that some of his employees had become dishonest in Thomas's and his absence. It wasn't long before all of the dishonest people were terminated. Alfred did not hurt any of them physically like Thomas would have, but he did assure them that if they gave him any trouble, he would kill them. They took him seriously.

New gangs had moved into the area in his absence and they were always trying to extort money from Alfred. Alfred hired himself his own group of thugs to keep watch on things. It seemed that the more men his thugs took care of, the more of them showed up. Alfred decided to sell some of his businesses. He sold the butcher shop, the bakery, the livery, and the general store. He kept his interest in the bank, the tavern, and the houses of ill repute. These businesses were where the money was anyway.

The gang problem kept increasing. Alfred did his best to get along with them, but sometimes it was impossible. Some of them just didn't want extortion money, they wanted to take over completely. It seemed that a gang war was always going on. Alfred did his best to keep his hands clean. He had good men, paid them well, and they would not rat him out. Alfred was becoming a hard man. He hired more men and went on the attack. Over a two month period, thirty men were killed. Nobody missed them. They were not the bosses. Alfred finally found out who the bosses were.

They were upstanding men in the community just like him. He planned their demise. In a little over three months, his adversaries were dead. Things seemed to be all right for awhile, then Alfred found out that one of the men killed was a son of a very powerful politician. The word was put out that he would not stop until his son's murderer was brought to justice.

Alfred decided it was time to move on. He sold the rest of his businesses and moved to Boston. Once there, he started calling himself Danny Danaher.

Danny had plenty of money and he started out by investing in several legitimate businesses. He associated with the important people in the city and became very well known. After a year in Boston, his friends talked him into running for city council. He won the election by a landslide. His business enterprises expanded too. He was very well liked and was invited to all the important social gatherings in the city. Several of his associates wanted him to run for Mayor of the city, but Danny told them that with the name Danaher, it was very unlikely that an Irishman could be elected Mayor. He wasn't Irish, but no one knew that. He declined, but he would back the next decent candidate.

David Cross had been a councilman and was well liked in the city. When he decided to run for Mayor, Danny knew that he was the man for the job. He was a man who could be easily manipulated. Danny and his friends backed him. The election was close, but David won. When the position of Deputy Mayor was created, he appointed Danny. Danny gladly accepted. When Danny became Deputy Mayor, a man named Tom Flannery was appointed to fill the vacancy left by Councilman Danaher. Tom Flannery won the next election by a landslide.

Tom Flannery appeared to be a fine gentleman, but he was thief, murderer, extortionist, and many other things on the wrong side of the legitimate law. He and Danny became good friends. With a Mayor like David Cross, it was easy for them to do as they pleased. Election after election, Danny's people backed David Cross and he was easily elected.

When the War Between the States erupted, several of Danny's friends wanted him to accept another Commission and join in the fight to save the Union. Danny was tempted, but told them that he had served his country in the war with Mexico, and been wounded twice. He could best serve his country by remaining in Boston and helping maintain order at home. Danny knew that this would not be an easy war as not everyone thought the same way as Abraham Lincoln.

Danny always acted upset when the casualty lists came, but actually, he could care less. When the 54th Massachusetts marched off, he stood and cheered like everyone else, but he could care less. He was making money. Making money was what life was all about anyway. He had all the money he wanted and the women of his choice. What more could a man want?

Danny didn't always approve of the things Tom Flannery did or how he did them, but he was making lots of money. His organization had Judges, lawyers, and police. He had no worries. That is, until that lawman from out west came to town. That lawman wasn't too concerned about doing things according to the letter of the law. When it got too hot in Boston, Danny left.

At first, Danny wasn't sure where he would go. He knew that the old politician from New York whose son Danny had killed, was long dead. He checked with some old friends still in New York and found out that everything was long forgotten. Danny went back to New York City and started calling himself by his real name, Alfred Nelson. He had worn a moustache and a beard for years, but he shaved them off when he got to New York. He figured there would be wanted posters on him and shaving would make him harder to recognize. Some wanted posters had only descriptions of them while some had artist drawings of the wanted person. Alfred hadn't seen any posters yet. He would stop in at the Post Office and a Police Station from time to time and check.

Alfred had plenty of money so there was no need for him to be involved in any kind of business venture. He stayed in a nice hotel and just walked the streets from time to time. The woman he had been living with in Boston was now gone. When he left Boston, he gave her $5000 and told her to move on. She wasn't in the least bit upset. She knew that her man was not a totally honest person and she had paid attention to what had been happening in Boston. She figured it was a good time to leave and the $5000 would help her get a good start. She was still fairly young and attractive. It wouldn't take long to attach herself to another wealthy man. She decided Washington D.C. was the place for her.

A couple of weeks went by and Alfred finally saw his wanted poster at a Post Office. The description of him on the poster was fairly accurate, but Alfred didn't think that the drawing was very good. He knew it would take a keen eye to spot him since he had shaved. What did surprise Alfred was the amount of money that would be paid for him dead or alive. He knew that the city wouldn't put up that much money. Someone must have that kind of money and really want him dead. Maybe it was the western lawman, but lawmen didn't have that kind of money. He would find out in due time. He would lay low for a few more weeks, and then come up with a plan to get rid of the western lawman and the Pinkerton who helped him. Alfred was not sure if his old friends would still be his old friends once they saw his wanted poster. $15,000 can ruin a perfectly good friendship. Killing those two could be very expensive. He would need to pay more than what he was wanted for. Also, for that type of job, the assailant or assailants would want money up front, probably at least half. What would stop them from taking his money and then killing him and collecting on him too? Of course his hired killers wouldn't have to know his real name, but men in that line of work are not stupid. They might figure it out on their own. It would take time to find the right person or persons he could trust.

~~~~

Frances Turner, Ox, as he was called in school, still lived in New York City. His life had not been a good one, but he was happy with it. Even though he spent a good bit of his time drunk or in jail, he seemed like a happy man. He was a fairly good thief and he could hold his own in a knife fight. He had killed a couple of men, but had never been charged with that crime. His time in jail was mostly for thievery or drunk and disorderly. He was doing thirty days in jail for drunk and disorderly when Alfred Nelson had been back in town for a couple of weeks. Something caught Ox's eye at the precinct the day he was released. It was a wanted poster. He took a close look at it. He knew right away that the man in the picture was Alfred Nelson and not Danny Danaher. He had wanted to get even with Alfred Nelson ever since the school fight over thirty years ago. For a moment, he thought he would tell the coppers that the man in the poster was not Danny Danaher, but decided against it. He would wait. One day he would run into the man, and that day would be his last. He would also be $15,000 richer.

A couple weeks later, Ox was hanging out near a tavern and waiting on a man. He knew this man to be wealthy and he had come up with a plan to rob him. He knew the man was inside the tavern and he positioned himself across the street and waited on the man. To Ox's surprise, Alfred Nelson walked down the sidewalk and entered the tavern. Ox forgot about the other man and concentrated on Alfred. He had his long knife with him that he had used when he had killed the other two men. He would follow Alfred home and kill him when the opportunity arose.

Two hours later, Alfred left the tavern. He walked on the sidewalk and entered a hotel about three blocks from the tavern. This hotel was not a flea bag either. Ox just couldn't waltz in and ask what room a certain man was in. He found a side door that was unlocked and slipped in. Once inside, he looked around for a janitor or a maid. They weren't usually working this time of day, but maybe he'd luck out. He did not find either, but he did run into an old woman who was very talkative. The old woman knew that Ox did not belong there and questioned why he was there. He came up with some story about how his family was on hard times and there was a man at this hotel who had offered him a job. The man had neglected to give him his room number and the clerk at the front desk told him to get out of the establishment as he looked like some some riff raff. Ox put on a good show. He almost brought himself to tears as he told his story. "Oh, you poor man, Mr. Nelson is in room 28," she said. "And good luck on your new job."

"You're most kind ma'am, and thank you," Ox said. Ox slowly went to Alfred's room. He had the knife in his right hand and held it behind his back. He stood in front of the door and knocked with his left hand. Alfred walked over and opened the door.

"Yes, may I help you?" he said.

"Remember me?" Ox said as he took the knife and plunged it deep into Alfred's gut. He twisted the blade some. Alfred never said a word or screamed, but Ox could tell by the look on his face that he knew who had stabbed him. Alfred fell to the floor dead. Ox stood over the body for a few minutes deciding what to do next.

Ox went down to the lobby of the hotel and to the desk clerk. "There's a dead man up in room 28," Ox said. "He's probably registered here as Alfred Nelson. That is his real name, but he's wanted for murder and other crimes in Boston as Danny Danaher. Someone needs to get the Police."

It took a good while, but finally the Police arrived. Ox had never answered so many questions in his life. He finally convinced them that for proper identification of the dead man, they would need someone from Boston to identify him.

Police Chief O'Hanly was overjoyed when he got the news that someone claimed to have killed Danny Danaher. He went on the very next train to New York City to identify the body. When O'Hanly first saw the body, he was pretty sure it was Danaher. There was one way to make sure. O'Hanly knew that Danaher had gold fillings in two of his teeth on the lower right side. He had noticed them in a few of the times he had talked with Danaher. "This is our man," said O'Hanly. "Tell that fella to file his claim and he'll be a rich man."

O'Hanly was so happy that Danaher was dead. He spent the night in New York, treated himself to a fine meal, and got very drunk. He had a bad hangover on the trip back to Boston, but he didn't care. Danaher was dead.

CHAPTER SIXTEEN

Maggie, Elizabeth, and Jeb were at the train station when Sean and Alan's train arrived. Jeb howled so much that some people at the station thought maybe a wolf was in the area. Both couples hugged and kissed till they were out of breath. They stopped at a restaurant on the way home because they knew once they got to the house, they wouldn't come out of their rooms for some time.

Sean and Maggie spent four days with Alan and Elizabeth before heading to St. Louis. The last day there, Sean and Alan had a long talk about Danny Danaher. He was still out there somewhere and they had to get him. There was also a good chance that he had hired people to kill Sean and Alan. They both decided to just take it easy for a while. With any luck something would turn up. As Sean and Maggie were leaving, Sean and Alan assured each other that if there was ever a need, for anything, they would be there to help.

They had hardly lived in the house in St. Louis before everything happened. It didn't take long for them to get used to it. They did spend a lot of time in their tub. Sean had let Judge Sharpton know he was back, but he was taking some time off. He also informed the Judge that he would most likely be giving up his badge. For now, he would keep it. He had hopes of finding Danaher. The Judge told him to take all the time he needed.

Sean and Maggie spent the first few weeks at the house just being with each other and enjoying each other's company. Sean spent a little time over at the "The Palace" and at times Maggie went with him. Susie and Dan were doing a great job running the place. Business was booming.

Two weeks later, Sean got a telegram from Boston. It was from Police Chief O'Hanly. Danaher had been killed and a man named Frances Turner was claiming the reward. Sean got a big smile on his face as he read the telegram. He went to his bank and made arrangements for the reward money to be paid. While he was downtown, he went to the telegraph office and sent a telegram to Alan. Then he went to tell Maggie. He was all smiles when he approached her. She knew something had happened. "Danaher's dead," Sean said. "Someone in New York City killed him and O'Hanly identified the body. I said that I'd still hang his dead body, but I don't feel the need now."

"That's wonderful news Sean and if that man identified the body, there's no need for you to even see it. Now you can put your mind at ease," said Maggie.

"I hope so darlin'," said Sean. "I just hope that son of a bitch didn't get anyone hired to kill me and Alan before he got himself killed. I reckon we'll find out if someone tries."

"Let's hope that he didn't darlin'," said Maggie. "He's dead. Let's move on with our lives."

"I love you Maggie," said Sean. "Maybe it's bout time you and me got serious." Sean gave her a big smile, picked her up, and carried her to bed. They spent the rest of the day and night in bed.

The next morning they got up and spent several hours in the tub before they went to a restaurant for a big breakfast. Jeb went with them. He was becoming a permanent fixture around town. Some of the places in town were becoming more civilized and didn't want dogs on their premises, but they knew Sean O'Rourke and made exceptions for him.

Another month went by with no attempts on Sean's life. He decided it was time to give Judge Sharpton his decision. He was going to quit being a lawman and be a husband and father. Someone else would have to take the reins.

Judge Sharpton was not surprised by Sean's decision. "I want to thank you for all you've done for the country," said the Judge. "You deserve to have a family without all the blood and killing. I hope the best for you."

"Thanks Judge," said Sean. "It's been an honor and if the need arises and you need me bad, I'll come." Sean shook his hand and left.

Judge Sharpton knew that Sean's shoes would be hard to fill. Good men were few and far between. He also knew that sooner or later, Sean would be back. A man like Sean could not tolerate outlawry. Being a lawman was in his blood.

Maggie convinced Sean that it would be a good idea for him to go to Abilene and pay everyone there a visit. Maggie was starting to swell up pretty good and she wanted him to visit Abilene before she got too close to delivery. Sean decided he would go, but he wouldn't let anyone know he was coming. He'd surprise them.

~~~~

There were a lot of new faces in Abilene. He hadn't really been gone that long either. When he got off the train, people he knew nodded their heads at him but he wasn't really sure they had recognized him. He stopped at a few stores on his way to Maggie's place. Phil Downs was at the newspaper and was very glad to see Sean. He tried to talk Sean into doing a big story on him. Sean convinced him that it wasn't a good idea. Sean had seen that Jason Hunter's store was not there anymore. He asked Phil about it and Phil told him that Jason was tired of the rowdiness and moved on. Doc Rawlins was still in town. He was glad to see Sean and not have to patch him up. Little Billy Thornton was still at the livery, but he wasn't little Billy any more. He had grown some. He still had all the dogs and they were still helping move the horses when needed. Walter Black still had his gunsmith shop and was making a fortune off of the cowboys.

Tom was behind the bar and when he saw Sean walk into Maggie's Place, he ran over and gave him a huge hug. Then he stepped back and shook his hand. "It's so good to see you Sean," said Tom. "Did you get Michael's killers?"

"We got'em," said Sean. "We got the whole lot of'em. So how's things around here now? I bet it's gets purty rowdy sometimes."

"The town does, but we keep a lid on things in here," said Tom. "Jim and Simon do a fine job keepin' things under control. We've got some new girls since you were here, but they're working out real well. I'll tell you one thing. This town better get itself some law. There's been plenty of shootings and thievery. Regular folks in this town are getting tired of having to step over drunk cowboys just to get to a store. Some of them boys just piss and shit in the street. Sometimes after a big herd gets here, you can't walk down the street the next morning without stepping in some puke where some cowboy threw up after drinking too much."

"Well, I am not available for the job of Marshal in this town," said Sean. "In fact, I give up my Federal Marshal's badge." Sean pulled his jacket open to show Tom that there was no badge on his chest.

"I'll be damned," said Tom. "I never thought you'd give up being a lawman. You are so good at it."

"Well Tom, I got a baby on the way and me and Maggie are going to have a normal family life for a spell," said Sean. Just as he said that, both Tom and Jim noticed that Sean was back. They went over to shake his hand.

"Good to see you Sean," said Jim. "Hope you got Michael's killers. How's that beautiful wife of yours?"

"Maggie's good and with child and we did git Michael's killers," said Sean. "And before Tom tells ya, I give up my badge. I'm gonna be a normal family man for a spell.

"That sounds good," said Simon. "Maggie's one hell of woman. You two deserve a good life together. You take care a her and yer youngin', and us boys here'll take care a yer place for ya."

"That sounds good Simon," said Sean. "How's that girl, Sara I think her name is, anyway, how you two doin'?"

"We're doing good," said Simon. "She stayed on here instead a goin' back to St. Louis. I'm hopin' we can be a permanent fixture some day."

"Is Cookie and Barbara here today? I wanna say hi to'em," said Sean.

"Go on back to the kitchen," said Tom. "They're back there cookin' away. Them cowboys really like the food here. I just hope that them two don't get it in their heads to leave and open up their own place."

"Well if they ever do, just tell'em to stay here and I'll pay'em more," said Sean. "They're worth it." Sean went back to the kitchen. Cookie and Barbara were both standing in front of a stove. Cookie had his hand on Barbara's ass. "You two still honeymoonin'?" said Sean.

They had not seen Sean enter the kitchen and were a little startled when they heard his voice. They turned and saw him and began laughing. Then they came over and both of them hugged Sean. Barbara kissed him on the cheek. "It's good to see you my friend," said Cookie. "How's Maggie? We sure do miss you guys over here."

"We miss you guys too," answered Sean. "Maggie's doing good. Should be seein' that baby in four ta five months."

"That's good news," said Barbara. "I know it'll be a beautiful baby with you two as parents."

"Yep, I sure got me a looker when I got Maggie," said Sean. "Well, I can see you're busy here so I'll leave ya be. I'll be here for a spell. We'll get together." Sean left the kitchen and went back to the bar. "I'm gonna just walk around town a bit and see what I can see," said Sean. "I'll be back in a bit."

"Watch yourself out there Sean," said Tom. "Every once in a while, some a them Texas boys think they're gunmen and want to prove it. There's been more than one shootin' out on the street over nothin'. The undertaker hasn't had to worry bout goin' broke."

"I'm always careful." said Sean. "I seen plenty a drunk cowboys. Kids mostly. First time away from home and fulla beans. I'll dent a head if I hafta." Sean gave Tom a nod and then took off walking.

He went to the livery first. Billy was there and so were some of his dogs. "Hey, young man," said Sean as he entered the barn. "How's the puppy business?"

"Doin' good Marshal," answered Billy. "How's Jeb doin?"

"He's good," said Sean. "He's had it purty easy the last month'r more. Hadn't had to chew up any bad men. And ya don't hafta call me Marshal anymore. I give that up."

"Are you joshin' me?" asked Billy. "Who's gonna take yer place?"

"Can't worry bout that Billy," said Sean. "Maggie'n me's gonna have a baby. I'm gonna be a stay at home dad."

"Well I sure hope we don't git over run with outlaws now," said Billy. "We git some mean lookin' cusses in town more'n we ever did."

"I see there's some mighty fancy rigs over there," said Sean. He had been looking at some of the saddles and bridles that were in the barn. "Purty expensive rigs for a plain ole cowboy."

"There's a lot a them professional gamblers around town," said Billy. "They like to take them cowboy's money."

"Well I reckon if them boys is dumb enough to play cards with a real gambler, it's their own dern fault," said Sean.

"There's been some men come in recently who look like gun-men ta me," said Billy. "They got fancy guns and holsters and keep'm tied down. I seen one man with a fancy shoulder rig."

"Well there's no law against bein' heeled," said Sean. "Maybe there will be some day. Well, I'll be seein' ya. Take care a them dogs."

Sean decided he would step into one of the other saloons in town just to see what it was like. None of the other saloons in town made the customers check their weapons like they did at Maggie's Place. There was a lot of cattle still in the pens to load and more herds were coming. There were a lot of cowboys in town. The saloon he entered was the one where Jug Carter's men had been beaten by the card cheats and then Jug's boys went back and beat the hell out of the cheats and everyone else who was in the place. Sean also ended up shooting the bartender that day after he had come after Sean with at shotgun. Bill Thompson had owned the place and his wife Elizabeth sold it. Sean didn't know who the new owner was.

The saloon was a little nicer inside than it used to be. The women weren't ugly but they weren't too good looking either. Sean figured that after a few drinks, the cowboys wouldn't care. The bartender didn't know who Sean was. When Sean walked up to the bar, he just asked Sean what he wanted and set it in front of him. There was no other conversation. Sean had himself a beer. It was somewhat cold and went down good. A couple of card games were going on. Some of the cowboys were playing with some gamblers. Sean just shook his head. He finished his beer and then decided he'd have some whiskey. He tried to get the bartenders attention, but he acted like he was too busy to help Sean.

"If yer too busy back there I can git my own damn drink," Sean said loudly to him."

"Just hold yer damn horses peckerwood," said the bartender. "I'll be there when I'll be there."

The bartender found out real quick that he had said the wrong thing. When he went past Sean again, Sean reached out and grabbed him. The bartender's apron ripped some as Sean grabbed him by both hands at his chest. "Weren't no need fer no name callin'," said Sean. "Now I'll accept your apology and you can git me a glass a bourbon."

"I'll be damned if I'll do either you son of a bitch," yelled the bartender. The whole place got very quiet now as everyone was wanting to see what would happen next. Sean could tell that the bartender was reaching for something behind the bar. Before the man could grab whatever he was after, Sean let go of the man with his left hand. Then he took his left hand and grabbed the hair on top of the man's head. Next thing everyone knew, Sean was slamming the bartender's face into the bar. He did it three times. Then he let go of the man and he fell unconscious to the floor.

Some well dressed man came running through a door that was behind the bar. "Just what in the hell is going on out here?" the man yelled. "Who did this to my man?

"That'd be me," said Sean. "You oughta hire yerself some nicer people. That there gent needs some manner lessons."

"And who in the hell'r you?" asked the man.

"Name's O'Rourke, Sean O'Rourke," answered Sean. The place got even quieter.

"Oh, so you're the famous lawman and gunman," said the man. "I know you own that other saloon. Did you come over here and beat up my bartender thinking it would help your business?"

"Mister, whatever yer name is. Yer bout as dumb as that asshole you got fer a bartender," said Sean. "Tell ya what. Since I knocked out yer bartender, I'll take his place fer a spell."

"My name is Camp, Camp Cordial," said the man. "If I let you bartend, you won't shoot anyone, will you?"

"I never shot anyone ever that didn't need shot," said Sean. "Camp, Camp Cordial. That's some name. Kinda got a ring'r somethin' to it."

"Well we can't pick our own names," said Camp. "Now please don't hurt anyone till I can get me another bartender here."

"Don't you worry Camp. This place is in good hands," said Sean. Camp went back to his back room office and Sean started tending bar. "Hey, how bout a couple you fellas come and git this lump a shit outta the way back here. I don't wanna be steppin' over'm." A couple cowboys carried the bartender out in front to the sidewalk and leaned him up against the wall of the saloon. Folks just stepped around him.

Sean was enjoying tending bar. He listened in on several of the cowboys conversation. One young cowboy was sitting there nursing his liquor. He was telling the other boys how he was gonna save up his money and buy all these fine things for his Ma. Then one of the young girls came over and grabbed him by the hand and lead him away. "Looks like Ma'll hafta wait a spell," Sean thought to himself.

After about an hour, a cowboy came over to the bar and was trying to tell Sean how good he was with his gun. "So yer really O'Rourke," he said. "I heard a you. I'm real good with this gun a mine. I practice and I'm gettin' faster all the time. I spect I'll be better'n you one day."

Sean looked him over. He had his colt tied down and the holster had been greased. He wore it low on his hip. "Is that so?" said Sean. "Why do you think you need ta be good with that gun?"

"What kinda question is that Mr.?" asked the cowboy. "A man needs ta be good with a gun to survive out here."

"So how many times did ya hafta use that iron on the drive up here?" asked Sean.

"I shot a rattler this side a the Red," said the cowboy.

"So you wasted a bullet on somethin' you coulda killed with a stick," said Sean.

"Ya know Mr., I'm thinkin' I don't like you," said the cowboy.

"Well ya don't really know me, do ya?" said Sean. "Let me buy ya a drink."

"Sure, why not," said the cowboy. "I can tell the folks back home that the famous gunman bought me a drink." The young cowboy hadn't noticed that Sean wasn't packing a star till just now. "Where's yer badge Marshal?" asked the cowboy. "Did ya just take it off while you was tendin' bar?"

"Nope, I'm not a lawman no more," said Sean. "I give it up."

"How come? Everone knows yer not a scared a nothin'," said the cowboy.

"Got a baby comin' and I'm gonna live a normal life fer a spell," said Sean. "I'm bout tired a chasin' bad men." Sean happened to be looking out the front window of the saloon. He saw what he thought was the bartender running toward the front door of the saloon. He had a double barreled shotgun in his hands. "Best duck down young fella," said Sean. "I think there's gonna be some shootin'."

Sean did not want to kill the man. When the man crashed through the swinging doors, Sean stood there behind the bar and just stared at him for a moment. The bartender cocked the hammers on the shotgun and raised it to fire at Sean. Sean ducked down behind the bar and laid on the floor. The man fired one barrel into the bar and then the other. He broke open the shotgun to reload, but before he was done loading, Sean had jumped up over the bar and charged him. He knocked the bartender to the floor and kicked the shotgun from his hands and stood over him. "Do you want to die now?" Sean asked him. Sean had not pulled a pistol yet. The man was quiet. "I said do you want to die?" The man still didn't answer. Sean pulled a pistol, bent down and put the muzzle of his pistol on the man's forehead. He slowly cocked the hammer.

"No please, please, please Mr. Don't kill me. Please don't kill me," the man pleaded.

Sean uncocked his pistol and holstered it. Then he gave the man a hand and helped him up. "Next time I see you, I'll expect you ta be more mannerly," said Sean. "Name's O'Rourke, Sean O'Rourke." Sean extended his hand to the man.

The man's eyes got real big for a moment. He wet himself some. He reached out and took Sean's hand. "I'm Bernard, Bernard Travis, and I'm pleased ta meet you Mr. O'Rourke. Sorry about bein' unmannerly. Won't happen again. Now if you'll excuse me, I think I'm gonna be sick." Bernard turned and left. He left the shotgun laying where Sean had kicked it. Sean went back behind the bar.

The young cowboy was there looking at where the buckshot had torn up the bar. "I don't understand why you didn't blow that man's head off," said the cowboy. "He tried ta kill you."

"Yeh, and if he would have, he'd a hung," said Sean. "He wasn't a bad man. He just made a bad choice at the time. He didn't need killin'. He just needed some manner lessons."

"I think I'd a kilt'm," said the cowboy.

"And then what?" said Sean. "Would you think you was a gunman? You never killed nobody have you? Killin' a man'll rip yer guts out. A man who thinks he likes killin' is no man at all. He oughta just blow his own head off and quit takin' up space that's needed by other folks."

"Well you've kilt lotsa men," said the cowboy.

"I have, and they needed it," said Sean. "They was bad men and they needed killin'. Some men I killed I said I liked killin'm cause they were so bad, but I really didn't like it."

"How bout Injuns?" asked the cowboy. "Have ya ever kilt Injuns?"

"Young fella, I was took in by the Cheyenne after my folks was massacred by some white outlaws," said Sean. "I had me a wife and child and another'n on the way. They was took by the cholera. We had scrapes with the Pawnee and Comanche all the time. I killed'em cause they was tryin' ta kill us, but I'll never kill no Injuns now unless their tryin' ta kill me. That fool Custer wanted me ta scout for'm sometime back. He knows better'n to ask me again."

"Yeh, that Custer was a damn Yankee," said the cowboy.

"I wore the blue myself there fella and I'm from Tennessee too," said Sean.

"Well I had two brothers fought for the stars and bars and they was kilt at Vicksburg," said the cowboy. "Just how could you be from Tennessee and wear the blue?"

"Cause young fella, I never had no slaves and I wasn't gonna fight so someone else could keep his," answered Sean. "Ownin' folks is wrong."

"They was just niggers," said the cowboy.

"Don't ever use that word around me cowboy," said Sean. "I'll pin yer ears back. Why do you call'em that anyway?"

"That's what everbody else I know calls'em," said the cowboy. "Now that the war's over, some of'ems gettin' purty uppity."

"Do you know any colored folk?" asked Sean.

"No, not really, but I see'em all the time in Texas," he answered.

"What's yer name cowboy?" asked Sean.

"They call me Twig Norton," answered the cowboy. "That's cause I'm kinda on the lean side."

"Well Twig, you should git ta know some colored folks," started Sean. "They're people just like us only they been mistreated fer lotsa years. I don't spect you'd want to be owned by someone and had ta work yer ass off for'em with no pay. Git whipped if ya did somethin' they didn't like. Supose'n you had a wife and kids and yer owner decided he was gonna sell off yer family. How'd that make ya feel?"

"I'd wanna blow his damn head off," said Twig.

"There ya go Twig," said Sean. "Wouldn't be nice bein' a slave would it?"

"I reckon not, but some folks says that's the way it's sposed ta be," said Twig. "They say them darkies are an inferior race and such."

"You need ta meet a friend a mine," said Sean. "His name's Jesse Strong. Nothin' inferior bout him. He's been my deputy lotsa times. He took a bowie knife and shoved into the top of a man's skull and the blade was stickin' out below his chin. He's the strongest man I ever seen, and he's a good man too. I'd trust my family's life with him."

"I hope that man what got stuck with the bowie knife was an outlaw," said Twig.

"He was Twig. He tried ta kill my wife," said Sean. "Well look Twig, it was good jawin' with ya, but I better git back ta bartendin'. You take care a yerself."

Sean was behind the bar for four hours till someone showed up to take his place. Camp complimented him on the job he had done and told him he could have a job any time he wanted. Sean gave him a smile and left. Sean went back over to Maggie's Place and got a meal. It had been a while since he had one of Barbara's meals. It was good. He got another plate.

He spent the night in a hotel instead of a room at the saloon, but he still didn't get much sleep. There were too many drunk cowboys roaming the streets. They would shoot off their pistols once in a while. Sean could hear some of them as they puked in the street. He was glad that he and Maggie were living in St. Louis now. He got up early and had breakfast at the saloon with Jim and Simon. Then he went for a stroll. Twig spotted him and came over to him. "Just thought I'd say adios," said Twig. "I'll be headed back ta Texas today. There's somethin' else I thought you should know."

"Well, what is it Twig?" asked Sean.

"I overheard a couple fellas at another saloon after you and me talked," started Twig. "I heard them say they was gonna kill you."

"What'd they look like?" asked Sean. "What was they packin'?"

"One was a big man. He had long yeller hair and was wearin' a buckskin jacket," said Twig. "He had a LeMat pistol on his right side and there was a Spencer rifle leanin' against his chair. The other fella had brown hair and a full beard and mustache. He had a Navy Colt on his left side and a Sharp's carbine . Both of 'em was wearin' black hats. Do you know them fellas?"

"I don't think so. I made me a lotsa enemies the last couple years," said Sean. "Now I thank ya fer the warnin'."

"Would ya want some help?" asked Twig. "I'd say them boy's is back shooters."

"I'd say they was too,'r there wouldn't be two of'em," said Sean. "No, you go on. I'll be all right."

Twig headed his horse south, but he had no intention of leaving. He was going to help Sean whether he wanted help or not. He had a Springfield carbine in his scabbard and he was a good shot with it. He rode to the edge of town and tied his horse to a small tree just outside of town. He grabbed his rifle and worked his way back downtown hoping Sean wouldn't spot him.

Sean was on the sidewalk and getting ready to enter a general store when someone yelled his name. "O'Rourke, you killed my kin. I'm gonna kill you," he yelled. It was the big yellow haired man and he was standing in the middle of the street. He had his buckskin jacket pulled back exposing the Lemat revolver. The Spencer rifle was in his left hand. Sean turned slowly to face the man.

"Where's yer partner?" Sean yelled back while staying on the sidewalk. He wasn't going on the street just yet to expose his back.

"I got no partner," yelled the big man. "Now git out here on the street so I can kill ya proper."

"I'm fine right where I am," said Sean. "Yer partner's not gonna see my back. Now pull that pistol'r git outta town, you big lump a shit." Sean knew the man was trying his best to get him out on the street so his partner could back shoot him. "Well are ya gonna git movin'r git dead?"

"Don't you wanna know who my kin was you kilt?" asked the big man.

"I couldn't care less you idiot," said Sean. "If I killed your kin it was cause they was tryin' ta kill me and they needed killin'. Now pull that shooter'r git outta town. The man didn't move. "Yep, you must be just like yer kin. Can't shoot a man a facin' ya. Who was yer damn kin, them thievin' and killin' Hawks?"

"My name's Elijah Hawk and now yer gonna die," yelled the big man. He went for his pistol. Before his hand even touched the pistol, he was thrown backwards with a hole in his forehead. The back of his head flew off and blood and brains went with it. Sean stood there on the sidewalk with the smoking gun in his right hand. He figured the man's partner was on a roof above him and was waiting for him to step out into the street. He waited for several minutes. People who had been out on the sidewalks and streets had rushed into the nearest building. Then Sean heard someone yelling. He recognized the voice. It was Twig.

Twig had spotted the other shooter on the roof and worked his way up on the roof and was behind him. "Drop that rifle or I'll put a hole through ya the size of a cabbage," Twig yelled at the man. The man hesitated and then turned to face Twig.

"Yer just some dumbass cowboy," said the man. "You don't got the guts to shoot a man." He was raising his rifle as he spoke. The next thing Sean knew, there was a shot and a man came flying off the roof and onto the street. Sean stared at the body for a moment. It didn't move.

"Is that you up there Twig?" yelled Sean.

"Yep, it's me," answered Twig. "I reckon that fella's dead isn't he?"

"Yep, you sure killed the hell outta him," said Sean. "Come on down now." Before Twig took a step, there was another shot.

"Son of a bitch, I'm hit," yelled Twig.

"Shit, there's another shooter up there somewhere," yelled Sean. "Never seen any smoke down here. Twig, stay down. Sounded like that shot came from your right. Keep watch to your right. How bad you hit?"

"Bullet hit me in the right leg just above the knee," said Twig. "Went right through. Not bleedin' too bad."

"Well wrap somethin' around it," said Sean. "I'll just stay right here for a spell. That shooter'll probly git jittery and show himself or take off. I'm bettin' he'll take off since his two compadres is dead."

Sean was right. It wasn't more than two minutes later when Twig spotted him. "He's runnin' Sean. He's gittin' down off the roof next door," yelled Twig. "I'll see where he goes." Twig dragged himself to the back of the roof. "He's got a horse tied out back Sean. He's mounted up and headed west outta town."

Sean took off running for Maggie's Place. Michael's Sharp's rifle was still there in the back room. The shells were still with it. He grabbed the rifle and a few shells and then ran out into the street. The street was still clear. Sean could hear the horse galloping away. He took off running to the edge of town. Finally he could see the rider in the distance. He got down in the prone position and slammed a shell into the chamber. He set the sights as high as they'd go. There was no wind. He took aim and waited till he had a perfect sight picture. Twig was standing now and watching. "Why the hell don't he shoot?" Twig said to himself. "Hell I can't hardly even see that far. That fellas gotta be damn near a half mile away now." A split second later, the Sharp's roared. The rider kept going. Sean counted to himself. Two seconds went by, then three. Before the count of four, the man was thrown from the saddle. He went down and didn't move. The horse kept going. "Holy shit! I never seen nothin' like that," yelled Twig. "You musta had some help from the Almighty on that shot."

"I'll take that kinda help anytime," yelled Sean. "Now I don't spect there's another shooter'r I woulda got shot at while I was out in the street. You just stay put and I'll git some help and git you down from there."

People came out of hiding now that shooting had stopped. Some other cowboys who knew Twig were still in town and they got him down off the roof. Doc Rawlins was there as they got Twig down. He had the cowboys take Twig over to his office. He's already checked the other two bodies and saw that it was too late to help them.

Sean walked back over to Maggie's Place. He put the Sharp's back where it was and went to the bar and had Tom pour him a glass of bourbon. Jim came over and he told him to take a wagon and get all the bodies over to the undertaker. "What about them boy's possessions?" asked Jim. "Before you always sold that stuff and put the money in that buryin' fund."

"Well, this time we'll sell the stuff, git that vermin in the ground, and give the rest to that young cowboy who give me hand," said Sean.

"Sure thing Sean," said Jim. "How far you reckon that last fella was when you dropped'm?"

"Not sure, but it was a fer piece," said Sean.

"Well, when I git done, I'm gonna pace it off," said Jim.

Sean finished the bourbon and asked Tom for a glass of Irish whiskey. Sean took a sip. "Oh my, that is good," said Sean. He took another sip.

"Any idea who them fellas was?" Tom asked Sean.

"That yeller headed one said he was a Hawk," answered Sean. "Don't know bout the others. Spect they're Hawks or kin of some sort."

"How in the hell did they know you were in town?" asked Tom. "And I thought most of the Hawks got wiped out."

"We did kill a bunch of'em," said Sean. "But what was left went back to Missouri. That was a fertile bunch. And I don't guess they knew I'd be in town. It was probly just a coincidence. They was in town and heard I was here. Well I'll be over at the Doc's checkin' on that young cowboy." Sean finished his drink and left.

"Well, how did it feel killin' a man?" Sean asked Twig when he entered Doc's examination room.

"I feel bad about it but not a whole lot," said Twig. "I'd do it again if I had to."

"So how's yer patient Doc? Is he gonna live?" asked Sean.

"He's damn lucky," said Doc. "That bullet didn't miss the bone by much. He'll be up and dancing in no time. Now young man, stay off that leg for a few days and change that bandage daily until it scabs over good. Come back and see me in four days. Sooner if you thinks there's a problem like infection or something."

"Thanks Doc," said Sean. "I'll make sure he behaves." Sean paid the bill and then helped Twig out. He had Twig hold onto him and they went back over to Maggie's place. They sat down at Sean's regular table. "I'm gittin' some Irish whiskey," said Sean. "What can I git fer you?"

"A beer's fine," said Twig. Sean yelled over to Tom and he brought over the drinks.

"So what was you gonna do back down in Texas?" Sean asked Twig,

"I was just gonna find another drive comin' this way and join up," said Twig. "Should be lotsa drives and they always'r needin' men."

"Ever though bout just gittin' a regular job," asked Sean.

"Cowboyin" is all I know," answered Twig.

"Well I got a good friend down in Texas. Name's Jug Carter," started Sean. "Gotta big spread now. I bet he could use a good man on his ranch. His place is not terrible far from Ft. Worth."

"I heard a him," said Twig. "They say he's one tough man. I heard some other ranchers don't like'm cause he lets the Kiowa have a steer once in a while."

"He'd rather live with the Kiowa than fight'em," said Sean. "That don't bother you, does it?"

"No, I reckon not. They're his beef anyway," said Twig.

"Well how bout I send my friend a telegram and tell'm he can expect you down there afore too long," said Sean.

"I'd be obliged to you," said Twig.

Sean and Twig sat there and talked for over an hour. Jim showed up with a big smile on his face and came over to their table. He couldn't quit smiling. "What the hell's wrong with you Jim?" asked Sean. "Yer smilin' like a possum eatin' shit."

"I can't help it," said Jim. "I paced that off out there and it was a little over twelve hundred yards. Twelve hundred yards!!! Jesus by God Christ!!! How in the hell can you shoot like that?"

"Let's just say that I can and let it go at that," said Sean.

"Well that's gotta be some kinda record'r somethin'," said Jim. "Anyway, I got them fellas horses'n guns and everthing else they had sold. They had $50 between all of'em. After payin' the undertaker, there's $150 left. All this is yours Twig."

"Yer shittin'me," said Twig. "How come this is all mine."

"Cause I said so," said Sean. "When I was a lawman and we killed some outlaws, we always sell all their belongins', pay the undertaker, and put the rest in a fund at the bank I call the buryin' fund. That way, if some outlaw needs put under and he's got no money'r nothin', we use the buryin' fund to get'm in the ground."

"Most lawmen I know keep everything," said Twig. "It's like a fringe benefit."

"Well I never needed the money Twig," said Sean. "Ya see, I own this saloon and another'n in St. Louis, plus I made lotsa reward money. So this money is yers. My way a sayin' thanks fer helpin' me."

"Well I truly appreciate it," said Twig. "And I wanna thank ya. No one's ever been this good ta me before."

"Well you deserve it young fella," said Sean. "Just don't spend it all on whiskey and women."

"I won't be doin' that," said Twig. "I'm gonna git me a new Winchester rifle and one a them pistols that's been converted to metallic cartridges. I intend to be well heeled. I'm thinkin' one day that I might git into the lawman business."

"That's somethin' ya need to really think about for a long time Twig," said Sean. "It's a hard life and there's no glory in it. The folks yer defendin' might hate ya, and the folks yer after will fer sure. Ya kill a bad man and then all his kin gotta come after ya. Life expectancy's not very long fer a lawman. You think real hard on it before you take the jump. There's a hell of a lot more bad men than there is lawmen. I had two deputies killed and me and every deputy I had has been shot all to hell at one time'r another. I was only a lawman fer just over two years. Anyway, think real hard on it. You got sand Twig. You might make a good lawman some day, but fer now, just live some. Yer young yet. Hell, I been talkin' too much. Whatever ya might do down the road is yer business. I wish ya the best."

"Well, I gotta git healed up and git down ta Texas fore I do anythin' else," said Twig. "I hope Jug Carter"ll gimme a chance ta show him what I can do."

"He will," said Sean. "I gauran by God tee it."

CHAPTER SEVENTEEN

S ean let Twig Stay in the back room at Maggie's Place until he was well enough to ride. His meals and drinks would be on the house. The back room was empty because Jim and Simon were living with their women. Sean sent a telegram to Jug Carter telling him about Twig. He also said that if Jug didn't need any men or couldn't afford another man, Sean would pay his wages.

After a full week in Abilene, Sean headed back to St. Louis and Maggie. There had been no more incidents in Abilene. Sean had telegrammed Maggie telling her when he'd be back and she was waiting for him at the train station. She was smiling like Sean had never seen her smile before. He ran to her and they kissed like they were newlyweds. He pulled back from her to get his breath and Maggie spoke. "I have some wonderful news, my husband and lover," said Maggie.

"I figured you did with the way you was smilin'," said Sean. "I have never seen you smilin' like that before. Now what's up?"

"I went to the doctor while you were gone," said Maggie. "He says he can hear two heart beats. We're going to have twins."

"Oh my gosh," cried Sean. "Is he sure?"

"He says he is," said Maggie.

"I don't spose he can tell if it'll be boys'r girls'r one a each," said Sean.

"There's no way he can know that," said Maggie. "We'll see when they pop out."

"I reckon we will darlin'," said Sean. "Maggie, I love you."

"I love you too darlin'," said Maggie. "Let's go home."

Sean and Maggie had been staying in touch with Alan and Elizabeth. Four months after Sean and Alan had gotten back from Boston, Sean and Maggie received a letter from Elizabeth. They had adopted Jimmy Dugan and Mary Campbell. Alan had quit the Pinkertons and was being a full time husband and father. Things were working out very well. Would they come for a visit soon? Maggie and Sean wanted to see their friends, but thought they should not travel that far with Maggie due in less than two months. They had made a wise decision. A month and a half later, John Michael O'Rourke, and Betty Margaret O'Rourke came into this world.

Here ends The Sean O'Rourke Series, Book 6, *Blood Flows in the East*. Continue reading for a preview of The Sean O'Rourke Series, Book 7, *Sam Waters, Marshal of Lonesome*.

The Sean O'Rourke Series
Book 7

Sam Waters
Marshal of Lonesome

by

Michael E. Cook

PROLOGUE

Sam Waters grew up on a small dirt farm in Louisiana. His family would have starved to death if his Pa hadn't been such a good hunter. Sam became a good hunter also. Sometimes when times were real hard, Sam's Pa made a little money catching runaway slaves. When Sam was older, his Pa took him with him. Sam learned well. By the time he was fifteen, he was going out on his own after runaways. He would go as far away as two states and was considered one of the best salve catchers in the state. Sam never thought one way or the other about slavery. It was just the way it was and that was it. He always brought the slaves back in good shape because some owners paid a bonus for that.

When war came, Sam wore the gray and rode with Nathan Bedford Forrest. He started out as a private but after this second engagement, he was given a commission. By war's end, he was a full Colonel. Sam always armed himself with three pistols and a carbine. One pistol was always on his left side and two pistols were strapped to the saddle horn. The carbine was in a scabbard. Sam cut the flaps off of his holsters too. He had lightning speed with his pistols and more than once had saved his men and himself when they had been ambushed.

Sam was at Fort Pillow when the Negro soldiers were executed. He didn't participate, but he did nothing to stop it either.
At the time, he just thought that war was war. In war you kill the
enemy. The dark soldiers were the enemy.

After the war, Sam went to Texas. He purchased three pistols
that had been converted to metallic cartridges and a Henry rifle.
He went all over the state looking for work. He was in west Texas
almost to the border with New Mexico when he was set upon by
three Apache warriors. He took an arrow through his side but
managed to kill the Apaches. An Army patrol happened by and
Sam went with them back to their fort to see their doctor. Sam
had cleaned himself up before the cavalry patrol had arrived. The
doctor was impressed with what he had done. All he had to do was
clean him up a little more and put on some fresh bandages. Sam
had scalped the Apaches because the scalps were worth $20 each
and he had no money. He sold the scalps and the weapons taken
from the Apaches and headed for the nearest town.

The small town he rode into was called Lonesome. He wanted
a woman, some whiskey, and some food and he wanted it in that
order. He spent some time with a beautiful Mexican girl named
Juanita. When they went downstairs to eat, Juanita's boss started
giving her a hard time. He expected her to move on to other customers. Sam had words with the man. Then two more men came
over. There were more words and the three men were killed. Sam
had someone go for the local law. That's when he found out that
he had just killed the lawman's kin. More words were exchanged
and the lawman and his deputy were killed.

Sam didn't know it at the time, but the lawman and his kin
had been riding roughshod over this town for a good while. The
townspeople were so glad Sam had killed these men that they

offered him the job of Town Marshal and he would have the saloon as his payment. Sam excepted. Juanita became his woman. Around six months later, Sam was out chasing bank robbers. When he returned, he found that Juanita had been taken by three men. They took her into Mexico. Sam tracked them. Juanita was found in a farmer's field. She had been severely beaten and raped. She had been left in the field for dead. She was not quite dead when the farmer's daughter found her, but she died shortly after. Sam found her grave and met the farmer who had tried to help her.

Sam tracked the men for a long time. Each place he went to, they had already passed through. He learned that one of the bad men had yellow hair and his face had been badly scratched. His name was Sol. He was a short stocky man and he had a big scar on his chin. Sam knew that this man had hurt Juanita badly. He would give this man what he had given to Juanita and more.

Sam thought he was getting closer to the bad men when he met some Juaristas. The outlaws had tried to steal some horses from them and had been chased across the border back into Texas. The trail went cold in Texas. Sam decided to head back to Lonesone. On his way home, he discovered that the telegraph had made its way to Lonesome. Now he could stay in contact with other lawmen across the country. Two years later, Sam got word that the three men who had taken his woman were riding with the Kid Evans gang and were in Kansas near Abilene. Sam went to Kansas and joined up with Federal Marshal Sean O'Rourke. O'Rourke was after the gang for several crimes, including murder, bank robbery, and cattle rustling. The gang had also abducted a woman, Kathleen Jameson. The gang was actually after Maggie,

Sean O'Rourke's wife. Maggie and Kathleen looked enough alike to be sisters. The gang did not know they had the wrong woman.

Kathleen was badly abused by her captors. She did what was needed to stay alive. Kid Evans had set up an ambush for the lawmen and was hoping to kill O'Rourke's woman while O'Rourke watched. There were six men in the Evans gang. Three of them had run out and Kid didn't know it. Sam and O'Rourke easily killed two of the gang and then discovered that three of them had fled. Kid was totally unaware of any of this. The whole time Kathleen had been a captive, she had been able to conceal a two-shot derringer. She could have easily shot Kid and another man at anytime, but they would have killed her too. Kid had her laid out on a blanket by a stream and had raped her again and was going to again after he had taken a dip in the stream. He still did not know that the lawmen were closing in. Kathleen could stand it no more. When Kid turned to go to the stream, she retrieved the derringer and shot him in the back of a knee. When he turned, she shot him in the other knee. Kid was trying for his pistol when Kathleen saw this huge beast charging their way. She wasn't sure what it was, but she soon found out. It was O'Rourke's huge dog Jeb. Kid tried to fight of the dog, but the dog easily overpowered him. Jeb bit off Kid's pecker. Jeb then backed up, sat, and watched Kid. Jeb spit out the pecker and went at kid again. This time he bit off his cajones. He backed up again and spit them out. Kathleen was beside Jeb now and hugging him. Kid wasn't done for yet. He tried for his pistol. When he got close to his gunbelt, Jeb attacked again. He grabbed ahold of Kid's wrist and shook. Kid's hand came off. Kathleen and Jeb sat there and watched Kid bleed to death.

Sean, Sam, and Sean's Deputy Jesse Strong made sure Kathleen was doing all right. Jesse stayed with Kathleen while Sean and Sam went after the three men who had fled. Two of them were killed and now Sam had Sol all to himself. Sam's woman Juanita had been severely beaten and raped by these three men. Sol had been the worst one. Juanita had broken limbs, broken ribs, her face beaten terribly, and one of her eyeballs was hanging out. The yellow haired man had also severely beaten Kathleen. Sam would now have his revenge.

Sol's horse had gotten away from him and Sol was now out of ammunition. Sam closed in. He shot Sol in both knees, both shoulders, and both elbows. Then he took a knife and took Sol's left eye.

Sol didn't scream or yell while this was happening. Then Sam backed off several hundred yards to watch the buzzards and coyotes eat their fill. A small pack of wolves came by. Sol creamed when the wolves started on him.

When Sam got back to Kathleen and the others, Kathleen was so glad that Sam had done these things to Sol. She attached herself to him. Sam and Kathleen became more attached each day. When Sam left Abilene for Lonesome Texas, he went with a new wife.

CHAPTER ONE

Before Sam Waters left Abilene with his new wife Kathleen, they paid a visit to Walter Black, the gunsmith. They wanted some heavy duty weaponry for Kathleen. After what she had gone through, they both decided that she needed something more than the derringer she had always carried. They had Walter take a twelve gauge double barreled shotgun and cut it down. The wooden stock was removed and replaced by a wooden pistol grip. The barrels were cut down to six inches. The original wood of the forearm was removed and replaced with a hand carved piece of wood that was almost like another pistol grip. It was a deadly weapon for very close range. They took it out of town and fired it a couple of times to see if Katherine could handle it. When it roared, the recoil knocked Katherine backwards a good bit, but she handled it well. Her other weapon of choice was an Army Colt, .44 caliber, with the barrel cut down to four inches. She made pockets in some of her dresses that were deep and reinforced. She would keep the shotgun in her right pocket and the revolver in her left. With the dresses and petticoats that she wore, no one would suspect that she had anything of that size in her pockets.

As they boarded the stagecoach to leave Abilene, Sam bid farewell to his friend Sean O'Rourke and his wife Maggie. They had become very good friends while in pursuit of the outlaws who had abducted Kathleen and had raped and murdered Sam's woman over two years ago. They assured each other that if there was ever the need, they would be there to help.

~~~~

The trip from Abilene to Lonesome was long and dusty. Kathleen and Sam were glad that they sometimes had layovers in some of the towns. There was a two-day layover in San Antonio. Sam took Kathleen and showed her the "Alamo." "You gotta know about the Alamo if ya live in Texas darlin'," said Sam. "If ya don't, you might be considered blasphemous."

"Well I know all about the Alamo sweetheart," said Kathleen. "Let's see, who was the famous frontiersman who was killed there? Oh yes, it was Daniel Boone."

"No, no, no, darlin'," said Sam. "It was Davey Crockett."

"I know Sam," said Kathleen. "I was just kidding."

"Well watch who you kid with down here," said Sam. Kathleen looked at Sam and smiled.

While they were in San Antonio, Kathleen turned a lot of men's heads. That was true of everywhere they stopped where there were any men at all. She was a beauty. There was a lot of hat tipping and such, but there were no rude remarks. Some young cowboys who looked like their tongues were about to fall out, were looking hard at Kathleen and might have said something, but thought better of it when they saw Sam. He had pulled his jacket open exposing his pistol and he also gave them a look that put the fear of God in them.

At the next relay station west of San Antonio, they had a delay while they waited on an Army escort. Some Comanches had been raiding and several places had been burned and several people were killed. The escort stayed with them for a good ways and there was no trouble. The rest of the trip to Lonesome was uneventful except for all the dust.

~~~~

As the coach pulled into Lonesome, Sam could see that there were several new buildings being constructed. He could tell right off that one of them was a saloon. He had no idea about the other ones. His deputy Daniel and the Mayor were there to meet the stage. Sam had not told them about his new wife when he sent the telegram saying he was returning. He introduced Kathleen to them. They were very courteous and helped carry their luggage over to Sam's saloon. When they first got to the saloon, Kathleen noticed something right away. "Sam, your saloon doesn't have a name," said Kathleen. "The sign just says Saloon."

"I guess we'll hafta come up with a good name now darlin'," said Sam. They carried all the luggage to Sam's room. Daniel seemed like he was getting impatient about something.

"All right Dan, ya got something stuck in yer craw. What is it?" asked Sam.

"I just need to speak with you as soon as you and the Mrs. get settled," said Dan.

"All right, meet me at the office in about three hours," said Sam. Dan nodded his head and he and the Mayor left.

"Well darlin', this is where I stay," started Sam. "It's not much, but we can do whatever ya want. We can git us a house, or I can build you a new house. Whatever you want."

"We have all the time in the world now Sam," said Kathleen. "Right now that bed looks good. How about us trying it out." A couple of hours later, Sam took Kathleen and introduced her to all of his help at the saloon. Everyone seemed very pleased to meet Sam's new wife. When the introductions were done, they went back to the room and Kathleen began arranging things. Sam gave her a goodbye kiss and went to the office to talk with his Deputy. On his way there he was greeted by several of the townspeople that he knew. There were also a lot of new faces.

Dan was sitting at the desk when Sam walked in. He jumped right up and began talking. "Sam, I want you to hear all this first thing. I'm not going to stay in this town," Dan began. "I've been offered a job with a law firm in Chicago. I can't turn down an opportunity like this."

"I understand Dan. Hell, that's what you went to law school for isn't it," said Sam. "What's yer dad think 'bout this. Bet he wanted ya ta stay here and build a practice."

"That's what he wanted, but I really don't like it here in Texas in the first place," said Dan. "Dad'll just have to get over it. And there's another thing I think you should know. I don't know if it's that important or not, but I think you should be aware of it."

"Well, spill it out. What is it?" asked Sam.

"There's a new County Sheriff now," started Dan. "The old one and his deputies mysteriously disappeared or just left. There's a rumor that the new Sheriff used to be a bad outlaw."

"I've heard about some outlaws givin' up their bad ways and becomin' lawmen." said Sam. "They might make good lawmen 'cause they know how a bad man might think. So was there an election while I was gone? A County Sheriff gets elected by the county unless there's a situation where one needs to be appointed. I never knew anything about some election comin' up before I left."

"There wasn't any election and that's not all Sam," continued Dan. "He's got five deputies and from what I here, they're just thugs and gunmen."

"Five deputies, why the hell would he need five deputies, and how could the county afford that many?" said Sam. "I just bet somethins' not right. Who's the Mayor over there at Hadleyville? Is he an honest man?"

"I couldn't tell you that Sam," answered Dan. "I haven't heard anything about him."

"Well what's this new Sheriff's name anyway?" asked Sam. "Maybe I heard a him."

"It's Chuck Sumner," answered Dan. "I looked at some old wanted posters, but that name didn't come up."

"Just cause there's no poster don't mean a man's not a bad man," said Sam. "I reckon I'll just see how things go. So if you're gonna head to Chicago, did your old man say anything bout me hirin' a new deputy? And where you been hearin' all this anyway?"

"Just been drifters and folks coming into town. Freighters and drummers too. They say them new deputies been running anyone out of town that they don't like the looks of. And no, my dad didn't say one word about another deputy, but I think you should bring that up next time you two meet," said Dan. "I'm taking the next stage headed east. I've had my things packed and have just been waiting on you to get back. I do hate to leave you shorthanded, but it has been quiet around here while you were gone."

"Is there a girl up there in Chicago awaitin' on ya?" asked Sam.

"Now why would you ask me that?" asked Dan.

"Cause I'm not stupid Dan," said Sam. "A good woman can help a man make his mind up purty quick sometimes."

"Well, there is a girl up there," said Dan. "She was the sister of a friend I made while in law school. We had dinner a few times and we—, well anyway, we became close and she is thrilled about me going up there."

"I reckon you kept in touch with her while you been playin' lawman," said Sam.

"I have and that's all I will say on the matter," said Dan.

"Well I hope she's a good woman and I wish you all the best," said Sam.

"And I thank you Sam. I have learned a lot from you and I hope the best for you and your wife," said Dan.

"Tell your old man that I'll be payin' him a visit in the mornin'" said Sam. Dan nodded, laid his Deputy badge on the desk, and left.

~~~~

That night, while they were in bed, Sam started laughing. Kathleen woke up and looked at him. He was still sound asleep. He was laying there with his eyes closed, and he was sound asleep. She tried to get back to sleep, but every so often Sam would break out laughing again. Finally she woke him up. "Sam, wake up darlin'," said Kathleen as she shook him. Sam finally woke up.

"What is it sweetheart?" asked Sam.

"You've been laughing a lot in your sleep," said Kathleen. "You must have been having some dream."

"Oh yeh, I was," said Sam. "I was dreamin' bout, well, I better not say. It might bring up some bad memories."

"Look husband of mine, I'll always have those bad memories," said Kathleen. "They'll never leave. I just have to go on with my life. It's our life now. Now you tell me right now."

"All right darlin', I was dreamin' bout that yella haired son of a bitch that hurt ya so bad. Do you remember all the things I said I was gonna do to'm?"

"Yes Sam, I do," answered Kathleen.

"Well, I done them things," started Sam. "I shot him in both knees, both shoulders, and both elbows. Then I took my knife and took his left eyeball. I twisted my knife some before I pulled it out. That son of a bitch didn't scream or yell the whole time all this was goin' on. Then I backed off to watch the buzzards and coyotes eat their fill. Some wolves showed up. There was three men there and a dead horse. Two a them men were dead but old yella hair was still alive. I made bets with myself on what the wolves would start on first. There was six a them wolves."

"Well Sam, what did they start on first?" asked Kathleen.

"I bet on the horse bein' first and I was right," answered Sam. "They started on the horse like I thought they would. Then they got ta fightin' and the leader of the pack stayed on the horse. The others went after the men. Ole yella hair didn't scream'r yell the whole time I shot him up and took his eye, but he let out a yell when them wolves started on'm."

"So what about all this made you start laughing?" asked Kathleen.

"I guess it was because that bastard didn't yell'r scream till them wolves got on'm, or mebbe it was that I bet that the wolves would start on the horse first. Them wolves knew that yella hair was a bag a shit and would taste like shit." said Sam. "I'm not really sure now."

"Sam," said Kathleen.

"Yes darlin'," said Sam.

"I love you. Now go back to sleep," said Kathleen.

~~~~

The next morning after breakfast, Sam went to talk with the Mayor. The Mayor was expecting him. "What can I do for you this morning?" asked the Mayor.

"Well, I been doing some serious thinkin'," started Sam. "I'm gonna hire me a deputy soon as I can find a good man. Secondly, I think it's time the town started payin' me a salary."

"What do you mean?" asked the Mayor. "We gave you that saloon."

"Yep, you did, but that saloon wasn't yours to give in the first place," said Sam. "The deed for that place is in my name. I got rid a them assholes you towns folks didn't have the guts ta git rid of. That saloon's been mine for over two years. I consider myself a business man and the Town Marshal."

"We can fire you," said the Mayor.

"Yep, you can, but that saloon is still mine," said Sam. "You even think bout pullin' some shit and tryin' ta take it away and I guarantee you that you'll end up bein' mighty sorry. You fire me and I'll just be Sam Waters, businessman. Just think about the money this town saved not payin' me and my Deputy all this time. This town is growin'. It can afford ta pay a Marshal and a Deputy. Now, are you gonna pay up, or are you gettin' a new Marshal?"

"I better talk to the town council," said the Mayor. "Maybe we won't need you anyway. The new County Sheriff has five Deputies. They should be able to look after this town too."

"Yep, this town's in the county, but the county seat is a far piece off," said Sam. "We're awful close to the border, but you do what you think is best." Sam nodded and left the Mayor's office. The Mayor was mumbling to himself as Sean left.

Kathleen was arranging things in their room when Sam got back to the saloon. "So how was the Mayor this fine mornin'?" Kathleen asked him.

"He's a fool," answered Sam. "Probly always will be."

"So I guess you didn't have a good visit with him," said Kathleen.

"Well, I never told you how I got to be owner of this place," said Sam. "I guess it's time ta tell ya."

"Sure, go ahead," said Kathleen.

"When I first came here there was some bad men runnin' this town," started Sam. "I was in this saloon enjoyin' myself and this fella who was the owner started givin' the woman I was with a hard time. We had some words. A couple a his thugs got involved. I had ta kill them three. Then I found out the Town Marshal and this fella was kin. Anyway, the Marshal and Deputy showed up and I had ta kill them too. The towns folks were so glad them fools was gone that they offered me the job of Town Marshal and said I could take over the saloon as payment. I jumped right on it."

"So what's the problem now?" asked Kathleen.

"I told the Mayor it was time the town started payin' me a regular salary instead of just havin' the saloon," said Sam.

"Well that's only fair," said Kathleen. "The town should pay you. I'm sure the Mayor has investments in this town and just doesn't rely on his Mayor's salary. So what if he won't pay you?"

"Well, then I'll be Sam Waters, businessman," said Sam.

"So what does a Town Marshal get paid?" asked Kathleen.

"Depends on the town," answered Sam. "Could be as much as $100 a month or as little as $30." I don't much care. It's just the point a the thing. If the town wants a lawman, they should pay for one."

"You don't have to convince me darlin'," said Kathleen.

~~~~

Later that afternoon, the Mayor and town council member met with Sam. They were at the Marshal's office. "We've agreed to pay you a salary of $50 a month," said the Mayor. "Any more than that and we'd have to raise taxes or something."

"Well I appreciate this Mayor," said Sam. "Now what about a Deputy?"

"We'll pay a Deputy $40 a month," answered the Mayor."

"Mighty big of you Mayor," said Sam. "So what is your salary Mayor?"

"That, Marshal, is none of your business," said the Mayor.

"Oh, but you're wrong on that Mayor," said Sam. "You're a public official and the public has the right to know. Now what is your salary?"

"All right, all right, I get $150 a month," answered the Mayor.

"Sounds like mighty good pay for what little you do around here," said Sam.

"Look Marshal, I didn't come here to get insulted," said the Mayor.

"Well you started this Mayor," said Sam. "Now I'll bid you all good day. Go do whatever it is that you do to earn your pay." The Mayor and the council members were grumbling as they left Sam's office.

"Look Mayor," one of the council members said as they left Sam's office, "Sam's a good lawman. We need him here. We're awful close to that border."

"All right, I was just trying to save the town some money, that's all," said the Mayor.

"Save it for what?" the councilman asked.

"Never mind," said the Mayor. They went their separate ways. Sam told Kathleen all about it when he went back to the saloon. She seemed pleased.

About an hour later, Sam and Kathleen were sitting out in front of the saloon when three riders came into town. They stopped at Sam's office. One of them dismounted and went into the office. When he was convinced no one was there, he mounted and the three men rode down the street toward Sam. They stopped in front of the saloon. Sam could see that these men were well armed and he saw the badges they wore. He could tell that these men were not ordinary lawmen. He told Kathleen to get inside. She left, but stayed close to the door so she could hear what was said. The one who had dismounted spoke. "We're County Deputies and we been trackin' a horse thief and rapist," said the man. "We're lookin' for the Town Marshal."

"That'd be me," said Sam. "Sam Waters is the name." Sam pulled his jacket open and showed his badge and pistol. "You boys git down off them horses. I don't like anyone lookin' down on me." The other two men dismounted. They tied their horses to a rail and stood in front of Sam. Sam stood now and sized them up. The one who had been doing the talking was a tall man, over six feet. He had long black hair and a full mustache. He had a tied down Colt on his right side and another pistol stuck in his belt. He stood in the middle. The man on the right looked like one mean son of a bitch. Sam thought he looked like someone who would kill his Ma if he didn't like what she made for supper. There was a big scar on his left cheek. His black hat was tipped back and Sam could see that he was bald headed. The man had a Colt on his left side for a right hand cross draw and a shoulder holster on his left with a smaller pistol in it. The other man stood there with a brand new looking Winchester in his hands. Sam couldn't see a side gun, but chances were, he had one somewhere. This man had long brown hair and a full beard. Sam's eyes went back to the middle man. "If you was trackin' a man, why didn't ya send a telegram and tell me what ta look for?"

"We thought we'd just stop in and meet you," said the man. "We heard a you. We heard you rode with O'Rourke back in Kansas for a bit."

"Sean and me worked together one time," said Sam. "Now tell me bout this man yer after."

"He's no man. He's a breed," said the man. "He's Apache and Mex. Might be somethin' else in'm too. He raped a white woman just north a Hadleyville and stole a horse ta git away on. The woman's dead, so I reckon it's murder too."

"Well nobody like that around here," said Sam.

"Now just how would you know that if you been spendin' yer time sittin' on yer ass in front a this saloon?" asked the man.

Sam pulled back his jacket. "It's time for you fellas ta leave town," said Sam.

"We're not goin' nowhere," said the man. "We're duly appointed County Deputies."

"That's right. You're County Deputies," said Sam. "This is my town. I'm the Town Marshal. What I say in this town goes. Now you three hit the road and I mean now."

"I reckon we'll do what we please," said the man. "Come on boys, let's get us a drink and then we'll have a look around this town." Sam spoke before they had a chance to move.

"You, with that Winchester, lower that thing down to your side and I mean right now," said Sam.

"The hell I will," said the man.

"Which one a you wants ta die first?" asked Sam.

"What the hell did you say?" asked the man.

"You heard me. Now move on," said Sam. Sam eyes told the three men he meant business. The bald-headed man's right hand moved just a hair toward his pistol. Before the three men even knew it had happened, Sam's pistol was about six inches from the middle man's face. "Now I'll ask you one more time. Which one a you wants ta die first?"

"The Sheriff's gonna wanna meet you real soon," said the man. "Come on boys. We better go. Probly got someone inside with another gun on us. We'll be seein you again real soon."

"You tell that Sheriff he's welcome here any time as long as he behaves," said Sam. Sam kept his pistol aimed at the tall man's head while the three men mounted. Sam watched the men all the way out of town. Then he holstered his pistol. He waited another ten minutes before he went inside.

Books By Michael E. Cook

<u>The Sean O'Rourke Series</u>

Book 1: *A Killer For The Common Good*

Book 2: *A Killer For The Common Good—LAWMAN*

Book 3: *O'Rourke's Revenge*

Book 4: *O'Rourke's Law or No Law at All*

Book 5: *Quiet Times*

<u>Coming soon</u>

Book 7: *Sam Waters—Marshal of Lonesome*

Available in paperback and eBook formats
at Internet retailers everywhere.

ABOUT THE AUTHOR

Mike was born and raised in south central Ohio. After high school, Mike joined the U.S. Marines and served two tours in Vietnam. After military service, Mike attended and graduated from Ohio University, Athens, Ohio, majoring in Psychology. Mike retired from the snack food industry in early 2014. Mike grew up loving two things, baseball and Westerns. Now that Westerns are not as popular as they once were, Mike is hoping to get the popularity back. "Everyone needs a good Western. It doesn't matter if it's all bullets and blood, cowboys, horses, and trail drives, lawmen and outlaws, Indians on the warpath, or homesteaders versus ranchers or mother nature."

Mike and his wife of almost 42 years, Eleanor, live on their 31 acre mini-farm in Southwest Central Ohio. They have two grown children and three grandchildren.

Contact the author at: cookorourkeseries@gmail.com